For Sharon

CROWN ISLAND

LEE A. JACOBUS
HAMMONASSET HOUSE

Hammonasset House Books

Mystic, Connecticut
http://www.hammonassethouse.com

Copyright © 2010 by Lee A. Jacobus

Library of Congress Cataloging in Publication Data
1.Fiction–General 2. Fiction–Literary
3. Fiction–Connecticut

I. Jacobus, Lee A., 1935-
II. Title

PR2301.J43   810.01
ISBN-13 978-0-9801894- 5-2
Manufactured in the United States

CHAPTER ONE
April 3, 1971

To the people of Quarrytown Marie Wainwright was an enigma. She lived on Crown island alone, the last of her family, a celebrity who kept mostly to herself, but still a youthful and beautiful woman.

Peter Chello talked with her several times since he dropped out of the University, and each time she surprised him because of her warmth and her interest in his work. Others who worked on the island over the years found her mystifying, and brusque. But since her husband and daughters had drowned, people became more charitable. They saw her now as more brave than distant. She had been dealt a cruel hand by the gods, and even those in Quarrytown with reason to feel resentful softened and spoke of her kindly.

When she hired him to replace her granite pier head and slate walkway, she sat him down in the Quarrytown Café and talked for more than an hour about the beauties of life on Crown Island, the way the light played on the water, the way the trees would soon be in bloom, the way the Granite Islands sat like a stately convoy reaching toward Long Island. There was poetry everywhere one looked, she said. And as they spoke Peter felt that she was not just talking with an employee, a stonemason from a family of stonemasons. She was talking with someone who understood the poetry of a beautiful vision. He knew just what she meant, but until now he'd never had anyone he could talk with about the beauty of the harbor.

On his first day he nosed past Kidd's Island, around the rocks where cormorants sat at low tide, until he began the approach on the south side of Crown Island. Then he saw the white house large and solid, with a fine verandah, two brick chimneys, and a widow's walk between them. Not far from the dock sat the sailboat from which her husband and children were thrown. The Petrel had not been back in the water for years. He thought he'd never see it again.

He beached his skiff in the sand and examined the steps leading up from the pier, then went to the door, but no one answered. All he heard was muffled barking. Where could she be? He thought for a moment of the calamities in her life. She had written her first book, *The White Wraith,* about her parents' death in a plane crash and her second, *On an Island of Hope,* after her family died. What was she writing now?

Back at the pier someone was swimming in the dark water toward him. All he saw at first were splashes of white, but soon Marie turned her face to breathe and then reached for the lowest step. She emerged like Venus, dripping a tumult of water. She wore a stark white bathing suit and a white cap that she peeled off, shaking the excess water on the stones. Her dark hair flowed around her shoulders as she greeted him.

"I wanted to get my swim in," she said with a smile.

He hardly had the presence of mind to say hello. She was intensely beautiful in this morning light.

"There's a towel down there." She pointed toward the stone seat behind him. "You're very sweet to come out today," she said taking it from him. He watched her dry herself and wrap the towel around her shoulders. "I've been putting off fixing these stairs for years. I hope it's not too late."

"No," he said. "No, It's not too late. You need good Quarrytown Granite."

"I've always disliked this slate. Have you had your coffee break yet?"

"I don't usually . . . ."

"We'll need to discuss what I want," she said. "And I've not had my breakfast. I always swim first, and have breakfast later. You'll come up and have something with me while we talk."

"You swim every day?"

"When it's nice. I swim over to Parker Island or Extra Island, then I like to swim slowly home."

"It's dangerous out there. You could get run over."

"I've been doing it since I was a child."

He felt embarrassed but moved up toward the house with her. She dripped on the slate as she walked, and beads of water sat on her arms and legs. Her hair hung in clusters across her shoulders and he found himself excited by her closeness, the way she seemed so comfortable in her body, the way she touched his arm as she leaned on him.

"Maybe we could have a swim one day," she said. "You must be a strong swimmer."

When they reached the house Marie's dog stood wagging its tail by the door.

"That's Jasper," she said. "You'll like him. We name all our dogs Jasper. Do you think that odd? My grandfather started the tradition. You know how traditions are."

He wasn't sure what to say. The people he worked for sometimes gave him cookies or cupcakes or tomatoes to take home after a job, but none of them had ever asked him to sit and have coffee with them. Marie surprised him. He felt himself stirred just by being near her. How could anyone think she was weird? Packy Caserto told him that she was a weird lady and that he'd seen her at night standing out in front of her house in the moonlight wearing a white dress with a white scarf over her head.

" I guess coffee would be great," he said. "With milk. And one sugar." He started to put on his shirt while she moved from the cupboard to the coffee maker, and she waved her hand. "Don't bother. Relax. We'll get more done if you relax."

She took a man's shirt from a hanger by the back door, and left it loose as she moved about the kitchen. The coffee maker began to gurgle. "I'm not sure exactly how I want the walkway to be, but I know I want it changed."

He sat and watched her lean on the counter. She never took her eyes off him and in a moment he looked away. He tried not to think of the letter in his pocket.

"Okay." He examined her drawing. It was close to some of the ideas he had himself. She stood on tiptoe reaching for coffee mugs. Her legs were long and smooth. She turned and smiled at him. She placed a nut roll on the plate before him and poured coffee for both of them.

"How's your father?"

"He's in the wheelchair now. I'm not sure he'll be able to do the heavy work any more."

"Is it permanent? The wheelchair?."

"He's going to have a limp, but he'll walk again. He was almost killed in the quarry, you know." She nodded. They sat opposite one another. "Do you ever get lonely out here?"

"Yes. Sometimes. I talk to Jasper a lot."

"You're writing a new book."

"I should be. Have you read any of my books?"

"I just finished *On an Island of Hope.*"

"Ah. Did you like it?"

"I really liked it."

"Thank you." She looked sad for a moment, but then she smiled again. "I'm in a strange period for me I think. The muse seems to have abandoned me."

She didn't say anything for a few minutes. The silence made him feel out of place. He looked around the room. The kitchen was yellow with glass-paned cabinets. Several skillets and copper pots hung above the stove. But apart from their own cups and plates there was no sign of anyone eating. Even the plate rack next to the sink was empty and the dishcloth beside it seemed dry and stiff. He couldn't help but wonder what her life here alone was like. He wished he could say something that would make him feel easier and less awkward.

"Do you miss college?"

"The University?" He thought a moment. It wouldn't be easy to explain his feelings. "I can go back," he said.

"Yes, but do you miss it now?"

"I guess," he said. But he knew he did miss it.

"It would be a shame not to go back. Especially if you like Classics. I loved school."

"Me too," he finally admitted. He tried not to think about it. His father kept saying he should go back, but Peter knew that Tom Chello was glad he was home. The business was not called Chello & Son for no reason. "I should go out and get to work," he said. "This was nice."

"I just wanted to be sure we were thinking alike on this project," she said. "I want to preserve the flowers, but I also want the walkway to be beautiful. Not just serviceable."

"No, I want that too. I want it to last as well as being beautiful. It's important."

She rose when he stood up. Her hair was dry and she fluffed it slightly. Her skin was warm and fresh looking. He realized he liked the way she smiled and the way she moved around the table as she walked him to the door. Jasper sat calmly near the stairs. "I'll be out in a little while myself. Take your time."

Peter went down to the walkway. The slates were set badly, eroding at the edges, crumbling and shattered in spots.

Whoever did that work had no sense of aesthetics, no sense of craft. He walked down taking notes on the floral gardens as well as the trees that helped shade the path when the sun rose. The old pear trees needed pruning. When Senator Wainwright lived here, the walkway was wide and beautiful. Peter wanted it to be that way again. He looked back at the house and saw Marie smiling at him.

CHAPTER TWO

Tom Chello was going stir crazy and needed to get downstairs and out to the barn where he could at least use his hands. Buddy Dooley and Packy Caserto lifted him in his wheel chair and brought him where he could fiddle with the complex molding that Dr. Candelucci wanted in his addition. Tom had to do something, even if it did not amount to much.

Peter worked on ideas for Crown Island. When he was satisfied, he went out to Marie with a nice sheaf of drawings. He'd done an elevation of the pathway with day lilies and tulips bending toward it as they would be when he finished the job. He suggested how he could fit Quarrytown granite so as to make the bends as fluid as possible.

"These drawings are lovely. You've got a talent."

"Thanks. Which one do you like most?"

"I like them all. But you can't do them all, can you?"

"Not really." He pulled one of the drawings out of the group. "This is one that would be really nice. Especially the way the trees are now. And it's visually interesting."

"Can you really do it that way?"

"I don't see why not. My father thinks I use too much stone, but I can make this look beautiful and also be efficient in the process."

"Good," she said. She looked up from the table. Her smile was warm and as radiant as he remembered when he first saw her rising from the water after her swim.

Peter hauled his supplies from the skiff. He hung his shirt on a flowering Hazel, careful not to get caught on a thorn. Then he took a spray can and marked out the outline of the walkway. When he finished and compared it with his drawing, he went up to the front door and knocked. Marie came from the sitting room with a book in her hand.

"I just wanted you to walk the pathway with me," he said. "I want to be sure that you like the way I've marked it off before I do any stone work."

"Oh, nice," she said, as if it were an excursion. She looked admiringly at him as he stood there and, self-conscious, he ran his fingers through his hair and smiled back at her. "I'm reading *Phaedra*," she said as they walked across the verandah.

"We were going to read that in Classics," he said.

"Yes, I think you'd like it."

"That was a while ago, but yeah. We were gonna do a stage reading of parts in class."

"Oh, maybe you and I can do that some time."

He didn't know what to say. "So this is all right?" He was trying to concentrate on the job, but he found it difficult with her so close to him.

"Fine. Go ahead," she said.

He saw that she had her finger in her book, and when they parted she went back into the house reading where she had left off. He would have preferred that she walk the entire pathway with him, but she had simply stood on the verandah and looked down at the markings and agreed that it was fine.

He pounded in some short stakes along the length of the path, careful to keep it clear of the plantings, and he widened the walkway gracefully as it came up to the verandah steps. He looked back and began to envision the finished path. He checked his work carefully. He wanted this path to last a lifetime.

When he came up from his skiff after placing his tools in the bow, Marie Wainwright was on the lawn watching him. She had a scarf over her head and around her neck. The book she was reading was still in her hands. "Are you done for the day?"

"For now. Tomorrow I'm going to take out the old stones and make room for the new."

"Come in for tea," she said.

"Tea?" Peter couldn't remember the last time he had tea.

"Yes, I'd like you to stay for tea. Do you have to rush?"

"No. Not really." She had a teapot on the glass table on the verandah. She had placed some cookies on one of the large plates he had seen in the cabinets.

They talked about books as the sun bent lower over the water. They could see across the Sound to Long Island. The clouds were low, bright cumulus streaks against the blue. Several sailboats seemed to play with one another in the distance. Down the coast, Peter saw a barge making for the quarry railroad pier head. Distant Island was almost out of sight, and Parker Island, off to the right and in a line with the sun, was just a silhouette. There were fifteen or sixteen homes on Kidd's Island, another ten on Parker Island, four on Distant Island, and fifteen or more on Mother's Island. Crown Island was the largest of the islands, and it had just one home, the Wainwrights'. There was no question in his mind but that Crown Island was the most beautiful of the islands now that he had a chance to see it. The ridge behind the house protected it against the peering eyes of Quarrytowners on the mainland, and the trees, which survived countless storms, made the island a lush and private world.

He resolved to begin reading again the way he had when he was at the University. Marie was the first person he had met since school who read the way he liked to read himself. The thought that they might read together thrilled him.

"You work with your father," she said. "Chello and Son. That's nice. Is that what you wanted to do?"

He was surprised by the question. "I guess," he said. But he could hear the uncertainty in his voice. She just looked at him. "We've been working together since I was in high school," he said. "It was started by my grandfather. It's a good business. And I like working with stone. When I look across from my skiff and see the walls my dad built and how they've lasted so long. I don't know, but it makes me feel good."

"It must make you feel proud."

"I like the idea of building something, working with my hands."

"Ah," she said, touching him lightly. "And interesting hands they are."

CHAPTER THREE

When Peter first set out for Crown Island, he had a nagging letter in his pocket from his girlfriend, Alice Carlson. She was in Galway with relatives for the summer. She complained that he never wrote to her the way she wrote to him. The letter made him feel guilty, and not just because he could not write a romantic note to Alice.

In high school, the idea of Peter's taking over Chello & Son and Alice's coming home to teach in Burnford and live in Quarrytown seemed completely natural. Alice knew just what she wanted out of life, and her certainty reassured Peter. It made life simpler. Every opportunity was right there for them, a great place to live, a good way to make a living, and a fine prospect for the future. Nancy and Tom Chello wanted the very future for Peter that Alice desired.

But all that was before he got the chance to go to the University and see how other people his age viewed themselves. He knew a number of his classmates would probably join a parent in a business, but if so they never said a word about it. In fact, while he was in college nobody ever talked about what they would do when they graduated.

Until his father's accident he was not entirely sure that he wanted to come back and run the company. He had begun to think that it wouldn't hurt to try something entirely different. Like his friends, he was caught up in the now, and excited about what he was doing. And the thought of suggesting to Tom Chello that he might like to spend his life doing something other than working with him as part of Chello & Son was difficult to contemplate. He knew it would break his father's heart.

He wasn't sure how much Marie understood about his

commitment to his father. And he couldn't be sure exactly what Marie Wainwright thought about his leaving college. She seemed to understand his needs and his reasons for dropping out. But he also detected a sense of disappointment in her comments to him. She seemed to wish something else for him.

Peter never mentioned Alice to Marie or Marie to Alice. He'd learned that the first semester Alice was away and he happened to show up at a post-game party with Louisa Matella, a girl from his high school class, and in a letter to Alice he mentioned her as being nice. That was like pulling the pin of a hand grenade. It didn't seem appropriate for him to tell Marie Wainwright that he had a girlfriend any more than it was appropriate to tell her that they planned to marry and raise a family in Quarrytown.

He was beginning to understand about jealousy and women.

Peter had a restless night. His mother made him nervous and his father's demands were too much, so he went out to the Nickel Plate, a dank saloon on Water Street in Burnford. It was near the recreation baseball diamond and where the ball teams usually wound up after a game. Sometimes the drunks got into a little rough housing there, but not that night. He had some beers and got a buzz going and got talking with little Tony Clemenza, a fellow who bartended there once in a while, but never really did anything on a regular basis. Clemenza umpired some of the games and was a talker, so Peter didn't have to work too hard when he sat there drinking and eating pickled eggs. Clemenza was driving a school bus now, and he had stories about some of the locals that you wouldn't believe.

He ended the night vomiting in the alley beside the Nickel Plate and leaning against the wall until he thought he was steady enough to drive home. He was afraid Chief Pultner might be sitting up the street from the Nickel Plate, but luckily he got away with it this time.

The next morning, Peter had a miserable hangover and

wasn't sure he heard what Marie said to him.

"The Greeks were wise about a number of things, and fate seems to be one of them," she said to him when he walked up to the house. She had been waiting for him and he was late.

He wasn't sure what she was talking about and he was distracted because he wondered whether or not he still smelled of beer.

"Fate?" Peter asked. The sunlight was behind the house and they both stood in the shade. The air was cool off the water and the sound of the trees was like music. He heard a phoebe call from a nearby dead branch. "Fate?" he said again, still not sure. "You mean like the Greeks?"

"Yes, some people think it a quaint idea, but in so many ways I think it's a cruel idea. It has been very cruel to me. What do you think?"

She seemed so bright, so alert. His mind was boggy and for an instant he wished she'd just leave him alone to dig for a while. But after a few moments of struggling with the idea, he began to sense himself growing aware of Marie's gaze and her expectant expression.

"I guess," he said. "You mean your family. I guess it can be cruel."

"You don't think about fate?"

"About fate? I suppose it's just what it is." That sounded a little lame, but finally he got himself awake enough to think about what she was saying. "I don't know if I believe in fate. Luck, maybe. Could that be the same thing, though? Another word for it. Maybe. Maybe bad luck is what you call fate. You think?"

"Sometimes. But not always. What happened in the quarry may have been fate. You did a good thing helping your parents. You know, they say your name is your fate."

"You mean you think I should play the cello?"

"No, but that would be nice, wouldn't it? No, I mean you simply follow the path laid out for you, don't you? Your father made it simple for you, just as my parents made it simple for me. I'm out here on Crown Island, and now you are with Chello & Son."

The next day Peter came early with his wheelbarrow and his heavy tools. After he prised out many of the old stones in the walkway, he heard Marie plashing through the water to the stair head. He turned to see her come out of the water up the stairs and take off her swimming cap. The water dripped from her body as she shook her cap to one side. Peter watched as the water pooled on the slates he had not removed. She had a happy expression on her face and he saw again how beautiful she was. She wore a dark green two-piece bathing suit. He smiled at her and showed her his work.

"Lovely," she said. "Come have some coffee."

He shook his head instinctively. He wanted to keep going, but at the same time he knew that if Marie Wainwright wanted him to have coffee with her, he would have coffee. Something was happening to him and he was not quite sure what it was. His years with Alice had taught him not to take an interest in other women. Alice was very demanding and he was smart enough not to fool around in Quarrytown. Everything got back to Alice when she was in Kingston and even when she was in Galway she knew who Peter talked to and whether women like Franny Bond took an interest in him.

But she couldn't know about Marie Wainwright. For one thing it would have seemed totally impossible to her that Marie would have even noticed him. How could she? She was a prominent islander in a world apart. Peter tried to fight his feelings for Marie, but he was also aware of how deep his feelings were becoming.

"Well, we need a coffee break, don't we?" Marie said brightly. "I need a little breakfast and you've done a good deal already." Jasper walked down the pathway a few steps and sat watching them both. He was a patient dog.

It was useless to protest, so he put his crowbar next to

his spade and reached for his shirt.

"I like you better without your shirt," she said. She gave him a mischievous grin. "You're more Greek that way." She came to him and touched his chin so she could read his profile. "Or, actually, more Roman. With that lovely curly hair. Definitely Roman."

When they got talking, Marie told him that she had been a classics major in college, which accounted for her reading and her interest in the Greeks. He read *Oedipus Rex* in high school and thought it was excellent. "In our Classics course at the University we read mainly Roman poetry, especially Propertius, and Ovid," he said. "It was a course about Amor, love. It was kind of interesting. But I never got to the plays we were supposed to read."

"Well," she said happily. "You and I will read a play together. I would love to have someone to read with me. Would that please you?"

"Yes. Yes, it would." He hardly knew what he was saying, but he knew he meant what he said. He didn't know anyone who took any interest in plays of any kind, much less old Greek plays. And the thought that Marie wanted to spend more time with him in such an intimate activity was so delicious that he knew he would read with her anything she wanted.

And that began a custom between them. Each morning after he worked for a time on the walkway she insisted that he have coffee and read aloud with her. She chose the books, usually plays, but often poems, especially the poems of Ovid, and they read to one another until Peter had to protest that he needed to get back to work.

"I'm paying you," she said one morning. "You needn't worry about our reading together. I'm including it in your check. It gives me great pleasure."

When he next stopped in the Café, Buddy and Packy quizzed him on what life was like on Crown Island. It was such an exotic place for Quarrytowners that it had a magical quality and took on a shape in the imagination that no island could truly live up to. Peter managed to describe it in terms that made their esteem for the island grow. If anything, his description made it seem even grander than it was.

When they asked him about Marie Wainwright he told them simply that she was okay with the work he was doing and that she sometimes came out to watch him. He did not mention that they had tea in the afternoon and coffee in the morning, or that they spent some of their time telling each other their life story and some of their time reading plays and poems by long dead authors. Nor did he mention that when Marie rose from her morning swim and came up the pathway that she often took his arm as they walked to the house, that she sometimes tilted her head toward him and dripped seawater on his arm and shoulders. He mentioned nothing to them about how his feelings were stirred when he saw her walking from the sea toward him, or about his fantasies when he thought about her.

For Peter, Marie was palpable, a woman unlike any he had known, a touchable, thoughtful, and tender woman. He realized, when he was away from her, how important she had become in his life. He found himself thrilling to the thought each evening that he would be back on Crown Island in the morning.

Peter began the process of lowering the walkway, hauling away the earth, and then laying down a careful bed of powdered crushed stone. Marie worked nearby, pruning flowers, trimming shrubs. She planted hundreds of impatiens while he labored near her. At times he became self-conscious of the odors of his body as the sun drew the sweat down his chest in long beads. Sometimes Marie sang to him and he liked to hear her vocalize tunes that he recognized as sentimental, but sweet. He began to realize that Marie was cheerful most of the time.

One day, she had spent the morning digging in her garden while he laid the last of the crushed stone bed carefully in the path. That afternoon she called down to him to come and have lunch with her. Peter stopped bringing his own sandwiches and thermos because their custom was to have lunch and talk or read together before he did the afternoon's work. This afternoon was slightly different.

"I've been practicing," she said. "I want you to hear what I've been working on."

They went into her music room, where she had her library of music, and her Steinway. It was a majestic instrument, enormously long, shiny, and dark. She sat down, played a few notes, and began to sing a song by Debussy, and while he did not understand the French he realized that it was about love, "amour."

She sang effortlessly and smiled at him in a way that made him feel intimate with the music. He had never heard singing like this, but he knew he would like to hear more. She sang another song and Jasper came into the room and sat by her with his head on his forepaws. He seemed to enjoy the music as much as Peter.

"It's beautiful," was all he could say.

"I don't play enough," she said. "If I had you for an audience more often I would play all the time. It gives me joy."

CHAPTER FOUR

Peter's father had trouble with the physical therapist. "Christ, it's a prison up here," he told her. Peter watched him and saw the therapist's reaction.

"It doesn't look like a prison to me," she said.

"He's downstairs a lot now," Peter said. "One of the guys helps me."

"Otherwise I'd blow my brains out," Tom said. "Weren't for the Red Sox, God knows what I'd do. When am I gonna get out of this goddam thing?" he asked, indicating the cast on his right side.

"Soon," she said. "Then you'll be a lot more comfortable. I think the doctor is going to take it off the end of the week. That means you'll have to work a lot harder on the bars. You are going to have to follow orders on this."

"Yeah, yeah," Tom said. "You know me."

"I'm afraid I do." Then she turned to Peter. "Why can't he move downstairs?"

When it was settled that they'd move him downstairs and have Buddy build a ramp so Tom could get to the garage, the therapist left and his father leaned back in his wheelchair. "I talked to Charley," he said. "You ain't got the stone for the island yet."

"I'm getting it. I talked to Charley this afternoon. He didn't tell you?"

"Talked to him yesterday. What's doin' out there?"

"Far as I can see everything's fine."

"You billing her?"

"Everything's fine." He didn't want to talk about Crown Island with his father.

"Fine, huh? You sure everything's fine?"

"Of course. I'm making sure I don't have to do it over again. My theory is you do it right and do it once."

"She bothering you at all?"

"Miss Wainwright? No. I think she's happy with the job."

"Keep her happy," he said. "But not too happy."

When Peter went downstairs his mother was waiting for him. "You going out tonight?"

"Just for a while," he said. "Don't worry, I'm not going to be out late. I have to get stone out to the island soon."

"How's your father?"

"The therapist wants him to move downstairs. We'll do it tomorrow. Buddy and me. Put him in the living room. It's what the therapist says we need to do."

Nancy Chello didn't look happy. "The living room?" she said.

"The dining room's too small for the hospital bed. And it's going to be good for him."

"I suppose," she said.

"It's just temporary."

"Right. He's beginning to look better."

"And acting more normal."

"I talked with Susan Carlson. Alice is starting to develop an Irish accent she says. You should call her. You can call, you know."

"I can never figure the time difference. I get it backwards."

"And she says you don't write. I don't see any of Alice's letters any more, either. Is there something wrong with you two?"

"No, she sends her letters to the office. I try to write. But I've been so busy. With the office stuff, and the payroll, and the payments on the equipment and the work I'm doing on the island. It's a lot to keep straight. I don't have all that much time to write Alice. But I do. I do."

On his way to the library he stopped at the CVS and bought three postcards with local scenes of Quarrytown harbor. He wrote a brief note on one of them, telling Alice how much he was thinking of her. Then on another he back-dated the card and wrote about how his father was getting along and how the therapist wanted him to keep active. In his heart, he knew that Alice didn't really care about any of that and all she wanted was for him to be romantic in his letters to her. But it wasn't that easy at the end of the day to come up with stuff that sounded reasonable.

Peter arrived at Crown Island with the stone he had chosen for the walkway. He told Marie he needed a day in the quarry to pick out the right stone for the job. Peter knew it would take a couple of days to unload the stone, so when Marie came up the path–walking among the flowerbeds–from her swim he told her he could not have coffee, but when he finished moving his quota of stones he would want to have lunch.

She pulled his work glove off, took his hand and turned it over to study his palm. She traced his lifeline and saw that it was unbroken and long. "You have strong hands," she said. He looked at them and saw they were rough and dirty from his work. "And your lifeline is very promising." She held her hand palm upward on his. "Like mine. We are long lived. Wouldn't it be nice if we were able to be happy as well?"

"Why wouldn't we be happy?"

He held her hand in his and looked down at it. "Your fate is to be loved," he said looking into her eyes. He was trying to be romantic. It didn't seem so difficult.

"Do you see that in my hand?"

"I see it in your eyes," he said, hoping that he sounded convincing.

"Do you see a hero come over the water to bring me cheer and love?"

"I see satisfaction." He touched the soft mounds at the

base of her fingers. "It may be joy, it may be fulfillment." He wanted to see something profound in her hand, something to make her feel that life was positive and that he saw a future filled with good fortune.

Still wet from her swim, she raised her hand and cupped his face, touching him tenderly. "You're very sweet to me," she said. "Very reassuring. I'll see you at lunch." She walked up to the house, bending now and then to pick a flower or straighten a plant. He could not take his eyes from her, watching her as if she were dancing through her garden. She captured his imagination and he wondered if he were really living through these days on Crown Island and if Marie were truly there, talking to him, a presence that made him aware of himself in ways that were new and wonderful.

The books they read together had reignited a sense of delight that he had almost lost. He had always been the reader in the family. His father was sometimes made suspicious by the books he stacked on his bedside table, but his mother was pleased to think that he read so much. The problem he faced at home was that he had no one to talk with about his books.

Shortly after noon, when he had unloaded more stones and placed them near where he planned to use them, he walked up to the house where Marie was setting the table on the verandah. The sun was high and the weather again was clear and dry. A few dark clouds hovered over the distant part of the Sound, near Long Island, but they would pass later in the afternoon and perhaps contribute to a dramatic sunset, but little more. These days had been unusually warm, but not hot.

"I have lemonade," she said as he came up to the table. "And ham sandwiches." She laid out a bowl of kalamata olives and brought out the rest of the meal passing him a bright green napkin. He didn't know whether he should risk getting it soiled, then he followed her example and placed it on his lap. She had changed into a white shirt and tan shorts. She was bare-footed and her gold necklace caught the sun as she pushed the olives across for him.

They talked about music at first, but then Peter asked her how her book was going. He had just taken out her two novels to read again.

"Do you believe in the muse?"

"I don't know. I've never tried to write."

"I do. I have always felt visited by the muse when I write. I think you may have brought the muse back to me."

"I don't know how, but I hope you're right. I'd love to read another of your books."

She took an olive and peeled it away from its pit before eating it. "You're very reassuring," she said.

Marie sometimes took her early morning swim with Jasper, who stood on the new stairhead watching for her return and when he saw her, he jumped in and went to meet her. When she rose from the water Peter had to stop his work and watch as she walked tenderly up through the flower beds. He was afraid he was falling in love. According to the card in the library she was only in her thirties. She was beautiful and her energy and charm made him feel more alive.

In *The White Wraith* he pictured the heroine, Cynthia Stiles, as Marie, and when she fell in love with the dark haired actor Alexander Rhinelander he imagined himself as a tall handsome actor in a Eugene O'Neill play, and wondered what it would be like to hear great applause. At one point, Peter thought that if Marie wanted him to go off with her, he would do so gladly. Like Alexander Rhinelander, what would he not do for a woman he loved?

A few days later, when he began setting stones close to the house in the walkway, he heard Marie typing in the upper room. He stood up and looked toward the window. He had not heard that sound since he had been on the island. The typing was rapid and intense, punctuated by short pauses. He imagined words flowing from her fingers, weaving themselves into sentences and thoughts evoking emotion from their eventual readers. He turned and added his own sounds with his father's chisel and hammer trimming the granite to make the stones fit aesthetically. With his head filled with ideas, Peter finally finished the walkway. The island was a paradise of flowers and birds.

Marie was typing vigorously when he was done. He gathered his tools and placed them in the skiff. He took his brooms and worked them over the stones a final time. Then he went down to the skiff and stood there in his boat looking at the stairs to see that they were well done. He studied them for a while, then took the first step and slowly walked back to the house, observing each careful fit, each shaped movement of the stones, and all the sloping patterning that would help make the walkway as permanent as a man could make it. Then he went inside and knocked on the wide banisters. The typing had already stopped and Peter imagined Marie sitting there thinking, visualizing her characters before moving on.

"So you've finished," she said, when she came to see what he had done. They went down the wooden steps of the verandah, and standing on the last step, Marie looked out at the gently swerving walkway. "It's quite like poetry," she said.

Peter hardly knew how to reply. "It's stone."

"Lyrical stone," she said. As she spoke, she took his arm and they walked down to the water, very slowly. They paused again and again as Marie marveled over the grace of the walkway. She cradled his arm and he felt her breast against him. Anyone cruising by would have thought them a couple having a romantic afternoon. "Now I will never be able to look at stone again the way I did. You've changed me."

Peter knew it was she who had changed him, but he said nothing.

"I want you to come back to the house," she said. "I have another project that I think you might be interested in taking on. It would mean a great deal to me."

It was then that Marie began discussing the idea of

adding on a large room that would be her library and workspace. "I'm working upstairs in a bedroom, and I never have the space I need, never have the books I need at hand." She drew a plan on a large sheet of paper. "Here's what I've been thinking of doing. I've drawn it so many times in my head that it seems almost real to me even now. Have you done anything like this before?"

Peter looked at her idea. "Sure. You'd need to make some changes, but it's the kind of thing I've done before."

"Would you do it for me?" she asked. She looked him in the eye and he knew he would do anything she asked.

CHAPTER FIVE
June-July 1971

Now that his cast was off and the ramp was in place, Tom was able to get around with his wheelchair. Peter rented a special van that could take him out to a job, if only to see what was being done. He was interested in Crown Island and asked more questions than Peter could answer. He wanted to know what Miss Wainwright was like, whether she approved the job he did, why it took him so long, and what it was she had in mind for Peter to do now.

"I could use you myself," his father said. "I can get Buddy, but I'd rather you."

"She wants me to put the addition on." Peter showed him the preliminary drawings he had made of the library.

"Oh," his father said, waving his hand in dismissal, "if Miss Wainwright says she needs you, then there's no question. How long you figure to take with this addition?"

Peter didn't know. "Could be until October. Depends on what I find when I see how I'm attaching it. Those old houses surprise you."

His father snorted. "That's a fact. You think she's gettin' soft on you?"

Peter redesigned the library and drew both a plan and an elevation so Marie could see what it would look like when he got it finished. He insisted on making the front a large bow window and angling the windows so the light would flood the room, but still make it possible to read throughout most of the day by natural light. When she saw the drawing, she looked up and told him, "It will be an inspirational space."

They got the foundation in without blasting, although it was not an easy job. The granite base of the island accepted the poured concrete, and since there was no intention of making a basement space, there was no need to dig below grade. Peter got Buddy to help him with some of the more difficult work and made a point of their eating lunch together on the skiff and avoided talking with Marie while Buddy was on the island. Once the space was framed and the rafters secure, Peter was on his own. He worked carefully through the mornings, breaking for lunch with Marie, who began reading to him as he sat with his iced tea. She read the love poems of Ovid, then the poetry of Propertius. He knew some of their poems by heart. He recited:

> *You, who in Cupid's rolls inscribe your name,*
> *First seek an object worthy of your flame;*
> *Then strive, with art, your lady's mind to gain:*
> *And, last, provide your love may long remain.*
> *On these three precepts all my work shall move:*
> *These are the rules and principles of love.*

Peter knew these rules and principles but they were still abstract to him. In his letters to Alice, he sometimes described the projects he developed on Crown Island without mentioning Marie's name. But he knew Alice was not interested in hearing about his working with stone or building with wood, and she would be incensed if she knew how he felt about Marie. Alice was filled with her own excitement of Galway evenings in Eyre Square watching Irish dancing in Cullen's and Irish Nights in the Great Southern Hotel with her cousins

By the end of July he was working entirely on the interior finish of the library. Marie had specified an expensive light cherry wood for the shelves that went around the room. Peter ordered it and waited, working on the walls and ceilings, installing the oak flooring. He had plenty to do while he waited for the wood to arrive.

By then, Marie began to talk about her life, pausing now and then to admit to her loneliness. "I have none of my father's abilities, and most of my mother's insufficiencies. They keep me here on my island, I'm afraid." She smiled wanly at him. "I suppose it's no crime to be lonely, and when I am not writing and when you are not here I am lonely. I admit it. Do you ever find yourself lonely, Peter?"

"Sure. Sometimes. Not here."

"Even when I am upstairs writing? Not even then?"

"I'm working then. I like hearing you work."

She rose and held out her hand to him. He took it and they walked the length of the verandah and looked out across the Sound. "Would you take me out on my boat this afternoon?"

"You mean the Petrel?"

"Yes, I've had Harold check it out. I know you're a good sailor."

They took his skiff to the mooring and got into Marie's sailboat, a wooden hulled twenty-seven foot Herreshoff design. It was a graceful old-fashioned sailboat. Peter took them out in his skiff, tied it to the mooring and climbed into the cockpit.

They had the sail up, the mooring cleared, and pointed themselves out to the deeper water in a little more than an hour. Marie brightened, and what Peter thought might have been a moment of darkness passed from her expression once the boat was under way. The sail began luffing between the islands until he set it straight and then watched it fill and take them out over the smooth water. He wanted to make for the open spaces as quickly as possible so that no one who knew his father would see him on a boat with his employer at a time when he should have been taping wallboard.

Marie's white scarf was wrapped around her face and over her hair. It rippled in the breeze and she smiled happily at him. "You are beautiful. Do you know that?"

He didn't know what to say. "I think you are beautiful," he said.

"Then we are both beautiful, aren't we?"

He laughed at the thought. "I guess we are, then," he

said.

She came to him and put her arm across his shoulder as he maneuvered the boat and picked up speed. It was at that moment he felt that they were two people quite alone, quite independent of the world, quite free to be and do what they pleased. It was unlike any feeling he had ever had. He did not want it to stop.

"This is the first time I've had the Petrel in the water since the accident."

They were clear of the islands, heading into the open water of Long Island Sound. The wind held light, but steady, and the boat moved effortlessly ahead.

"I thought it was time. Can you understand what I'm saying?"

"I think I know." He didn't want to speak directly to the accident. "Was there a storm when it happened?"

"No. No storm. They collided with a large powerboat going much too fast with no running lights. My daughters were found. My husband never was. They were coming back from a sunset cruise. It had become dark. I was on land, writing. There were times when I wished I had been with them. Maybe I could have helped."

"Not likely," Peter said. "You couldn't have helped. You might have died with them." He felt uneasy when she seemed depressed. What could anyone expect after losing an entire family at one stroke. He was very careful with the boat, watching the sky where a few dark clouds seemed louring. They were distant, but he was not anxious to take a chance.

Peter kept on a course for Long Island and eventually brought them in sight of the ferry station. The arriving Ferry loomed ahead of them, pounding toward the dock. People on the upper deck waved to him and he waved back. Marie stood close to him, touching. She seemed to be in a strange rapture. He studied her expression for a moment and saw that she was at peace.

"Should we pull up and stop here?" he asked.

Marie took the helm and headed the Petrel for a dock where several graceful sailboats were moored. "I know this place," she said. "We can put our feet up for a while and watch the world from a new direction."

She took them skillfully into a marina and threw a rope to a young man who helped secure the boat. They went down to the end of the pier and up into the Eagle Yacht Club's bright open restaurant on the water. They ordered tea and looked back toward the islands, which were completely invisible. A haze settled in and the clouds closed over enough to make the water a steely gray. This side of the Sound had become choppy.

"My father sometimes sailed over here. We would race the Petrel in those days. He was a very successful racer and I crewed for him. Those were gay times." Her happy memories seemed to bring a cheer to her expression and Peter thought she was more lovely to look at than at any time he had seen her. She seemed more tender of spirit, more warm and happy. He felt a strong urge to touch her, and when he did she placed her other hand over his. "You're very dear," she said. "You've made me very happy."

When they finished their salads Marie told him how the news of the accident came back to her. Marie had collapsed and ended up in the hospital in Elm City, hardly aware how she had gotten there. Her editor had flown from New York to arrange the memorial service in Quarrytown. But Marie did not quickly recover. She lived on the island in seclusion, which was how the rumors of her hermit-like behavior and her sense of despair had developed. She told him that she began to feel like herself only when she could write again. And she had only just been able to write, she said, "because you brought my muse back to me."

He held her hand. He had no idea how he had helped her, but he was glad that he had.

"Crown Island is curious," she said. "At one and the same time it is a prison and a paradise. I live with ghosts part of the time, spirits of people I loved dearly, but nonetheless spirits. When I am writing, it is a place apart, a world of its own, and I am as content as I think any person can be. I think there will never be a place that will be as dear to me, or that I will be able to live in that will make me feel as whole as I feel now. I suppose there is no way I could make you understand that."

"I like Quarrytown, too," he said. "I'm not sure I'd want to live on an island all the time, but I think I understand how you feel."

He felt an overwhelming surge of affection for Marie. As he held her hand he realized this was not a fantasy.

But as he sat there in a reverie, he saw the first drops of rain. "We've got to go," he said. "It's beginning to rain and we should get back."

Marie squeezed his hand. "You're right. I've probably worn you out with my talk."

"No, you didn't. I'd like to hear more, but we have to go."

Peter headed the Petrel back to the Connecticut shore just as the rain began to get serious. The wind was strong and easterly, so he made a powerful exit from the harbor and moved decisively back toward the Granite Islands. The light failed much more quickly than he'd expected, but he could still make out the landfall.

Marie found two yellow slickers and gave one to Peter. The water was rough with the beginnings of the storm. "I should have seen this," Peter said. "I wasn't thinking when we set out." Marie did not seem fearful, but the clouds grew darker and the rain stronger. When they pulled close to the Granite Islands they saw lightning strike far down the eastern shore-line. Peter did not want to be out on the water when the lightning reached Crown Island.

"Don't worry," he called out to her over the sound of the surf hitting the boat.

"I'm not worried. You're doing fine."

"We need to get in as quickly as we can." Lightning struck somewhere in front of them as he spoke and thunder exploded over their heads. He was afraid for the first time. The Petrel maintained its course. It was built to deal with this kind of weather, but he was concerned that he had let Marie's safety be threatened. Marie's story about the death of her family had made him aware of irony even as he struggled with the wheel to keep the boat on course.

Finally, he saw the island ahead. The lightning moved steadily toward them. The thunder crashed above them and the sea rose in their faces, but the Petrel remained steady. He had furled the mainsail and brought the boat in with the engine running steady. When they approached the mooring, Marie took the wheel. His boat was not there. It must have come loose in the storm. "My skiff is gone," he said.

Marie seemed to understand him, but her reply was lost in the sounds of the wind and water. She seemed to be telling him to catch the mooring, which he tried to do twice without success. Finally, leaning far over the bow, he affixed the chain and made sure it was solid.

Marie was drenched. "We're going to have to swim for it," she said, taking off her slicker and shoes. He looked at the distance and saw that it was only a hundred yards or so. He put his slicker below, along with his shoes. He thought of leaving his trousers below, and while he realized how embarrassing it might be, he knew he had to do it. They would slow him down, and they might be dangerous. He could come back for them when he found his skiff.

Finally, with spray on all sides, the lightning bearing near, and the noise of the water closing all around them, they leapt into the water and felt themselves borne immediately toward the island and both of them made for the cut where Aldridge Wainwright once worked on his boats. Marie got there first, clambered to her feet and reached out to him as he came in from the roiling water.

"It's beautiful," she said, when she got her breath.

"And dangerous. I'm glad we're here."

It was after nine o'clock and they were in the middle of an intense storm. "You can't go home tonight," she said. "You'll sleep here. We'll find your skiff in the morning." She went into the first floor bathroom and came back with towels. "Here. You're soaking." She began drying herself off and he wrapped a towel around his waist. He took his shirt off and dried himself with a second towel. She wrapped a towel around herself and dropped her shorts to the floor and then took off her yellow shirt and dried herself.

Jasper came to greet them from the large living room. The light switch was dead. Peter looked out the kitchen window to Maples Point. No lights. Quarrytown was dark. "We'll use a hurricane lamp," she said. She lighted a candle and held it as she opened a cupboard and took out an old-fashioned oil lamp. "These have been here since the beginning. And they work."

Peter moved to help her. She took the mantle off and set the wick. She used the candle to light it and as she did Peter's lips brushed her cheek. She turned smiling at him and kissed him softly and openly. He bent to her and felt her hand caress the back of his neck in such a fashion as no one had ever done before. As she put the mantle back on the lamp she touched his cheek again. "Should I have done that?"

"Yes," he said. "Yes." He was fearful that she would pull back in regret.

"You're very beautiful."

He kissed her again and held her close to him. He felt awkward and angry at himself for his inexperience. Yet he was here with Marie, and Marie held him and kissed him with a kind of passion he had only imagined.

Marie ran her fingers through his hair and held the lamp as they went up the stairs to the large bedroom that looked out at the lights of Long Island. Wordlessly, she took him to her bed and they made love. He tried to appear expert but the way he and Alice fumbled with each other was different from this. Marie seemed aware, but said nothing. And just as she was his teacher in love poetry, she was his teacher in love.

That night they made love several times and fell asleep in each other's arms. He told her he loved her and she told him she loved him in return. It was beyond all his fantasies. Even when she began crying early in the morning, before it grew light and as the rain still ran down the window panes, he was so deeply moved that he held her close to him and tried to be her protector. He had no idea why she cried, but he grew fearful and held her tighter.

"I'm all right," she said. He could barely make out her features in the dark. "It's just a release. It's like coming back to life. Can you understand?" She touched his hair and his face and kissed him gently. "I so hope you understand."

When they woke, the summer rain had begun to let up. Marie ran her finger down his nose and touched his lips. He kissed her finger. "Are you all right?"

"I'm fine," he said.

"You're not shocked?"

"It was wonderful."

They made breakfast together and Peter faced the prospect of going home. The power was back on in the harbor and things seemed normal. But Peter felt forever changed.

He put on an extra bathing suit hanging in Marie's hallway and went down to the dock to scour the vista for his skiff, but saw nothing. He walked around the side of the island and looked out toward Parker Island. Nothing there, either. He tried to imagine how the winds were blowing last night and which way they would have driven his boat, and after a short while realized that if it had washed up, it might be on Extra Island. He walked to the other side of Crown Island and after a search saw his beached skiff just as he hoped.

After struggling with the soggy fuel line and the stubborn engine, he got it started and went back to the Petrel.

He climbed aboard, checked the mooring to be sure it was secure, then went below for his trousers and his shoes. They were wet, but with the rain still intense, it made no difference. He got dressed, went back to the house and gave Marie a last kiss and held her for a long moment. Then he turned his skiff to the town dock.

CHAPTER SIX
August-September 1971

In August, when Alice came back from Ireland she brought Peter an Aran Island sweater, a book of Irish folk tales, and a picture of herself with eight of her eleven cousins, all on her mother's side. They were named Brennan and Raftery and Hughes and all of them were red-cheeked and most were red-headed except for the dark-haired Brennans who stood a head and shoulder above the rest. Peter sat in the Carlson's living room the day after Alice came home and listened to her stories about pub crawls and how they lighted Merchants Row in the evening with colored lamps strung across the street as if they were having a fair. She described the Uillean pipes in Cullen's and the way the waitresses dressed in The Great Southern. She talked about hearing Irish spoken in the evening on Claddagh Quay and how they took a class trip to Oughterard looking for some lost gravesite that was still mysterious to her. But mysterious or not, it was an adventure. And she brought back all the news to her mother, Susan, about what the cousins were up to and how they kept a picture of Susan's mother on the mantelpiece as a remembrance. It brought tears to Susan's eyes and when Peter looked over at Harry Carlson he thought he detected a touch of boredom.

"Galway was great," Alice said. "The courses I took were really hard, but I'm glad I did it. I was scared at first."

Alice was so filled with the excitement of her semester abroad that she hardly seemed aware of him. Before she left she had said that this would be a test of their love and that she knew they would both pass it. He said he knew that too. Now he was not sure. Alice was a pretty girl, like her mother, with a bright, open disposition and a cheerful smile when she was happy. But like her father, when she was unhappy, her countenance darkened into a somber indifference that Peter could never penetrate. Fortunately, her time in Ireland had brought out the best in her.

Alice was aware that Peter wanted to go back to the University someday. She seemed reluctant to talk about it at first, but eventually she listened as he explained things. He might go back when his father could take the business on again. That might be two years, or it might be a little more. He wanted Alice to know that he was glad he did what he did, glad that he could keep Chello & Son going. If he hadn't he didn't know what his parents would have done or how they would have lived. Alice seemed to understand. In fact, she seemed to take what he did as being the most natural thing in the world. She touched his hand as he explained things and she smiled at him. "It was the right thing to do," she said.

They had only two weeks together until Alice began the new semester in Kingston. She had some complications because of her classes in Galway. She was sure things would work out, but because the overseas program was relatively new, nothing was going to be easy. Peter tried to follow her discussion, but had a difficult time. What he did see, however, was that Alice was happier than when she had left Quarrytown, and she seemed more aware of herself. She had absorbed a tinge of an Irish accent, which had put him off at first.

In one way she had not changed. She did not ask him anything further about his work or his deepest concerns. She assumed that he was the same person she had left in February.

When they were first alone, she complained about his letter writing.

"You never wrote to me," she said.

"I did write."

"Maybe once a month." She looked at him hopefully. "Peter, you'll write me at URI, won't you?"

"Sure."

"And you'll come on weekends?"

"When I can. Sure. And you'll come home."

"I won't be able to come home that much if I'm going to graduate on time. So I have to depend on you. I'm going to need plenty of support and plenty of caring from you if I'm going to get through this semester. I student teach my last semester. So that will be different."

"Sure."

"That's what you always say. You've got to mean it."

"I mean it."

Their last evening was supposed to be an evening out, but Alice had to get clothes ready and Harry had to pack the car, so instead of their being alone, they spent their time at the Carlson's, with Alice's father occasionally praising the space in the car because he couldn't believe he could get "all that stuff" into it. Peter was secretly glad that there were so many distractions. He kissed Alice goodbye and when she pouted at him, he told her he loved her still and that he would write. He heard Harry Carlson in the living room complaining about how much stuff they had to take as he left the house.

The long wait for the cherry wood that Marie ordered for the library shelves was over, but now that it was delivered, he had a great deal of work to get the finish exactly right. Marie was paying him for excellent work, not acceptable work. His father wondered why it took him so long, while his mother marveled at the fact that Miss Wainwright wanted him to work so steadily over such a period of time.

The job progressed while Marie worked on her book each morning until late lunchtime. Peter made a point of arriving early so they could have a cup of coffee after her swim. Marie was careful to kiss him inside the house and not where people could see them, although she said she did so only to protect him. He did not want to be protected, despite her reasoning. "You may change your mind," she said.

"Never." He kissed her on the verandah where any passing boat could see them. He imagined that if they were seen people would think of them as lovers–or possibly just as a married couple. He did not care.

Marie's recordings and her typewriter were steady and intense, and he set up his table saw in the middle of the library to work with the beautiful wood she had ordered. Its surfaces were smooth and rich and he respected the wood the way his father had taught him. He beveled edges carefully and counter-sank the nails as he constructed the shelving. He installed a railing high in the hexagonal space and attached a cherry ladder fitted with brass rollers so that Marie could reach the top shelves on all sides, including those over the windows and over the large door ways.

He had the shelving in place late in September. Alice's letters from URI were filled with complaints about her roommates and her problems getting credit for the work she did in Galway. Peter managed to write back, although not each week. He hit upon the scheme of including a poem in each letter. It helped him fill out the pages. Alice always asked him to write more, but his natural inclination was to write less. He avoided visiting on weekends by telling her he had to work overtime for his father and describing how his father still needed a wheelchair and still had to be careful of himself. Her own pressure kept her at school.

His happiest moments were in the late afternoons on Crown Island.

He told Marie that he had to keep a minimum of progress on the library. He was working on the interior finish now. The roof was on, the windows in, and the shingling was carefully matched to the rest of the house and carefully painted. If he got his minimum done, he felt less guilty when he lay in Marie's arms on her long cushioned sofa while she read to him, or when he sat with a cup of coffee listening to her play the piano and sing the songs she loved.

Through the summer, they read Ovid's *Metamorphoses*. Then Virgil's *Aeneid* and then his *Georgics*. They read plays together aloud, *Agamemnon, Antigone, Medea, The Trojan Women,* and *Bacchae*. Marie read with lovely expression. She had performed in some of these plays in college. He also browsed her bookshelves and read in Plutarch. Those were the only times he did not regret leaving the University where he could have read such books. For him, and for now, Crown Island was his college.

Marie had seen Peter driving past the Café with Alice in the passenger seat the Sunday before Alice went back to school. Alice was talking about where they ought to look for a house when they got married and Peter noticed Marie turn toward his truck as he approached the Café. Marie wore a yellow scarf and held a paper cup of coffee in one hand and a book in the other. She saw him and he could not wave. He felt a tightness in his stomach and knew it was the physicality of guilt.

"You have a girlfriend named Alice," Marie said when he came to the island on Monday. "You never told me."

"She was away in Ireland."

"But she's still your girlfriend."

Peter didn't know what to say.

"It's all right," she said. "I wasn't claiming you forever. I'm very glad you have a girl your own age. Are you planning to marry her?"

"We've talked about it, but . . . ."

She raised her hand to stop him. She was smiling at him. "Peter, I don't love you less for that. You will want to marry. You should marry and have children. I could never have children again. I couldn't."

"If you don't want children . . . ."

"You must have children. You deserve to have children. Does Alice know about us?"

"God, no. I've never mentioned you to her. I've hardly

mentioned working on Crown Island. Alice isn't curious about what I do." He watched Marie's expression. "I'm trying to think of a way to break it off with Alice."

"No. You can't break it off. You shouldn't break it off."

"What do you mean?"

"You'll leave me. When your work is done."

"No."

"You're very sweet," she said, kissing his forehead. "And very sincere. But I know more about the world than you. I know how you'll leave. And I'll have to let you go. But not yet." She put her finger on his lips. "You are very important to me. And love is very important to me. I want you to promise me that you will leave me when it is time, but not before."

"I can't promise that."

"Before we hurt each other," she said.

"We are not going to hurt each other. Have I hurt you? Have you hurt me?"

"Not yet," she said. "Not yet."

"I think I should tell everyone about us."

"No," she said quietly. "No." She leaned and kissed him.

He lay there thinking he should be more heroic, more like the characters in the dramas they read together. His threat to tell the world was an idle boast. He had done his best to keep their love secret. "I'd like it to be different," he said finally.

She laughed. "Could it be more beautiful?"

"I don't think so."

"Then why would you want it to be different?"

He turned and kissed her. She was right. He did not want it to be different if it were not more beautiful. And now he felt their love was a beautiful thing, something impossible except in the fantasies he had woven for himself in those early weeks working on the island. Such fantasies, he had told himself then, never come true.

A few days later, his father wheeled into the work shed

while Peter was unloading some of his gear after work. Tom was getting stronger, but still moving slowly and in pain. He quizzed Peter about how things were progressing on Crown Island. "It's going pretty slow," he said. "When'll you be done?"

"It's going about as fast as I can do it."

"Maybe you should ask Buddy or Beady to come out and help you."

"No," he said, trying not to respond too quickly. "No, I can work on it alone. Miss Wainwright understands. I'm doing a good job. Beady's with Packy on Kidd's Island and Buddy's tied up with the Steiner problem. I'm on top of it. The library finish work has to be good because the wood is expensive. I also faced the foundation with stone, so that took me a little time. I hope I'll be done in October." But as he said the words he could not imagine himself finishing any project that would take him away from Crown Island. What would he do if he could not get back to see Marie?

"What is she like?" his father asked. His father looked at him doubtfully. "Does she treat you okay?"

"Sure."

"Not snooty?"

"No, she just writes when I'm there. Or works in the garden. I hear the typewriter going most of the time. She's writing a new book."

"And she's a lonely woman."

"She says she doesn't get lonely," Peter said.

"I think she does." They stood silently for a moment. His father looked around for a tool. He seemed about to say something more to Peter, but then held back. "I wanna thank you," he finally said. "For what you did."

"I'm just glad you're getting better. Maybe next year I can go back."

"Yeah." His father turned and busied himself looking for some scrap trim.

Peter walked out of the shed and downhill to Granite

Street. He wanted to get in his skiff and go back to Crown Island, but he just wandered down to the dock and stood looking into the water. Steve Clements was loading an evening cruise in *The Lost Penny*. Japanese lanterns hung from the rigging and lively music came from the boat. It was a party. People were happy and some of them were probably in love. Peter wanted things to be different from the way they were.

CHAPTER SEVEN
October 1971

Tom Chello knew that Peter sometimes read books that Marie Wainwright lent him. His father was suspicious of books, especially with names and authors that sounded strange and unfamiliar. He had asked Peter about Oedipus, a name he could not pronounce. Peter told him how Oedipus had killed his father and married his mother, and when Tom heard that he looked horrified. "What kind of book is that?" he asked. "How could he marry his mother and not know it?" his father asked him. Peter tried to explain. "And why did he kill his father"

"But he didn't know. He was living out his fate even though he was trying to do everything to avoid it. He even moved away from the people he thought were his real parents so he wouldn't kill them."

"We're your real parents," his father said very solemnly. "You can be assured of that. And I don't think I want those kinds of books in my house." Peter thought he was serious.

Peter's afternoons with Marie were a treasure. After work, they read together, talked together, and listened to music together. "I'll be finished with the library in a few weeks. I don't want to leave."

"I have nothing more for you to build."

"I wouldn't have to build something to stay with you."

She smiled, but he saw that it was a knowing smile, a tolerant smile. "Couldn't I help you with your writing?"

She shook her head.

"You never read your work to me."

"No, my sweet. It's part of my ritual not to read to

anyone. It's for the same reason that I never talk about what I'm writing. I'm afraid of losing it."

He did not understand, but he knew she meant what she said.

Their afternoons began around three o'clock. She was happy when the writing went well, just as he was happy when his work went well. He spent time cleaning up, ordering his tools for the morning. Peter did not tell Marie that sometimes in the evening he went to the Quarrytown Library to read about Greek and Roman religion and history. Then, when they read together, he felt less ignorant and she seemed more pleased when he spoke sensibly about Greek culture.

Their afternoons were romantic only in the sense that they were close to one another. Often they would lay side by side touching. But they rarely made love in the afternoon. Peter's parents grew accustomed to his being out late. Sometimes he told them he was going to the Nickel Plate Saloon to see some friends or down to the park to see a game, but some nights he took his skiff out to the island. He had the skiff moored to a distant stake where it could not easily be seen from the gazebo on the dock, where, before he was hurt, his father sometimes sat talking and smoking with other men in the evening. When he arrived at Crown Island, he pulled his boat up onto the sand so it could not be seen from the water.

Those evenings felt stolen, but delicious He talked with Marie about his feelings.

"I want to love you in the open," he said.

"I know."

"But you won't let me."

"No."

"You think I'll leave you."

"Yes. But not now."

"I don't think I understand. Does it have something to do with fate or something like that?"

"I've had some experience with fate. I think I understand

fate. But I also think I understand love better than you do. I've stolen you, don't you see."

"You couldn't have stolen me. I was a willing victim." He smiled at her.

"You think so now. But the truth is that I have stolen you from time, and soon I will have to give you back. I have no choice. The gods will it."

"The gods are cruel."

"If you've learned nothing else from our reading, you have learned that. The difference between us is that I have learned how cruel the gods are from life as well as from literature. No matter how cruel the gods may be, I will not be cruel to you."

"We can't be cruel to each other."

"If I don't give you up, I will have been very cruel to you." She kissed him to stop him from talking. "An evening will come," she said. "And it must come. And we will be unhappy, but tonight let us be as happy as we can be."

Peter knew from Roman poetry that after lovemaking all creatures were sad, but he never felt sadness. His heart was joyful when he took his skiff away from the island. He only felt unhappiness in the thought that he could not stay and wake in Marie's arms the way he did the night of the storm. It would have been so much better. But no matter how he protested, Marie always insisted that he leave and return in the morning.

It was more and more difficult to write to Alice. He had so little to say to her that it was painful to try to fill a single page. Peter would look at the blank paper and write in large strokes. He knew he could never write fewer than two pages in any letter. When he did, Alice complained that he didn't love her.

"I do love you," he told her when she came home for a weekend. But Alice seemed not to hear him. She told him about her roommates and their local boyfriends and how they took over their room and she had to read in the library until late at night, or else she would get nothing done. Alice seemed to have many problems and many complaints. When Alice began discussing their plans for the future, Peter had very little to say to her.

"After next semester I'll be finished," she said. "Then you should be looking for a house for us. I still have enough from my grandmother's inheritance. We can use that for a down payment even if we have to rent something at first. After that, we can save my salary and then we'll have enough for a better place. Then we can have our babies. I'll have maternity leave by then."

Alice expected to teach at the middle school, where she had been a student and where she knew the system. Mrs. DiCarlo, her seventh-grade teacher, said they would need teachers when she graduated, and she kept in touch so she would not be forgotten. As she spoke, Peter began to think that Quarrytown was a very small place. Crown Island felt larger.

Over the weekend, when they went to the movies in Franklin to see a French film, Peter began talking about its connection to Medea, but Alice had never heard of Medea. She complained about the subtitles and decided they shouldn't see any more French films unless they had the intelligence to speak in English. After the film, they dropped in on a party at Packy Caserto's new apartment. He had finally moved out of his mother's place. Packy had the Beatles going full blast on the stereo. Most of the guys drank too much, and Alice worried him, too, with the way she put down the beers. She got talking with a girl from UConn who was going to become a high school teacher. They both compared notes, and both seemed a little drunk. After a few minutes Peter went into the kitchen, grabbed a beer, and talked with Packy. Packy and his older brother Beady were replacing windows in a house on Kidd's Island, and talked about the weird things they found when they dug around in the old walls.

"There's treasure on Kidd's Island," Packy said.

"We never saw any."

"It's buried, stupid. Pirates used the island."

"Somebody would have found it by now."

"I told you, it's in a cave below water line."

"That's got to be a shallow cave, then," Peter said. "How deep can the water be around Kidd's Island?"

"In places it's deep."

"You've been snorkeling out there or something?"

"I bet there's treasure even out on Crown Island. I'll bet that's why they call it by that name. I heard someone once found crowns and half-crowns out there."

"There's no treasure there," Peter said. "Those coins were planted." He had no idea if they were or not, but he was desperate enough to lie to keep Packy from nosing around Crown Island. "Besides, if there were any old treasure there it would be pieces of eight and Spanish doubloons, not English crowns."

"Yeah, I guess. Kidd's Island is more likely."

Peter and Buddy had fantasized for years about finding Kidd's missing treasure on one of the islands. When they were twelve or so, they dug up parts of Kidd's Island and got chased off by residents who complained to their fathers.

After the party, Alice led them back to her house. She was trying to pretend she was completely sober, but she almost fell off the seat of the pickup when he opened the door. Her parents were long since in bed, so they tip-toed down to the family room. They closed the door and turned the radio on low. Elvis was singing "You Don't Have to Say." Alice turned it off and turned on the TV and stood a few moments looking at the picture come into focus. She turned the volume low so that it sounded as if they were just sitting there watching a movie.

Alice told him her roommate was having sex with her boyfriend and wanted to know if she and Peter had gone "all the way." "What did you say?" Peter asked.

"I wasn't sure what to say." She lost her balance as she sat on the couch next to him.

"You promised your parents you wouldn't, though."

"I know. I didn't tell her that."

"What did you tell her?"

"That we were having sex, too."

They had come close more than once, but they had always held back. His lovemaking with Marie gave him even more reason to hold back again, but when they began to kiss and fondle, Peter knew that Alice had forgotten her promise.

"You want to?" she asked him softly. He hesitated. She pulled back. "You want to, don't you?"

"Of course, of course."

They made love with the flickering of the TV lighting the room and the soft dialogue and background music of a romantic film blurring their own sounds and their own passion. Later, she cried softly and rested her head on his chest, and just said, over and over, quietly, "Oh, Peter, Oh Peter."

When he was home, Peter thought about Alice's refrain, "Oh, Peter," and knew that life had suddenly become much more complex. Alice had fashioned his fate by establishing her expectations of him so firmly and so soon. They were sweethearts and they would follow through on the plans Alice had spelled out for them. What happened tonight was just another step in those plans. In his own way, Peter had been faithful to Marie by not telling Alice about their love. And because he could not tell Alice that another reason existed for them not to make love, fate pressed him onward.

Peter understood expectation as well as obligation. His mother loved Alice and encouraged Peter to make plans for marriage. Alice was clear-headed and practical, and her relationship with his mother was so close at times that Alice could have been the daughter she never had. When home from school, Alice seemed to be in his mother's kitchen more than in her own. She and his mother talked about cooking and clothes. Alice made special dishes and brought them to his house to share. She made blackberry jam, layer cakes, macaroni salads, three-alarm chili, special ravioli, and tomato sauces, all of which his mother said were exquisite. Over the years, Peter's mother had come to love Alice in such a way that he knew if he did not follow through on their plans he would not only break Alice's heart, but his mother's as well. His circumstances, which had seemed so simple only months ago, now took on a faintly Greek cast.

Alice went back to college a much happier woman. She pledged him to write and told him how much his letters meant to her. When she left, he wondered what their life would be like, how he would live without Marie and their afternoons and evenings of sweet pleasures.

"You have found a marvelous woman," his mother told him. "She's a solid person, if you know what I mean. Real down-to-earth and solid. No pretenses."

"I know."

"You hold onto her, you hear?"

"Right."

"Don't do anything stupid."

"I'm not going to do anything stupid."

"Your father seems worried about you."

"You don't need to worry. Nobody needs to worry. I've got some work to do."

She did not say so at first, but Peter's evenings at the library, and the books he brought home with him, confused her. She asked him early on why he was going to the library so much, and he told her that he needed to read some good books so he would not remain ignorant. He instantly regretted saying that to his mother.

"I sure don't have time to read anymore. At the end of the day I'm too tired. I fall asleep in front of the TV. How you can read all that Greek stuff. It's all Greek to me," she said laughing.

But Peter was saddened. Marie was the only person he could share his thoughts with.

Monday was a brilliant, sunny day. The wind was light, but gusty and would have been perfect for another sail. Peter was about to suggest that they take the Petrel out later in the afternoon, but then remembered that Marie could not sail today. "My publisher and my editor are coming. They will be here for lunch and stay overnight."

"From New York?"

"Yes. We're going over my new book. There are some things I want to be sure they do correctly."

After they had coffee, Marie went back upstairs and began typing. She put on some of her favorite music. Peter went into the library and worked on finishing trim and hardware. Some of the fits were not as snug as he wanted, so he went over his past work and got the details right. He worked out a lighting system in the shelves that would help Marie on cloudy days or in the evening when she needed to find a book. He fed the wiring carefully under the trim.

The book people arrived on the *Albertus*, the small ferry Steve Clements operated regularly up to the end of October. They were both younger than Marie, but older than Peter. The man, Charles Stallings, Marie's publisher, wore a dark blue suit and a dark striped tie. When he approached the open door he called out Marie's name and she came running down the steps as happy to see him as she seemed to be when Peter came to the door.

"That's one of the last quartets I hear," he said brightly.

"Right."

"Inspiring stuff," he said. "Last time I was here it was Wagner. Much darker then." He laughed. "Oh, I love coming here. It's otherworldly."

"Hello, dear," Sybil Forstner, Marie's editor, said. She gave Marie a hug and Stallings kissed Marie on the lips.

They all talked busily and Marie whisked them into the kitchen where she had some cold soup and sandwich makings.

They chattered cheerily and Peter heard Marie's accent in the man's speech, while Sybil Forstner sounded like a professor on TV.

He continued the wiring, which had to be precise and careful if it weren't to be seen from the outside. He had wrapped the wiring in a thin tubing so that it would handle more easily and so it would be virtually invisible. The tubing was held in place by special clips that he adapted from a commercial design. When it was done, the effect would be very dramatic.

When he moved to one of the next shelves, he saw the three of them sitting at the marble table in the kitchen, although they could not see him. He watched them laugh and gesture with such confidence and intimacy that he began to feel how different he was from them. His task was to work carefully and surely, and to be sure to avoid these people. He would not have understood them.

Charles Stallings said something about a writer whose name Peter could not make out. Sybil said that the writer would have liked the quiet and the beauty of Crown Island. Marie talked about one of his books, but Peter could not follow the conversation. There was apparently a new translation of his book on swans. He couldn't hear it clearly because his own work was noisy. But they raved about him and he knew the writer must be good and he should know him. He found himself sinking inwardly as he worked the wiring into its proper place. There was so much that Marie knew that he would never know. He wasn't sure if he had ever heard any music by Wagner, or what they meant by the last quartets.

He broke for lunch and took the skiff to the mainland. When it was lunchtime, Marie and the publishing people were deep in conversation, drinking from her best glassware, totally unaware of anything outside their circle. So he went into the Quarrytown Café and ordered a sandwich and read the house newspaper. Franny Bond came over and refilled his coffee. "How are things out on the island?" she asked. She had a conspiratorial expression on her face, but Peter decided to ignore it.

"Work, work, work," he said. "I had to take a break."

"I'll bet," she said, and left him alone.

Packy Caserto came in with Buddy Dooley and they put their coffees down on his table. "What happened to you and Alice the other night?" Packy asked.

"We got tired."

"Oh yeah, I bet." Packy snorted maliciously. "So you both thought it was bedtime, right?"

"Don't fool around," Peter said.

Buddy started whistling the "Wedding March."

Packy laughed and went off for their sandwiches. "Don't see you for lunch a long time now," Buddy said. "You still on Crown Island?"

"Yeah."

"What's up with that woman? I saw her at the post office a couple of weeks ago. She's never in town. Bet she's a nice piece of ass." Packy smirked.

"Come on," Peter said. "She's had a lot of tragedy in her life."

Buddy came back with their sandwiches. "How's the white witch out there?"

"Jesus, she's not a witch."

"She's out there on the lawn in the dark sometimes," Packy said. "I saw her a couple of times coming back from Distant Island. She just stands there. I waved once, but she never waves back."

"She's too important to wave back," Buddy said. "She's a big deal. You know that."

"Yeah, she's really stuck up," Packy said. "Ain't that right?"

"I don't know," Peter said. "I just work there."

"What's that addition? A dining room or something?"

"It's a library."

Buddy laughed. "What the hell's a library? Who needs a library? We got a library right here in Quarrytown. What's she need a library for?"

"She's weird," Packy said.

"She's a writer. She needs a room for her books."

"I bet she'd be a great lay," Packy said. "Probably really needs it, too. You know what I mean?"

Peter wasn't going to say a word. He tried to look unconcerned.

"Good bod," Buddy said. "I wouldn't mind gettin' into her pants."

"Maybe I'll drop by and offer my services," Packy said. "She's gotta be desperate for it."

"Maybe she's queer," Buddy said.

"Nah, the lezzies'd be out there all the time. She's prime, baby."

"She ever put the moves on you?" Buddy asked.

Peter shook his head.

"Did I ever tell you about Mrs. Stearn on Moss Point Road?" Packy said. "Jeez. I come to work one morning–I'm putting in a new bathroom downstairs–and I hear this call from the hall upstairs and I come to the foot of the stairwell and there she is in a white bathrobe calling down to me and as she's telling me what she wants me to do, the robe opens up and, wa-la, there's everything on view. I look up and she goes on talking and leaning on the bannister like nothin's happened, and I say I'm sorry? and she goes on about how the water in the upstairs bathroom is not as hot as she wants it and she expects me to come up and do something about it."

"So what'd you do?" Buddy asked.

"Well, you know she's not a bad looker, and I figured maybe there's something I could help her out with and I go upstairs and she doesn't bother to fix her robe, so I can't get my eyes off those tits. Man, I didn't know she was that built, you know? And I find that she's got the bathtub filled with soapy water and she asks me is that hot enough. So I put my hand in it and it's good and warm, just right. I tell her it's great. She feels it herself, then says do I think it's the right temperature for a bath, and I say, yeah. Hop in."

"So what'd she do?"

"Christ, she drops the robe and steps in, real ginger like, and sits down. Then she says, 'Do my back, will you?' So I look around. Who knows, the husband could still be there. I didn't want to get shot or anything. Donny Stearn is a mean mother when he wants to be. So I figure no one else is there and she's looking up at me wondering what I'm going to do, so I take the washcloth from her and start rubbing her back, and I get a hardon you wouldn't believe, and she sees it. And I think, O shit, and what does she do but while I'm rubbing her back with the soapy water she reaches around and grabs the front of my trousers, getting them all wet, and I yell. And she says, 'What's wrong, I just wanted to see if it's real,' so I tell her it's very real, and she"--Packy leaned over and talked much softer so no one else nearby would hear--"she says to me, 'If it's so real, why don't you take it out and show me,' and I think, what is this, some kind of trick. Maybe she doesn't want to pay me for the job. I don't know. I never got into anything like that before and it could have been anything. I mean, I don't know what's going on, and before I can do anything, I'm still rubbing her back and she tries to unzip my pants, and all the while she's getting me soaking wet. She can't get the zipper because there's too much soap on her hands, so she gets up on her knees and pulls me by the belt buckle so I fall into the tub and half drown, and while my head's into the goddam soap suds, she's pulling my pants down and I lose my hardon because I'm fighting for my life in the water. I'm thinking, this lady's going to drown me if I'm not careful, but suddenly I come up for some air, and she's got the pants down and I'm bareassed in the water with her and the goddam water is splashing all over the floor and I'm thinking Christ there's going to be a flood if this keeps up. And what does she do but start laughing. No shit. She's laughing like hell and I try to get my balance in the tub and she's got my cock in her hand and pumping like mad and I come all over her and she laughs like hell. 'This is fun,' she says but she doesn't let go and I am almost dying from the come and then I feel her pulling off my shoes and taking the pants and she puts them into the tub with us, so I can't hop out and get dressed or anything."

"Why would you want to hop out?"

"So she gets me to take off my shirt, and I start laughing now, because I'm so happy I didn't drown, and I am also very happy that I decided to come upstairs and see what I could do to help her. And we're sitting there in the tub, the two of us, laughing like mad and she grabs my cock again and I feel her tits and she starts laughing all over again. Then she splashes me and I splash her and the frigging water is all over the floor, soapsuds everywhere. She's got this fancy bath oil shit that foams up like shaving cream or something. You never saw anything like it. I say to her 'This is great,' and she kisses me. She actually kisses me and then she's back at my cock again and I come again and she won't stop and I'm yelling and she's laughing like mad. So she stands up in the tub and looks down on her tits, all covered with this soapsud stuff because I've been rubbing them and she tells me, 'Lick it off.' I say, 'What?,' and she says, 'Lick it off my tits,' just like that."

"So what'd you do?"

"So I licked it off. It tasted good, like some kind of flower stuff. I don't know what, but it wasn't bad, and what a kick. She was like coming herself so I kept on licking, and I got it up again and she tried to put me in, but the tub was too small, so we are climbing out and she loses her footing and I grab her and keep her up and then I lose my footing, and we end up with me sitting on the toilet and her across my lap and everything fits just like it should and what a ride we had. Jesus, I thought with the noise she made the Hendersons next door would be in with the fire marshal any minute, and she would not stop, just kept on going.

And was she slippery. I try to hold on to her ass, but she slips away, and her tits are bouncing all over me as she's humping up and down and I'm coming and she's coming and both of us are like wailing and when we are out of breath, she leans back and shakes her tits at me and grins. 'What a performance,' she says. 'Wow.'"

Packy stopped and began eating his sandwich. Both Peter and Buddy were open-mouthed. "So what did you do?" Peter asked.

Packy took a hit of coffee. "We got up and she took a washrag and washed me off, then washed herself off and then she got the towels and we dried each other off, real careful like. I patted her tits and her bottom real careful and she just dried me all over and then she wrapped the towel around her head, took my clothes and threw them into the drier and then she takes me downstairs, both of us butt naked, and we have a nice lunch. Just like now. Only the two of us are leaning over the table and she kisses me like she really likes me, and I think, this is one hell of a job I got here. Maybe she's got some more work for me. Maybe we can take another bath in the new bathroom when I get it done."

Packy looked out the window to the Long Island Sound. He looked at the expressions on Buddy's and Peter's faces. "But you know what happened?"

They shook their heads.

"We get all dressed. She tells me she's never felt so good. She touches my cock once more for good luck, I guess, and then she goes out and starts up her 280SL and drives off. And when I come back the next day she's out shopping or something. And every day after that I'm working on the new bathroom, and I don't see her except when she comes in and says she'll see me later and then she's off. I get the picture pretty soon. It's like I never existed. She just got what she wanted and that was it. I thought we could have a little thing going there, but you know there was never anything there. She just got excited one day and

I guess she did what they say in the ladies magazines. She acted out a fantasy. I read that in the unisex place where I go. When I read it I figured out just what it was all about. I thought I was balling her but she was balling me."

"You never told me any of this shit."

"We weren't working together. You were away."

"Yeah, but jeez. You get any of that kind of shit out on the island?" Buddy asked Peter.

Peter shook his head.

"Man, I'd be up for that," Buddy said.

"Yeah, well we better be up and outta here or Tom'll have our ass."

Peter sat there while Packy and Buddy trailed out and down the steps to their pickup. He got himself another cup of coffee and tried to believe Packy's story. Packy was a notorious story teller, but sometimes the stories he told were true. This one sounded true to him, but you could never tell with Packy. He was not a bad looking guy. He was strong, and he was pretty big. Who knew?

Sitting there alone, Peter reflected on the conversation of Marie's publisher and editor that made little or no sense to him. He hadn't heard much of it in a consistent way. He had to move around the library and sometimes all he heard was their laughter. They were staying overnight and Marie told them she had made up two rooms with wonderful views, and Peter wished he could have been with them. Stallings, the publisher, mentioned some important writers Peter had not read and some he had never heard of. He took out his carpenter pencil and wrote down two of the names he recognized, Babel and D. H. Lawrence, and then he stopped. There had been more names, but he didn't recognize them. He wondered why Marie had never mentioned these writers to him. How was he expected to know about these people? They must have been important or else the publisher wouldn't have mentioned them. And both Marie and her editor knew who they were. If he had stayed in the

University maybe he'd have studied some of them. But, then, if he had stayed in the University he would not have Marie in his life. Sometimes fate was a matter of choices. But you never really knew what your choices would produce.

He felt a subtle ache in the center of his chest when he despaired at ever knowing who these writers were or why they were important. He decided not to go back to the island today. Tomorrow he would stay away, too. It was too painful to be there with people talking about things that made no sense to him. He felt ignorant and abandoned because Marie had not introduced him to those people. When they were on the island she seemed not to be aware of him at all.

The library in Franklin had two books of short stories by D. H. Lawrence, but nothing by Isaac Babel. He tried to remember some of the other names the editor mentioned, but the librarian could not help him. He sat and read some of Lawrence's stories. They weren't bad, but some of them did not make a great deal of sense to him. One was about a boy riding a hobby horse thinking he was in some kind of race, but he couldn't tell quite what it was. He read a story about miners in England somewhere. It was so depressing he stopped reading altogether. How could this be so important? Or was he missing something?

Peter sat with the book on his lap and began to reflect on Packy's story. He had seen Alicia Stearn in the Quarrytown Café. She was very sexy looking and her visiting friends always seemed a little fancy for Quarrytown. Packy's story made him wonder about women like Mrs. Stearn. She was probably around Marie's age, but he could not be sure. They might be friends, but, then, he had never seen them together. All he really knew about Mrs. Stearn is that she was from New York and had lots of money. Her husband, Donny, now worked in Elm City at a bank. Peter saw him in church or going into the liquor store at 4-corners, or at the Christmas holiday sings and pageants. Once, Donny Stearn stood talking with Marie down at the town dock when she waited for the ferry. He knew a lot of people in Quarrytown.

Peter got home late and went right to bed. In the morning he got a cup of coffee at the Café and drove into Elm City and went to the University library. The woman at the main desk looked at his list of authors and gave him a call number for the stories of Isaac Babel. She also told him the book on swans was probably by Aldous Huxley and she told him to check the card catalog. He went to the card catalog and found Aldous Huxley's *After Many a Summer Died the Swan* and began reading it. It was good, but it didn't sound like the book they were talking about, especially since this was not translated from another language. Still, it was pretty interesting and he thought he should read some more books by Huxley. The name was definitely familiar to him, so he felt a little more comfortable with it. But the stories by Isaac Babel left him cold. They were curious, but he didn't see what the big deal was. Martha Gellhorn did nothing for him, and he couldn't see why she was important, if she was in fact the one they talked about. His experience in general with these authors made him feel left out. What was it Marie and her editors saw that he did not see?

He looked at his watch and wondered if he'd meet any students he knew. He'd been away and wasn't sure whether anyone from his class would be in the library at this hour. It didn't seem likely, and besides, he didn't feel he would have much to say to anyone he'd known when he was a student here. All he'd be able to say is that he was working and might be able to come back to school some day, but he did not know when. It was better, he thought, that he didn't have to talk with anyone who knew him.

He left the library and walked up the street to The Elm Bookshop and looked in the window. Marie's *On an Island of Hope* was on display along with other books about islands. Peter knew it was not really about islands, but obviously the bookstore didn't care. He turned and walked back under the great oaks in the town green to his truck. Two speckled pigeons waddled around his feet. He had nothing to feed them, but he was impressed by their hopefulness.

Marie was waiting on the verandah the following morning. She was still in her bathing suit. He arrived an hour late on purpose. He did not want to talk with her.

"What happened to you?" she asked.

He pretended to struggle with some of his tools.

"I missed you," she said.

"I couldn't get here," he said.

"I wanted you to meet my publisher and my editor. They loved the work you've done. Sybil especially loved the walkway. She's been on that path before. So had Charles. They loved what you did. They would have hired you on the spot if they lived nearby. Charles was absolutely astonished at what you did with the library. He said it was genius."

"I'm glad," Peter said.

"So I wanted them both to meet the man responsible." She held his hand as she spoke.

"You were so busy."

"We had a great deal to go over. I wanted to discuss my new book. It's called *A Perfect Love*. When I went to introduce you, you were gone."

"You were talking about all those writers."

"Oh, Charles always gets into that vein. He drops names. It's what he does."

"I looked up the one who writes about swans."

"Swans?"

Peter looked at her. They had talked about that writer so much he thought maybe he had got it wrong. "Yes, swans. I got Aldous Huxley's book, but your Mr. Stallings said it was a translation, which it isn't."

"Swans? Oh!" Marie began to laugh. What was she laughing at? "Oh, dear. Oh, dear. Not about swans, about

Swann. It's *Swann's Way* he was talking about. Oh, goodness. Oh, you sweet. It was Marcel Proust. Charles was reading a new translation of Proust, you poor thing."

Peter could not think of himself as a poor thing, although he knew from her laughter that he was ignorant enough to be thought comical.

"Oh, you're hurt, aren't you? Did I hurt your feelings over stupid Proust." She tried to kiss him, but he pulled away. "Oh, sweet. I did. I did hurt your feelings. What is it?"

He did not want to talk with her about it, but she insisted. She held his arm so he could not go into work on her library.

"You've got to tell me, sweet," she said. "I wouldn't want to hurt you."

"You laughed at me."

"But it was funny." She smiled as if she were going to laugh again. "You'll see it one of these days when you read Proust. I'll read some of it to you if you like. You'll enjoy it. It's all about love. We can read some of him together. Oh, my sweet Peter. Your feelings have been hurt and I'm so sorry."

Peter left her standing on the verandah and got to work on the library. He tried to bury his feelings in moldings and trim. It was exacting work, so it took him only a short time to get out of himself. He did not look for Marie nor think about her. He heard music upstairs, but no sound of typing. If she couldn't write that was fine. She deserved it. Except, Peter was the one who was disturbed. Marie was completely herself with her publisher and editor. And Peter remained himself, the Peter Chello who originally walked out of the University and onto the island long ago and who now thought about nothing more serious than how to repair a stone walkway. That path was different from anything he had expected it to be. He considered the vanity of thinking he could be something other than what he had been. All those hours looking at books in the University library had not really changed him.

Marie came into the library around one-thirty. "Are you feeling any better?"

"I'm fine."

"You don't have to hold back with me, Peter. I haven't been able to write a word."

"I'm going to lunch at the Café."

"Won't you have lunch with me, here? I'd really like you to stay."

"I shouldn't eat here."

"I don't understand. Why can't you have lunch with me?" She waited for him to answer, then said, "Peter, I know I've hurt you, but I want to make it up to you. I can't do that if you won't talk to me. Can I?"

She made it difficult for him. She came to him while he held a piece of trim in the corner of one of the bookcases. When she touched him he felt the warmth emanating from her flesh. Her presence was as intoxicating as ever. She kissed his hair as he turned his face to his work.

"Please," she said. "You're very precious to me."

"I wasn't very precious when your friends came."

"Another time I will know better," she said. She turned him to her and kissed him on the lips. He could not hold back. She took his hand and led him away.

She had prepared a seafood salad and opened a bottle of white wine. The light in the sunroom off the kitchen was soft. Reflected light from the water brightened the ceiling and made the room seem cool and fresh.

It took Marie some time, but she finally began to get the story of Peter's nights in the library, his frustration and pain, and his sense that nothing would ever make him worthy of her.

"You're very honest," she said. "I think that's more important."

"No, I'm not honest. I was honest. But I've had to lie to people who love me. I've had to lie to my father and now I'm lying to Alice. I wish I could be honest. You won't let me."

"You mean talk about us, don't you?"

"Yes."

"All it would do is hurt you."

"Wouldn't it hurt you?"

"What more can hurt me? I've lost everyone close to me. How could I be hurt more?"

"By what people might say?"

"It means nothing to me. If I've loved you . . . if we've been lovers and people know about us, you are the only one who will be hurt. I don't want that."

"It would be better than what I felt yesterday."

"What you felt yesterday can be undone. But it will take time."

"I don't know how."

"If you changed your mind and went back to the University you'd find all your feelings would change. You'd see what you are missing right now. You've got such a fine mind, and you love literature."

"I've told you why I can't."

"Yes, I know. But that won't last forever. I saw your father in his wheel chair in the post office. Things change. You'll have another chance."

He did not expect to make love that afternoon, but Marie took him upstairs and drew the curtains to create a romantic effect in the large bedroom. She undressed him carefully, stopping to place kisses on his mouth. In the bed he waited for her to come from the bathroom like one of the goddesses praised in Ovid's poetry. Afterward, he lay on the pillow looking up at the ceiling.

"You are so beautiful," she said, leaning over him. "And I'm so sorry for having hurt you."

CHAPTER EIGHT
November 1971

Two weeks after Peter finished the library, Marie took the final draft of her novel to New York where she stayed long enough to talk with her editor. After that she flew off to Provence. When she explained how she followed a ritual after finishing a book, she showed Peter a photograph of her friends' rambling house and rose gardens in Avignon near the Rhône. Marie said that in the fall it was especially beautiful. "I'll bring back some photographs, but we won't be able to write."

"Why can't I write you?"

She smiled and touched his lips. "Your father needs you, and you need time to work things out with Alice. I need time in France. These are the people who helped me in St. Bart's after Paul and the children died. They are a lovely family. This is their house." He looked at the photograph again with a sinking feeling.

When he kissed her good bye he held her close for a final moment, then let go. He wanted her to know he was strong and that he would wait for her to be back in December. It seemed eons away.

The day she left Crown Island, Peter buried himself in the exhausting work of repairing the Bursteins' seawall with Buddy Dooley and Packy Caserto. His father was not out of the wheelchair, but he was getting around better in the van and could still give directions. Peter could see Crown Island plainly from Maples Point and made out the silhouette of Marie's house through the trees as he worked. He found himself in a reverie, thinking of his first days patterning her stone pathway. He saw Marie in his mind's eye, walking toward him in her white bathing suit, shaking the water from her hair. But his work on the seawall was so exhausting he would hardly have been able to visit Marie even if she were on Crown Island. This seawall was more than one hundred fifty feet long, curving around the Burstein house, looking back toward the town dock. It had been neglected for years. As he worked on the far end of the wall, he saw the trees on the ridge behind Marie's house and, with the leaves fallen, he caught sight of her chimneys and the widow's walk.

He and Buddy spent several days in the quarry explaining how they planned the repairs and looking for ready-cut granite that might work for them. The quarry delivered the stone by rail to the water, then offloaded it to a barge, then they moved it from the barge into position with cranes. Repairing seawalls was a skill that Tom Chello learned from his father and that he taught Peter. As long as Quarrytown sat on the water, his father told him, this skill would permit him to make a living. Peter knew it was true, and he learned everything he could, watching the quarriers drill and blast the blocks they would use in the finished wall. Even with his hip ruined, Tom Chello knew what should be done. And Peter found a new source of pleasure in watching the seawall take new shape and become a thing of beauty. When his father patted him on the back after a particularly hard day's work, Peter found himself enjoying life and enjoying his father's praise.

This year Peter was scheduled to have Thanksgiving dinner with Alice's parents. He had already worked a full day when Alice got home and called. He showered, got a cup of coffee, and went to see her. Her face told him they had a problem, and he guessed right away. "You're pregnant?"

"I missed my period twice. I never miss my period."

"It was that night before you went back to school."

"I thought it was safe. What are we going to do?"

Peter knew what they had to do, but he didn't want to think about it. How to tell his parents—how to tell Marie?

"I wouldn't be showing much until April or May. I can do my student teaching somewhere nearby. They can work that out. Peter?"

"Yes, I'm just thinking."

"We can get married. I had to tell my parents. They said we can get married whenever we want, but soon." She waited for a second. "You want us to get married, don't you?"

As he studied the look on Alice's face, Peter felt an unexpected sense of relief. He had been working and worrying all the time, thinking first of Alice, then of Marie away in France. Marie had tried to tell him that there were limits to their love and that his fate lay with Alice and not with her. Until now he was not sure he believed her.

"Yes, of course," he said.

He told his mother first and to his surprise she was disappointed, but not angry with him. She told him she was proud of his wanting to get married right away. It was the honorable thing, she told him, but she also told him that he was getting a wonderful woman and that he would never regret it.

His father, too, accepted the facts. "You'll stay in Quarrytown." he said. As far as they were concerned, this now swept all uncertainties away and the future seemed secure.

They were married on Friday morning, November 5th, by Ricky Coddle in the Quarrytown Church with the trees blazing orange, yellow, and copper. The sun was bright and high and his friends had brought their powerboats to the town beach in front of the church and headed them inward, all decorated with streamers, saluting them with their extravagant horns as Peter and Alice headed out the front door man and wife. They were hastened into a limo and taken off to Summerland, where most of his friends had their wedding receptions. Peter knew most of the band, "The Hot Rocks," who played electronic versions of tunes he'd grown up with. Alice was blissful. She danced with her father, and Peter danced with Alice's mother, who was short and heavy, and very clumsy on the dance floor. He danced with his mother and she told him he would look back on this day as the happiest of his life. She had tears in her eyes.

The limo took them to New York City. They were honeymooning in a suite in the Mayflower Hotel on Central Park West for the weekend. Alice had to be back to school on Tuesday, and Peter promised his father that he would finish the Bursteins' seawall. In New York they went to Chinatown and wandered in among the crowds on Canal Street. A woman who spoke English in a stall selling strange vegetables gave them the name of a restaurant where they had dinner. They went to see a romantic film with Paul Newman at a movie theater up in Times Square, then went back to the hotel and made love. They made love again in the morning and then ordered breakfast in their room. Alice talked about their plans, how she was going to teach in Quarrytown and how they would raise their baby. "Could it be twins?" she asked at one point.

Alice's mother had given them tickets to a revival of "On the Town," with Donna McKechnie, who had been in the original cast, and Alice declared it the loveliest show she had ever seen. She loved the costumes and the way Donna McKechnie danced—"so gracefully" across the stage. It was a matinee and Peter led them out of the theater into Times Square where they stared at the ribbon of lights streaming the news around the building. The air was bright and chilled and Alice wanted to go to Bloomingdale's to buy a black sweater "that would go with everything." Peter had never seen her so happy as she walked over toward Fifth Avenue. They reached the Forty-Second-Street library which had a display on Greek and Roman drama.

Peter took Alice into the library and into the large rooms where books and playscripts and photographs of performances were displayed under glass. "I never heard of these," Alice said. "Are they good?"

"*Antigone, Elektra, Iphigenia in Aulis, Medea, The Eumenides*, yes, these are all great. I didn't know people were still doing them. He looked at the photographs of British actors and American actors in costume on stage as well as backstage photographs of directors and cast going over the rehearsals. He thought it must have been very heaven to be one of those people, saying those great lines to audiences filled with the excitement of anticipating the terrifying outcomes of those plays.

"What's the point of this?" Alice asked, indicating a group of masks beneath the glass of one showcase. "I thought they were supposed to be either smiling or frowning."

"In Greece they wore masks, but they were to indicate the characters. I'm not sure how it worked, but it was important for them to stay behind the masks or it would ruin the effect. Didn't you take any of this in college?"

He could see she was offended. "I took English," she said. "They didn't talk about these kinds of plays. I read *Death of a Salesman.*"

"Well, that's kind of like Greek. It's a tragedy."

"I hated it. So gloomy. Who could care about those people?"

Peter held his tongue. Alice swirled through the displays and when they headed out and down the steps she said, "I thought that was going to be interesting. All it was was stuff you couldn't even read."

When they got to Bloomingdale's Alice stopped and let a woman spray her with perfume, then let another woman rub some ointment on her hand, and yet another woman sprayed something on her hair and then ran a brush through it. One of the women told her how to find the department with sweaters, although she warned her that the selection would be skimpy now that the season was here.

Alice tried on eight different sweaters while Peter stood by. Much of the time he was in the way of other women who studied themselves closely in the mirrors. He avoided looking at them, but they moved close to him and examined garments on the racks nearest him. Alice tried on sweater after sweater and asked his opinion. As far as he was concerned, they were all alike. In his mind a black sweater was a black sweater, but for Alice each one was very different and she couldn't make up her mind among three that she thought were best.

"Oh, which one, Peter. You decide. Do you like this one?"

"Yeah, it's great."

"Or this one?"

"Well, that's good too."

"This one's probably my favorite."

"Okay. Yes. That's a good one."

"Oh, you're no help."

"The last one," he said.

"Do you like the buttons or do you think I should change them?"

He had not noticed the buttons. They were small and black. He stared at them and wondered what he should say.

Peter paid for the sweater with his new credit card. It seemed hugely expensive to him, but Alice, annoyed, said that's what sweaters cost and if Peter had been out shopping more he'd know that. Back at the Mayflower, Alice turned on the television and watched an afternoon show she said was important about relationships. Peter lay down with a towel over his eyes and listened to several women complaining about how their boyfriends never took them seriously. The show was dedicated to the question, "What do women want?" and as far as Peter could tell, there was no clear-cut answer to that question.

After dinner, they walked up the broad steps to Lincoln Center with Alice wearing her new sweater. People sat on the rim of the fountain and others streamed toward the opera. A banner proclaimed Bernstein conducting orchestral music by Wagner. "Look," he said. "They're playing Wagner."

"Is he good?"

Peter charged two tickets to his credit card and brought them back to Alice with a flourish. "We're in," he said. "Good seats, too."

On the way into the auditorium Alice tugged on Peter's arm. "Look," she said. He looked, but saw nothing until Alice told him, "That woman's wearing my sweater." The woman was with an older man, short and bald, wearing a dark woolen jacket. "I'm not sure it looks that great," she said, and Peter just nodded. "Do you think it's no good?" she asked him.

"No, it's fine."

"But you just said it didn't look that great."

"I didn't say that, you said it."

"But you nodded."

"So?"

"So that means you don't like the sweater."

"It's fine. I like it. I meant it's not so great on her."

"I don't think it's that bad."

Peter threw up his arms. How could he get this right?

Alice opened the program and read out the names of the pieces they would play, *The Siegfried Idyll,* and overtures and preludes from *Tannhäuser, Lohengrin, Parsifal,* and *Tristan and Isolde.* Then there would be a performance of *The Wesendonck Songs.*

"Do you know any of these?" she asked.

"No, but they're by Wagner and he's good."

"I hope so. I hope the songs are good."

The music was good. Peter recognized the first piece, the *Liebestod* from *Tristan and Isolde* because it was one of Marie's favorites. Now in Lincoln Center, the sounds and harmonies were so rich that he found himself with his eyes closed, his head moving softly to the rhythms, feeling the depth of the music as he had never done before. During the *Siegfried Idyll,* Peter turned to Alice to tell her Wagner had written this for his wife, but Alice was sleeping, her head bowed slightly, her mouth open.

When she woke at the end of the piece, she sat up with a start. He pretended not to notice.

In the intermission, before the *Wesendonck Songs,* Alice

was angry. "You let me fall asleep," she said.

"You were tired."

"Yes, but you shouldn't let me fall asleep like that. Was my mouth open?"

"A little."

"Oh, God. I must have looked stupid. How could you do that?"

"I didn't do anything."

"You shouldn't let me sleep like that."

"I didn't know. I'll wake you next time."

She began moving toward the doors, "Not tonight," she said. "I can't stand this music. You can stay if you want."

"Oh, Lord," he said. "I'm not going to stay if you're going."

"I need some coffee or something."

They went across the street and ordered coffee and dessert. Peter had lemon cake and Alice ordered apple pie a la mode, with whipped cream.

"Is this the craving stuff you're supposed to have?"

"Don't be funny," she said. "Did you like that music?"

"Yeah, I thought it was good."

"It was boring. Boring, boring. How much did we pay for that?"

"Eight dollars a seat."

"Oh, God. What a waste."

They took the train back to Elm City in a somber mood. Alice told Peter how surprised she saw no one in New York who was "really well dressed." Even in Bloomingdale's people looked "really ordinary." Except for the women who sprayed everyone on the way in. They were "really overdone," she thought. Too much makeup and too much big hair. And the concert was a total washout. "On the Town" was the highlight of the honeymoon, she said. "Didn't you love it?"

"Yes," he said. "I thought it was great."

"Oh, Peter," she said when they got close to their

station, "we're going to have a great time."

The arrangement until the end of Alice's term was awkward. Peter stayed living home with his parents for the first three weeks while Alice went back to college. Technically, she couldn't stay in her dorm room as a married woman, so she did not tell anyone except her roommate. Meanwhile, Peter spent his free time at Alice's house fixing up a small apartment. Long ago the Carlsons had a paying boarder, but lately the rooms were used as a storage area. Peter helped Mr. Carlson clean the place out. Then he painted it and found some second-hand furniture, moved in, and started paying rent. He was still working on the Bursteins' seawall. His biggest immediate problem was that he did not know how to cook anything more complicated than hamburgers and pasta.

"At least you'll be nearby," his mother said. "And you and Alice are always welcome here. You know that." His father just said, "Now I get a little space around here, and you're going to have to get your own tools."

"I've had my own tools for a long time now. You know that."

"Well, we'll see," his father said. He clapped him on the shoulder and Peter took his pickup and drove his belongings around to Haycock Street and moved everything into his new apartment.

At first Alice's parents doted on him. They invited him to eat with them, but after a few dinners in which Alice's mother recited a litany of complaints about the changes in Quarrytown from when she was a girl, Peter decided to get some frozen dinners and have them alone reading a book. It was more peaceful and he explained that he did not want the Carlsons to worry about him, and he didn't want to sponge off them. In a short time they had a relationship similar to that of neighbors.

"I missed you so much," Alice said when she got back on Friday. "I had to write a paper for Psych. and it took forever. On the effect of art classes on eighth-graders. But I got an A. Would you like to read it?"

Peter read the paper but all it seemed to say was that art classes increased eye-hand coordination and color recognition. It was nothing like the papers he had written at the University.

They went to bed early after dinner and made love. Lying there afterward, hearing Alice sleeping quietly, he imagined himself happy. This was the life that he planned for years, the life that the gods allotted him.

Alice had asked him what he thought of the baby they were going to have.

"Do you want a boy or a girl?"

"Which do you want?" she said.

"I asked you."

"Do you want a boy?"

"Either one."

"That's no answer," she said.

"Sure it is. I'd be happy if it were a girl or if it were a boy."

Peter was very attentive to Alice, but Alice was easily annoyed by his caution. "I'm not made of glass," she said when he helped her get in her seat belt in the pickup.

"I just want to be careful. I've been reading about the first weeks of pregnancy."

"It's the last weeks I'm worried about. I hope you'll be in the room with me."

"Sure," he said. "Should we take classes or something?"

"I'm already taking classes, remember?"

He couldn't figure out why she was so touchy. Was this what pregnancy did to women?

On Saturday night he had to be very quiet because Alice had to do her reading for her Monday courses, so he sat in a corner of the living room reading a disappointing biography of Wagner. As he read, Alice sat at the kitchen table with a yellow marker highlighting passages in her shiny textbook. She chewed gum, snapping it occasionally, and at one point Peter put his finger in his ear to cut down the noise, but Alice chewed harder the later it got.

When she left for school on Sunday evening, she complained that they should have a place of their own in Kingston near her. But they both agreed that it was not very practical when she would be home by the end of the semester.

Peter had dinner with his own parents on Wednesday during the next week. When he got to the house his mother kissed him. He smelled lasagna in the kitchen, his favorite meal, and his father opened a bottle of red wine that Tony Sklar, a former customer in Essex, made himself. They all had a glass before dinner, then several glasses during dinner, all the while complimenting the excellent wine. "My grandfather made wine right here. Did you know that?" Tom Chello asked. "There were big vines right out in back where the flowers are now. They died when I was a kid. Some kind of fungus they said. But they had big purple grapes and my grandfather would put them in a vat and stomp them. He let me get in with my bare feet when I was about five and I'd dance around and the juice would feel great. I never did learn how to make wine, but I sure did learn how to crush the grape. It's an art," he said. "When you were six or seven I still had a couple of bottles of his wine left. It wasn't that bad."

His parents ate quietly. They asked him a few questions, especially about how he got along with the Carlsons. He explained the arrangement, emphasizing his sense of privacy.

"And are you happy?" his mother asked.

"Sure."

"Things are working out?"

"Next semester we'll both be in the apartment. Alice does her student teaching."

"Have you chosen any names yet?"

Peter laughed. "We don't know what we're getting yet."

One of Alice's first letters described her roommate's reaction when she told her she was married. She did not tell her she was pregnant, just said how great it was to be married. Alice began the countdown to the day when she could be home with Peter. She said she was very happy, but that her classes were too demanding. Her letter seemed a bit over-dramatic, but he folded it and put it in his pocket and went to work.

The next day, Peter went into Elm City to the University. He walked down a narrow street to the back entrance to the library. He wore chinos and a blue shirt and sneakers, so he looked like most of the other students on campus. The only difference was that he had no books in his hands.

Inside, the gothic interior, which he hardly noticed when he was a student here, made him think now of the cathedrals he had seen in Marie's art books. The ceilings in the main part of the library soared, and the weathered paintings on the walls made him think of Raphael's *School of Athens*, one of his favorite paintings. He remembered how the library catalog seemed to go on endlessly. People now sat on stools thumbing through narrow drawers of cards. As he looked at them, he thought that he might have been sitting there, too, if things had gone a little differently. He had a sense of loss greater than he had expected. When he was here as a student he took too much for granted. Now he was a stranger.

He found the shelves of Latin classics and opened a collection of Lucretius, Virgil, Tibullus, and Manilius and read a few poems, then put the volume back. The huge room was silent except for the occasional book dropping in front of a reader or the sound of a stiff page turning. Some men sat in large green chairs reading newspapers.

He took down a large illustrated edition of Ovid's *Metamorphoses* and looked around for a place to read. He took a seat near a dark-haired girl surrounded by several stacks of books and studied his volume. Marie had read to him from the

Metamorphoses several times. Now he had it in his own hands again and he began to turn the pages.

He found the story of Daedalus and Icarus. They had not read this together. He was surprised to see that Daedalus was an architect, that both he and his son were builders. The connection with his own life touched him. Peter could not resist the analogy with the maze in which he had found himself at that very moment and the maze that Daedalus had built for the monster child. Would he undo himself by flying too close to the sun like the child Icarus? Daedalus's advice rang in his ears: Don't fly too low to the water or it will pull you down. Don't fly so high that the sun will melt your waxen wings. Fly at mid-level–or risk destruction. Was this not, in essence, the very advice his own father gave him? He studied the illustration of Icarus falling through the air and recalled, then, the painting by Breughel that Marie had shown him. The plowman in that painting never noticed the fall of Icarus. But Ovid had.

Peter looked around him at the students, some of them younger than he, poring over their work, taking rapid notes, flipping through pages. Most of them had stacks of books by their elbows, moving from one to another. In one of the closed-off carrels he heard the sound of rapid typing. It made him think of Marie.

He rose and walked to the exit and showed the guard his open palms. He had brought nothing in and brought nothing out. The students who had exited before him all held books in their hands and all opened their briefcases or book bags for the guard to study. Peter felt naked as he passed through the exit gates.

He stood in the sun and took a breath. The air outside was clear and fresh. He pulled up his collar before heading back to his truck.

He drove straight through to Rhode Island and found Alice's new dormitory. He had no idea where she would be at this time of day, but he was sure that she would come back to her room before dinner. He would catch her then.

The parking lot by the Theodore Francis Greene dorm was filled. Peter parked on the grass under some dense fir trees. Only a few students walked by on the asphalt path. None of them looked at him.

Studying the bulletin board with messages and announcements tacked at random all over it, he must have looked baffled or lost. A dark-haired girl with textbooks in her hand came in, studied the board, then looked at him. "Can I help you?" she said.

He faltered. "I'm looking for Alice Carlson."

"Are you Peter? I'm Jennie. Her roommate?"

"Oh, right. She's mentioned you a lot."

"Come on up. You can wait upstairs."

They climbed a stairwell that had been defaced with spray paint over a huge dark satanic painting in reds and yellows and blacks. The effect was theatrical, like an entrance to Hades. Jennie did not seem to notice it.

"You can sit there," Jennie said, when she opened the room. She closed the window even though the room seemed overheated. Alice's bed had several stuffed animals on the pillow. Books were piled on her desk and laundry and towels seemed to cover almost every available surface. "Does she know you were coming?"

"No, I just came up to surprise her."

Jennie picked up some of her underwear and shoved it into a laundry bag. She got her clothing together quickly and smoothed out her bedspread and sat with her pillows behind her. "So you got married," she said. Her tone implied that she wanted details.

"Yes, a family wedding," he said. Jennie had not been invited.

"Were there a lot of people?"

"Some. Mostly family, though."

"So, is she preggers?"

"You haven't talked with her?"

"Oh sure. Sure we talk all the time. I'm getting married when I graduate in June. His name is Mel and he runs a jewelry store in Woonsocket."

"That's great. How'd he get to do that?"

"Mel's very mature. He works for his father. For now. But he's got big plans for when I'm out of here and we go off to Providence."

He could tell that she did not really think his being a stonemason or a carpenter was that great. She would be much happier if he worked in a jewelry shop.

"What are you studying?"

"Finance. I want to get into an investment firm when graduate. We have interviews very soon. I'm hoping to find something in Providence."

"Finance," he said. "That's nice." He had no idea what finance meant.

"We're going to try to buy a house on the East Side. That's where all the nice houses are. Do you know Providence?"

"No. I'm sure it's nice."

"You guys got married in a hurry, didn't you?"

"We made up our mind. Then we said, 'Why wait?'"

"That's romantic. Where'd you honeymoon?"

"New York."

"Great."

Peter kept the conversation going until Alice showed up a few minutes before dinner. "I saw your truck," she said. She ran into the room and gave him a kiss and a hug. "What brought you up here?"

"Just you."

Alice gave him another big kiss and hug, which Peter thought was for Jennie's sake. "You're such a dear," she said. "You're so thoughtful."

Instead of going to the dining hall, Peter and Alice went down the road to the highway and ate at a Wendy's. Alice went on about how Peter never visited her and now he showed up without telling her and it was a problem because she had so much studying to do. He thought he might have made a mistake. Alice seemed uneasy.

"I went to the University library today," he told her when they got their coffees.

"You weren't working?"

"No, my father had to go to the veterans hospital in Newington. They checked on his hip and gave him prescriptions. I took a couple of days off."

"You could have come yesterday."

"I had to do some thinking is all."

"You mean for the baby?"

"Not exactly. I was thinking maybe I could get the University to take me back. When I left, Dean Coulton told me they'd work things out when I was ready."

"What about your father? Will they give you back your baseball scholarship?"

"I'm not sure. But I was walking around the campus today, and when I got into the library to read–I don't know, it did something. I thought maybe I should figure out a way."

Alice put down her coffee. "How can you be at the University if we're going to have a baby?"

He shook his head. "I don't know. Did you think I was going to stay home with the baby?"

"Some of the time, sure. I can't stay home if I'm teaching. And if I'm teaching I'll be the one with the steady income. We could save what you make for our mortgage payment and live on what I make. I want us to have a house as soon as possible. Don't you?"

"Yes, right."

"And if you're in the University how could we do that?"

"I'm not sure."

"I think we ought to be sure. We've waited a long time. This is what we planned all along."

Peter drove home in the pitch dark, passing all the open farmlands that he'd admired on the way to the college. The road was bleak, empty, and long. In most ways Alice was right. They were going to have a baby. He would need to work to keep things together.

The thought of going to the University played across his mind. He imagined himself batting fungoes on the field, ranging out for fly balls, then settling down in the library with his books around him. Life was treating Peter the way it had treated Marie. But instead of taking his family from him, it was giving him a new family of his own.

CHAPTER NINE
December, 1971

The Great Muldoon, a New York television actor, hired Chello & Son to remodel the Jensen house on Extra Island as soon as they could start. The house was a typical Quarrytown structure with narrow windows, a center stair case, and a country kitchen. Muldoon, who appeared on the successful crime series called *Blow Out!*, wanted the first floor to be opened up, insulated, and outfitted for air conditioning and heat. Tom Chello told the actor that no one lived on the islands in the winter.

"What about Marie Wainwright?"

"You know her?"

"Sure. I met her in New York."

"Well, she stays on the island year round, but she's an exception. Her house was built originally as a hotel, then refitted as a home. It was always intended to house people year round."

"So that's what I want. I probably won't be here much in the winter, but I don't want to close the option. And I want to be comfortable in the summer."

Tom was strong enough to be carried into the skiff so he could go out in his wheelchair and supervise Peter and Buddy and Packy when they had the first floor ready for insulation. The house was sound and the work went very quickly. Peter had Len Moore paint the upstairs and help out with some of the flashing.

When Marie Wainwright came back to Quarrytown, she was interviewed in the *Quarrytown Times* with a stylish photograph. The article talked extensively about her stay in Provence and her growing literary reputation. She had become an important writer and her books were translated into Italian,

Spanish, German, and French. She said that she had seen *The White Wraith* in bookstores in Aix-en-Provence.

Peter went out to the island in mid-morning the next day. The early December air was clear and beginning to warm up. The first snows had not yet arrived, although temperatures had fallen into the thirties each evening. He wore a lumberjack parka and dark watch hat and felt the bite of the spray against his face. It was low tide and the climb on the new steps was slippery and difficult. As he went up the walkway he expected to hear typing, but the windows and doors were closed and all he could make out was the sound of quiet music.

"Peter," she said in surprise. "How I was hoping to see you. Congratulations."

"Ah, you know."

"Steve Clements told me on my way out here. Steve knows everything that goes on in Quarrytown. I think it's wonderful."

They sat in the library on the new leather sofa she had placed in the center of the room. They had a view of the empty water and the stark, bright December light.

"Alice is pregnant. We've got an apartment in her parents' house."

Marie smiled warmly at him. "You'll have a child. What a fortunate child that will be."

"Alice is out of school next week. It's what we've always planned." He shifted and felt the leather yield slightly. "I wish I could have talked with you. I wish I could have explained."

"No," she said, raising a hand in reassurance. "No, it was the right thing. I told you as much. You know I love you, but never that way, never the way you really need."

Peter's life had changed in a very short time. Marie looked at her hands for a moment, then looked up and smiled. "I think this will be a wonderful new beginning for you. How do your parents feel?"

"They're both happy for me. They love Alice."

"And you?"

"I would have married you if you would have had me. You know that."

Marie shook her head. "What we had was not that."

"But we were in love."

"Yes, but that doesn't mean we should marry."

He did not need Marie to say that. He understood from the moment Alice told him she was pregnant that forces in the world, forces of love, were even more powerful than the love he felt for Marie. The thought of having a child for whom he could help shape a meaningful life was almost intoxicating. If Marie were willing to face raising a family again, he would have found a way to make her his wife, but she said she could never risk it again.

The thought of losing Marie was awful, but in the final analysis, he realized that whatever Marie felt for him, her generosity of spirit was so great that she would let him go rather than rob him of what she thought was rightly his. Her words rang in his ear, "Oh lucky, lucky child who will have you to love."

She took his hand. "I want you to find your way now. You are going to be a father, and I know you'll be a wonderful father. I don't want to come between you and your family."

"I want you in my life. You've been my life in so many ways. I don't have anyone to talk with the way we can talk. When Alice first told me she was pregnant, I felt I was living life the way it was in so many of the books we read together. I thought I was heading toward a different fate, and then . . . ."

"The gods of fate are long gone."

"What gods are here now?"

"Perhaps stranger gods than any we've known before."

"I think the Gods keep us in our place," he said, suddenly. "They'll only let you fly a middle level path, like Icarus. I read more Ovid in the University library. I truly felt as if I was Icarus when I read *Metamorphoses*. The builder who risks and loses. But I don't think I really risked enough."

"We risked and won, Peter. Don't forget that, please. We did not lose. And you will not lose in marrying Alice and having children."

Marie's affection had not changed. He knew she still loved him, and he still loved her. Things changed outwardly, the world had changed for him, but Peter left Crown Island feeling encouraged, not disconsolate. He had in Marie a friend, perhaps no longer a lover, but the profound friend of those wonderful afternoons in the sunlight reading the Greek and Roman poets. No matter what might happen, he would not lose that memory.

They agreed that Peter could visit when he wished. And as he left he went to kiss her, but she held back. Her gesture was tacit, but clear. He touched her hand instead and went on down to his skiff. The sun was high over the water and the swans Marie sometimes fed had gathered around his boat and looked at him with an unblinking gaze as if they understood his fate.

That night he went to the Nickel Plate Saloon for a beer and found his father leaning over a hot cup of escarole soup in a corner booth with Buddy Dooley. Buddy had a Sam Adams.

"How'd you get here? How come you're not eating home?" Peter asked his father.

"Your mother's out."

"Clemenza and I carried him up the stairs. When the cat's away," Buddy said.

"She shopping?"

"I suppose."

Peter decided to get some soup and sat down across from his father by the window. Ice had formed in the corner and had only now begun to melt. "It's nice out," Peter said.

"Cold on the water."

"Yeah."

"You go out there to Crown Island?"

Peter was surprised. His father squinted as he waited for a response.

"Just to say hello."

"Miss Wainwright's back?" Buddy said.

"Yeah." Peter tried to look unconcerned.

"You tell her you're married?" his father said.

"Of course. She's pleased."

"Pleased, eh? That's good. What'd she want?"

"She didn't want anything, Dad. I just went out because I saw she'd got back. She might have needed some help."

"She knows your number, doesn't she?"

"Right."

"Then, she'll call when she needs help."

"I told her that myself." Peter wondered how far his father would take this.

"Otherwise, you should stay away."

"She's a friend, Dad. A friend."

Buddy began to look a little nervous. He obviously did not enjoy the tenor of the conversation. It was pretty clear that he could see what Tom was driving at.

His father raised his spoon in a skeptical gesture, pausing just an instant before drinking his soup. He didn't seem to believe him. He probably would never believe him. "You've got to learn one thing, kid. Those people out there are different from you and me. We're just the dirt under their feet."

"That's not true."

"They're very nice to you when they need something from you. But they'll toss you away like a piece of garbage when they're done with you. They live in another world. They think they are the important people and that we are just here to serve them."

"We *are* here to serve them, aren't we?"

"I'm nobody's servant. Never have been. I work for a living, which is more than most of them do."

"They work."

"Oh sure, her hitting typewriter keys is work? And what about the Great Muldoon out on Extra Island? You think making believe on TV is anything like work, like what you and I do? You think any of these people could take a piece of granite and make it do what they want it to do? You think any of them could pull a piece of Quarrytown stone out of the ground and dress it and polish it until you could read your future in it the way we do? Do you think they could do any of that?"

"No, but . . . ."

"And what do you think I feel like when someone like Mrs. Harrison on Kidd's Island changes her mind about how she wants the kitchen cabinets to look when I'm in the middle of the installation and when I've got a bill for $2400 due on them and she wants me to take them out and tells me I made a mistake when all I did was follow her instructions exactly? Eh? How do you think I feel when I'm being told I don't know shit and that I've got to do a job over that I did exactly right the first time. And when I have to stand there while the Mrs. tells her husband how difficult I am to work with when I've screwed up something that I didn't screw up? You've worked for those people. How do you feel when they treat you like shit because you don't know anything about how to hold your fork right at dinner, or you don't read the latest issue of *House and Garden*, or you've never been to the opera, or you don't know how to shop at Tiffany's? You feel good about that?"

"No, I wouldn't. But nobody's done that."

"You just don't notice. You let it go. You're too easy-going. That's your mother in you. But if you'd seen some of the stuff I've seen then you'd change your tune. They see the dirt on your boots and figure you're really made of the same mud that's caked on there. That's what we are to these people. When they need us they're all over themselves with polite shit. 'Oh, thank you, Tom.' 'That's lovely, Tom.' 'Wonderful, Tom.' But that's the end of it. You think I've ever been in a single house on any of those islands except to fix the molding, repair the roof, put on an addition, or work on the sea walls when they start to erode into the water? You think I've ever said a single word to anyone out there that didn't have to do with the job or the weather? Jesus, kid. What am I?"

Buddy was sitting there with his mouth open.

"You want to be invited out there?" Peter asked his father.

"That's not the point. I don't need to be invited anywhere. I'm not a party-goer in case you didn't notice. But I don't want to be treated like I'm some slime-ball, some untouchable that doesn't deserve to be talked to except when I've got a chisel in my hand. You know, that's why I don't go in the Quarrytown Café for lunch. I bring my own, usually. You know that. I showed you how. But there are lots of times I would like to go there and sit in the sunlight and have lunch and talk with folks the way I see them do. But they'd never come over and sit with me and talk, and I'd sure as hell never poke my face in where it isn't wanted. They live in their own world, kid, and they don't want us in it. Not even a little. We're trash as far as they're concerned. They look right through us like we never existed. Long as they don't need us to fix something, we are invisible. We don't exist."

Peter didn't know what to say. His father rarely talked about his feelings, except when something specific happened to him, and as far as Peter knew nothing had happened to warrant this. "You okay?" he finally said.

"Sure. Perfect. You just listen to what I say. You'll save yourself a lot of pain." He finished his dinner and pulled his wheelchair back. His hair was grayed and straggly. He had some speckles of paint on his right ear. He was still a strong-looking man, short, powerful shoulders, and a steady gaze. He was getting ready to wheel himself back to the men's room.

"What happened to him?" Peter asked Buddy. "He's got a hair up his ass about someting."

"Muldoon dissed him. Made Len paint the kitchen a different color and tried to blame Tom for the first color."

"Blamed me," his father said. "The asshole."

CHAPTER TEN

The next morning, he waited for his father, Len Moore, Packy, and Buddy on the town pier. They came along with the barge and Peter handed them down some hot coffee. "Let's hope he's in town and not out here. He was upstairs sleeping when I called this morning. Said he had to go out," his father said. After they got his father tied down in Peter's skiff, they moved slowly and carefully out to Extra Island.

Peter and Buddy unrolled the fiberglass insulation and fitted it between the studs on the first floor. Tom wheeled from the doorway to a work table in the kitchen and adjusted the fitting on a cabinet door. Len Moore painted the trim upstairs. Peter and Buddy worked wordlessly. They both knew what they needed to do, and how to do it, and with the two of them working in perfect synch they finished insulating the first floor by five p.m. "That's good," Tom said, looking around at the pink walls. "We can do sheet rocking and the taping tomorrow. Or at least start it."

"Sure." Peter learned how to tape drywall when he was in high school and did well enough to please his father almost from the first.

"What about the floors?"

"He likes these boards," Tom said. "They're chestnut, from an old barn he bought. They're worn oddly. So what we'll do is sand them a little when we've got the walls up. They'll be okay."

"Oak would be better."

"You can't argue with the Great Muldoon." Tom Chello made a sweeping gesture with his hand as if to confirm his view. "God knows I tried. But he says he knows what he wants, and he's paying, so he gets what he wants." He looked around. "You both did a good job."

Peter watched him hobble out of the chair on one leg and into the bathroom. He was worn out. It was going to be a long time before he could get back to work.

Later, Peter took his tools, climbed into the truck, and waved his father good bye. There were times when he thought there could be no better experience in the world than working with his father on a house like the old Jensen place. The two of them were alike in many ways. They looked alike to other people—even Marie made that comment when she first met him. And when Peter worked for a while with his father he began to take on some of his gestures, and tics.

"Christ, you're just like him," Buddy said to him only a day or so ago.

Yet, Peter did not agree with him about the way people treated him on the job, or the way they ignored him off the job. His father may have been right about that for himself, but things were different for Peter. His father's life had been radically different from his. Peter felt more at ease with the islanders—at least as they had treated him so far.

But as he drove back to his apartment, Peter also knew that in many more ways he was following in his father's footsteps whether he liked it or not. The Chellos had lived in Quarrytown for eighty years and more. Tom Chello was born here in the very house he still lived in on Toth Street. Most of the people they both worked for were essentially newcomers to Quarrytown. They were people who made money and thought the town was quaint and curious, and came in and bought a house that had not been altered for a century, then redid it with additions and decks and large new windows that changed its entire character and raised its price two or three times over.

One of Tom Chello's constant complaints was that when the time came Peter might not be able to buy a house of his own in Quarrytown. The Chellos, his father once declared, would be priced out of the very soil that had nurtured them since the beginning of the century. The new money was wonderful in the short run–it gave Chello & Son plenty of work–but it was anathema in the long run. It meant the town would eventually be filled with new millionaires like the Great Muldoon. "And the irony is," his father once said at their dinner table, "forty years ago people thought Quarrytown was the armpit of the shoreline. People were afraid to come down here to the harbor for fear they'd get spit on by one of the town drunks."

The next morning the Great Muldoon was sitting in the kitchen with an open carton of milk, a bowl of cereal, and a pot of coffee. He was on the phone when Peter and Buddy opened the door to start putting up the wallboard. "Come on in," he said. His mouth was full and he listened intently to the person on the other end of the telephone. "Give me a couple of minutes," he said, shoveling another spoonful of cereal into his mouth. Len Moore helped Tom Chello wheel himself in.

Peter and Buddy uncovered the wallboard on the porch. The moisture on the island was always a problem, but they had used an old blue plastic cover and bungee cords to keep it tight. They carried a couple of sheets through the front door.

"Tom wants us to stack it over here," Buddy said. They pushed the sheets against an open wall.

"I don't give a shit," the Great Muldoon said savagely into the telephone mouthpiece. "You tell him that fifty grand is chicken feed, chump change. I heard you. This is either a major project or it's nothing. I'm not going to budge for less than a hundred grand. Look, does he know who he's talking to? Does he? And what the hell are you pussy-footing around for? You should have been the one to shut him up right away. Jesus Christ. I have to do fucking everything. What do I pay you for? You go back and tell him how much it's going to cost him and make him cough it up. Who's he going to get, Tony Curtis? Sure. And I'm Charlie Chaplin. You tell him, Bernie, tell him just what I said. And don't goddam bother me again until you get him to sign." He slammed the phone down and drank some coffee. He looked up at Peter and Tom. "Goddam agents," he said. "You wonder sometimes what they hell they're thinking."

"Everything okay?" Tom Chello asked.

"Sure. They'll have to agree to my terms. Something like *Blow Out!* doesn't come around every day. I have to keep my agent in line. He'd sell me out for seven grand when he could get double that. You wonder about people, what they're thinking. How's the job going?"

"Good," Tom said.

"Is one of these your son?"

Peter went up to the table. "Right, I'm Peter Chello."

"Yeah, I saw you before," the Great Muldoon said, shoveling more cereal into his mouth. He nodded to Buddy. "They got any other color than pink for this stuff?"

"Haven't seen any," Peter said.

"But it works, right?"

"Sure. Get you up to R-19. You could stay all winter if you wanted to."

"I'll be in LA most of the winter. I just want to be sure that I could come out here if I needed to, like if I have to be in New York. I'd rather be out here. Know what I mean? Quiet. These people drive me nuts with their agita. I'm doing a made for TV film, something new. Supposed to be on an island in Maine, but they're building the set on the Paramount lot."

"That must be interesting," Peter said. "Building a set like that."

"Could be. You ever in LA when I'm there I'll show you around."

Buddy signaled to him and they moved the first piece of wallboard and hammered it into place. Tom watched them carefully. They took the second piece and repeated the process. When they got the next pieces of wallboard into place the phone rang and the Great Muldoon signaled them to stop for a minute. Muldoon screamed into the phone. "Screw that! I told you what the deal is. You tell him. That's all you got to do. Tell him and make him believe it. What are you, a mouse? You got him over a barrel for God's sake. You got him over a fuckin' barrel. No. Not a chance. Not a dime less. You tell him. I'm thinking a hundred grand maybe isn't enough. What does Jack Lemmon get? Well find out for God's sake."

Peter looked at him, waiting for a signal to get going again.

"Yeah, yeah, go ahead." Muldoon stood up and put his dishes and cup into the sink and ran some water over them. He looked out the tiny kitchen window. "Should I get myself a boat?"

"Sure," Tom said. "A nice Boston Whaler'd be good."

"What'd I have to spend on that?"

"Maybe ten, maybe a little more."

"Then I've got to take care of it. Can I use it in the winter?"

"Depends," Tom said. "If it freezes up, no. If it's mild, sure."

"This place freezes up all the way out to here?" He seemed genuinely surprised.

"It happens. But not recently. Supposed to be some kind of warming. If it really got cold you could walk to the island."

"That's all I need. I'm out here so that every asshole who watches *Blow Out!* can't walk out here and tell me how great it is and then ask me to sign my name on the back of a lousy napkin. Give me a warning if it's going to freeze over this year so I can buy a Doberman."

Peter and Buddy nailed another wallboard into place. The Great Muldoon came over and drank from his oversized coffee mug and watched them.

"Christ, that's all you do these days is put that pink shit in and then tap these into place?"

"That's it."

"My grandfather's place in New Jersey they had this

incredible stuff you had to knock out with a sledge hammer."

"Lath and plaster."

"Right. It's solid stuff. Even had horsehair in it. Not the way they build things now."

"Doesn't insulate, though."

"You don't think so?"

"I know so. You get in one of those old houses out here on the islands–and they got a couple still over on Mother's Island. Cold as hell. They got some wood stoves in there, but still can't get the chill off. It's like having a stone wall. No insulation."

"I don't know. This looks a little chintzy to me. Changes everything."

"Because you got used to the two-by-fours," Peter said. "The unfinished look. People get to like it on the islands."

"Maybe. I never thought about it. Right now this looks like shit."

"For a while," Tom said. "It'll shape up."

"I don't know. You think these windows are too small?"

"They're okay for out here."

"Maybe I'd like a glass wall over here," he said, sweeping his hand along the wall where they had begun sheetrocking. "Be very dramatic, wouldn't it?"

"And cold. That's the north wall.

"So?"

"Gets the most weather around here. You want to keep that window-free if you can."

"That's no fun. What'd it cost me to make this whole section a window. One big window."

"You mean a window or a big piece of glass?"

"What's the difference?"

"A window you can open. A piece of glass you can see through, but not open."

"Is it just the view you want?" Peter asked.

"I suppose."

"All you're going to see is the Quarrytown harbor. Maybe the lights at night."

"That'd be nice, wouldn't it?"

"Maybe. But everybody with a telescope could look right in and see what you're up to."

So what about the south side?" He walked across the open space to the opposite wall. "What do you see out there?"

"Sailboats."

"That'd be nice."

"Ever sit on the porch sometimes?" Buddy asked.

The Great Muldoon laughed as if Buddy were retarded. "Sit on the porch? Jesus Christ, I don't have time to sit on the pot. You hear the way these people push me around. I come out here for R & R and what do I get? Indigestion. I can't even eat my Wheaties without some dumb klutz telling me he's selling me down the river for peanuts. Sit on the porch? Christ sake, I'm a star and they treat me like I just walked in off the street like a nobody. You don't know what these people do to you."

"You could see the lights on Long Island some nights. When it's clear. Especially in the winter."

"There's a yacht club down the bend there. You could probably see the regattas when they start and finish. And the quarry boats load up down there. That's kind of interesting."

"Interesting? Really? Sounds like watching paint dry to me. I need a little action."

"You're not going to find it out here," Tom said.

"I guess that's a fact," the Great Muldoon said. "I came here because it's sleepyville *sur la mer.* Big time. I went into that ratty little café the other day. What a crew. People in there reading the paper. Christ, I think they were moving their lips most of the time. I guess that's just small town stuff I got to get used to. And where the hell do you get any groceries around here? I had to drive over to Franklin to the super market and it was like a bodega I saw in Ensenada once. Tiny, and wilted lettuce a specialty. How you guys put up with it. Then I had to wait for that leaky ferry and listen to all the bullshit along the way just to get my stuff back here. Don't you have a service?"

"Service?"

"Yeah, someone who'd do the shopping and bring it out to the island?'

"I wouldn't know," Tom said. "Maybe somebody does that. Why don't you ask at the Café "

Peter had stopped to watch the interchange and considered what his father had said about the islanders. Whether or not he was right about most of them, Peter could see that the Great Muldoon was in a league of his own. He doubted whether any one else on any island would be much interested in talking with the Great Muldoon, and it was obvious that he had little he'd want to say to them. After listening to Muldoon, Peter wondered how he could portray the interesting, roguish, and charming creature he projected on *Blow Out!* He had made a point of watching the show just to see if he could get to know the Great Muldoon a little better. But the disjunction between the character O'Reilly, whom he played, and the person, Muldoon, was so extraordinary that Peter got an entirely new opinion of what it meant to be an actor. In the case of Muldoon, he must be a genius. Until now he thought that he could tell what someone was like by the way he acted on TV. But now, he realized how wrong he was.

"How much would it cost to take out this area?" he asked. "Looking out to Long Island? That'd be pretty intense, wouldn't it?"

"I guess it would," Tom said.

"So how much?"

"Maybe fifteen thousand. I'd have to cost it out. But you'd want to do it soon if you want to get it done before the summer."

"You wouldn't do it in the winter?"

"Sure, but getting a big piece of glass out here won't be so easy, and getting it up without an incident, well, that's why I say the sooner the better."

"Fifteen thousand. Jesus. Every body wants a piece of me. Fifteen thousand for a big hole in the wall. I gotta think about it. Can I let you know?"

"I suppose, but you want me to sheet rock this place or not? You don't want me to sheet rock it and then have to take it apart later for a glass wall, do you?"

The Great Muldoon stared at the pink wall. "What would *you* do?"

Tom Chello looked at the wall then at Peter. "I'm not so sure that matters much."

"How about you?" Muldoon asked Peter. "Should I leave it solid or convert to glass?"

Peter wasn't sure what to say. "I suppose I'd leave it solid."

"How come?"

"Well, the weather for one. It can get tough out here. A seabird could break a big piece of glass, then you'd have trouble."

"That's true," Buddy said. "I seen some gulls go right through a picture window out here. It's a mess."

"But wouldn't it be dramatic to have a piece of glass go from the floor all the way up to the ceiling here?" Muldoon said, sweeping the wall with his hand. "I can see it now, looking at it from the water, looking through it at night, in the afternoon, anytime. Man, it could be a devil of an effect."

"So, you want to go with the glass here?" Tom asked.

"I need to know, though, just whether it can be done and keep the integrity of the house."

"Sure. We'd put in a header to support the upstairs. You wouldn't have a problem with that. We'd do that, then cut out the rest of the wall and put in the glass. Take maybe a week, hoping we can get the glass without too much of a wait."

"Do it," the Great Muldoon said with a flourish, then he ran up the stairs to shower and change.

"Can you believe that?" Tom said, when they heard the

shower running.

"You don't think it's a good idea?" Buddy asked.

"It's stupid."

"Why didn't you tell him?"

"It's his funeral. He's the expert. Let him find out himself."

"What do you mean?"

"Look, this house has been here how long? Since 1908. It's gone through the 1938 hurricane that swept a lot of more interesting houses right into the water, and broke down a lot more. This house was okay. You know why?"

"Because it didn't have much glass."

"You got it. The old-timers knew what they were doing out here on the water. You don't fool around with the storm systems out here. You know what he's gotta worry about? It's the kind of inversion where the air pressure changes. He could have that goddam glass wall pop right out on his lawn. In the middle of a storm. Then you watch him."

Peter and Buddy continued sheet-rocking the other walls and when they had things nailed in place they got out their stilts and began patching and taping the walls so they would be seamless and easy to paint. Tom Chello told Buddy to take the fiberglass out of the wall they were going to convert to glass and roll it up and put it aside.

The Great Muldoon called from upstairs for Tom Chello to phone over to the ferry so he could "get the hell out of here."

Few things angered his father more than being told to do an errand for a client. "I'll do it," Peter said.

"No. He told me." Tom Chello gritted his teeth and wheeled himself over to the telephone. Peter hated seeing him swallow his pride.

"Okay," the Great Muldoon said. He'd come down dressed in a dark woolen suit carefully cut to accommodate his height and girth. He loomed above both Tom and Peter. He put on a wide-brim hat that matched the suit in color. He had a soft-sided suitcase. Peter hoped he would not ask them to carry it down to his dock. "I'm going to the coast for two weeks. I think I told you that before."

Tom Chello's expression revealed surprise.

"Yeah, I told you that last week. We're reshooting some stuff and I have a picture deal that my agent has just about fucked up for me, and I won't be back until you get that wall as transparent as my crystal ball. I like it already. Maybe we should do the whole side of the house, up and down in glass. What do you say?"

"Let's just work on this wall. We'll get the rest of the house in shape so you can live in it any time of year."

"That's the boy," he said to Tom Chello. "I like that kind of talk."

The ferry honked once as it pulled toward the dock.

"Okay. Don't forget to watch *Blow Out!* I'll be back and I'll cut you a check for the rest of this job if you're finished by then."

Tom Chello said nothing. He turned away as soon as the Great Muldoon went out the door. Peter watched Muldoon saunter down the path to the boat. He heard his father's curses as the ferry moved off toward shore.

Tom surprised Peter by having Buddy put the insulation back in the south wall and telling him to start wall-boarding it. "How come?"

"I know how this works," his father said. "He's got this bright idea that just comes out of nowhere and he wants a stupid change and it's going to hit him sooner or later that it's stupid, and he's going to blame me if I follow through on what he's said. Besides, he didn't put it in writing. It's not in the estimate or on the contract."

"I don't know," Peter said.

"Just help Buddy with the sheet rock."

They finished the wall and Peter and Buddy taped and patched it the way they had the other walls and they cleaned up the first floor and brought in a sander for the floorboards. By the end of the week the first floor was perfect. Len Moore painted the interior an off-white that made it incredibly brighter than it had been when the Jensens lived in it. Sandy Buckworth came in and refinished the floor and when it was dry and walkable Peter knew the Great Muldoon was right in keeping it. Even if it were a little soft, it was a lovely looking wood. It was warmer and richer in feel than oak.

Tom Chello got a phone call at home over the weekend from the Great Muldoon. Out in Hollywood someone working on the Maine island project got talking with the Great Muldoon and told him he was nuts to put up a glass wall in a house on an island that was exposed to New England weather. "It's gonna cost you," Tom Chello said over the phone.

"How much?"

"Jeez, I gotta figure it. We got everything prepared for the glass, which is ordered and about ready to be delivered."

"Just stop it," Muldoon said.

"I'll see if I can," Tom Chello said while Peter hovered nearby. "But it's gonna cost you at least another two thousand. That is if I can stop the glass from being shipped out to the island. And if we can get the right materials for the wall so it will be solid again."

"Do what you gotta do. That's all I have to say. I want to see a solid wall on the south side of the house when I get back there. Got it?"

"Look, we'll do our best."

"Just do it. You understand me? Just do it. I can't deal with all the shit I've got to deal with here and also deal with your shit too. So get me the wall back to normal."

"We're working on it." Peter's father put the phone on the wall cradle and looked at Peter. "See, what'd I tell you?"

"We're going to charge him more for doing less?"

"It's insurance. Who knows what happens next? I don't want to lose money on this job. He gives us another two grand

and that'll cover all the nit-picking crap he'll put us through when he sees the finished project. You mark my words. I'm not going to be taken for a fool by him or anyone."

They finished the project on the sixteenth of December, a Thursday. The snow held off, just a light sprinkling on the Wednesday of the last week. The Muldoon house was amazing looking, open, bright, warm, and fresh. The Great Muldoon came back on the seventeenth and looked around and said, "Hey. It's great. I'm going to give a party and I want you to come."

CHAPTER ELEVEN

Alice was moving out of Theodore Francis Greene dormitory for good. Peter hauled box after box down to his truck and then waited while she packed the last of her clothes. "I'm exhausted," she told him. "All this and exams and everything. I had to do this all alone."

Peter understood the sound of complaint, but did not say anything. Alice needed to blow off some steam. On the drive home, she talked about how they had to move out of the apartment as soon as they could. "I don't want to live with my parents all my life," she said. "What kind of work do you have lined up now?"

"We're just about finished with the Great Muldoon's house. We've got a couple of days worth to do." Peter thought to mention exactly what he would be working on, but he held back.

"You don't have anything more?"

"It gets slow in the winter."

"What did you do last winter?"

"I was in school. Studying."

"I mean the company. What was the company doing?"

"Dad did some refinishing work in the church vestry. Then he remodeled a kitchen down on Bedrock Avenue. Not a big deal, really."

Alice seemed surprised.

"How can you keep going on that? You couldn't live on that."

"That's the way it's always been."

"How much do you have saved now?"

Peter wasn't sure. "About four-fifty. Muldoon owes us

for the Jensen house. I'll get about five hundred and a quarter. We'll have some money."

When Peter lived at home his father gave him spending money and told him his rent was included. Peter never really needed a separate paycheck until he moved into the Carlson's house. He and his father were still on uncertain ground about how he was to be paid, although he drew a salary now the way Buddy and the rest of the workers did..

"We can't live on just a salary. I won't be making any money until next year. I don't get anything for student teaching. You're supposed to get a share of the profits, aren't you? You've got to straighten that out with your father. Then you've got to get more work."

Peter was afraid to ask whether Alice's parents could help. He thought they could. Maybe give them free rent or something, but he did not want to raise that question. That was up to Alice.

"We'll be looking for work, but so will everyone else. Nobody does much construction in winter. And we can't do any stonework. It's got to be indoor jobs, painting, remodeling, that kind of thing."

"But you don't have anything lined up. How can you work like that?"

"We just do."

"You don't advertise?"

"Advertise? Nobody advertises."

Alice right away began to talk about advertising. She laid out a plan. She planned to have a three-part brochure made up at the print shop on Route 1 and circulate it in the Quarrytown Café, the library, the post office, and then put it in selected mail boxes. "You'll need photos of jobs you've done. Do you have any?"

He had four or five from people who liked the work he did. Marie had given him a photo she had taken of the walkway. It looked elegant, almost sensuous in the early morning light.

"Okay," she said. "You don't need more than three photos. I'll write some stuff up and we'll list the kind of work you can do. Stonework, walls, walkways, seawalls, remodeling, additions. Kitchens and bathrooms a specialty."

"Stone work is more a specialty."

"Not in the winter," she said sharply. "The money's in kitchens and bathrooms. What are we going to do when the baby gets here? Am I on your medical coverage?"

Their first days living in the apartment full time were unsettling. Peter was unaware that he had developed a routine that worked and that he had left Alice very little space in his day. Unloading Alice's things was easy enough, and going to work the next day was normal. But when he got back he found that the apartment had taken on a very different look. His clothes were in the tiny hall closet. Alice had taken all the space in their bedroom closet. His books were on the floor in the living room and her books were in the bookcase next to the desk, which she had fixed up as her work space. She explained how she had to produce study plans and work out schedules almost every night. He had kept extra tools in the kitchen, and Alice placed them on the landing outside the kitchen door, in an unheated space with a number of other belongings Peter had kept near his bed.

"How does it look?" she asked him when he came home.

He was filthy from work and stood uneasily inside the front door. "Amazing," he said. And without having to be told, he explained that before he could look around any more he had to take a shower and get the construction muck off himself. He stood inside the door and reached down to unlace his boots and put them to one side.

"I'm going to get a tray for your boots," she said.

When he got himself cleaned and dry, he searched for his clothes for a few minutes until Alice showed him where she had moved them. He got dressed and looked around. "Doesn't it look brighter and better?" she asked. "I hope we won't have to be here any longer than we need to, but I think it's okay."

Before Peter had a chance to say much, the door opened and Mrs. Carlson stood there admiring everything. "It looks wonderful," she said. "You kids will be really comfortable here. I can't believe how you've made it look so nice. And bright, too."

Alice stood proudly in the middle of the room. It took Peter a few minutes to become aware that Alice had invited her parents in for dinner and that he was now the host that Alice expected him to be. He and her father sat on the Carlson's castoff couch while Alice and her mother worked in the kitchen. Alice's mother was surprising. She followed Alice's instructions in making the meal. Peter's mother would never follow anyone's instructions in the kitchen.

"So what's the Great Muldoon like?" Alice's father asked him.

"He's loud for one thing."

"Oh, God, I knew that. I saw him eating out Steve Clements because he was ten minutes late getting the ferry out to him, and Muldoon got some spray on his new suit. He's got a mouth on him."

"I know. He wanted us to take down the south wall and make it all glass. My father wouldn't do it."

"Tom's smart about that."

"Mr. Muldoon is not at all what he's like on TV."

"You watch his show?"

"Sometimes. When I first went out there to work. I don't much like it."

"Last week's was good," Harry said. "I like the *Jeopardy* shows, *Wheel of Fortune.* Where you got to figure out the answers to problems and stuff. That's what I like."

Alice's father sold Chevrolets for a living. "Dependable machines," he said several times during the evening. He told them about a customer who "actually came in and kicked the tires of an El Camino. Can you believe that?"

"I never figured out why people do that," Alice's mother

said.

"As long as they keep doing it," Peter said.

"People are stupid about cars," Mr. Carlson said. "That's why they do it. Might just as well kick the license plate."

"People do that, too," Alice's mother said. "The lasagne's real good, hon."

"It is," Peter said. He touched Alice's left hand. "Very good."

"I sold three cars this week already," Mr. Carlson said. Then he gave everyone a run down on the equipment and models and how much they put down and what kind of argument they had among themselves when they made their mind up. "I sold them on the features right off. Then I let them sell themselves on the machines. You can't beat a Chevrolet."

Peter thought that might be a dig at him and his Ford pickup. He laughed quietly, but nobody noticed. Harry Carlson used to sell Buicks in Elm City, and before that he sold Chryslers in Franklin, and Fords in Guildford. Peter's father wondered just how the man managed to make a living.

When the weekend came and Peter thought he had a day off, Alice announced that they were going out for breakfast because they had to finish their Christmas shopping. Peter knew from her tone that he was supposed to feel guilt, but he didn't. The Chellos had always had a simple Christmas. He'd give his father a new tool and give his mother something she could use in the kitchen. The Mixmaster he gave her last year was a big hit because the old Sunbeam was clanking in a death-rattle. He didn't remember what his parents gave him last Christmas. Clothes maybe? It was not that important. What was important was the turkey dinner and the football game when all three of them sat on the couch and cheered whoever played.

"Well," she said, "we need to go out and get something. If they have anything left by now." She shook her head sadly.

Peter liked to shop decisively. But Alice loved to deliberate over color, size, style, quality, anything that needed decision making. They finally compromised on a Mr. Coffee for her parents and a nice tall cut-glass flower vase for his parents, although while he paid for it he wondered where they would get flowers through the winter. But Alice loved it and told him not to worry. It was the thought that counted.

" You're so funny," Alice said when they left one of the large department stores in Elm City. "You'd think you'd never shopped for anything before. You didn't even want to gift wrap things right there. Saves us a lot of time Christmas Eve."

"I always did my own gift-wrapping. I like it."

But all in all, their first Christmas shopping trip as a married couple went relatively well. Alice found what she needed and she relished taking Peter from one department to another and arguing the merits of one gift over another. He was easy to convince because he had few preconceived ideas about what people would want, or what would be nice. "Don't you have a list?" she asked at one point.

"I usually don't know what I want until I see it."

His Christmas shopping was last-minute in a rush, but it always worked out. People liked what he got for them, and he liked what they got for him. He knew Alice didn't need to worry about him.

"I found my sister's gift in October. I've even got it wrapped. I made a list and I've got everything now."

While Alice cooked dinner, Peter went out with his truck and found a nice small tree. Then he stopped into Caldor's and bought two strings of lights and a box of tinsel. When he got back Alice was worried because dinner was ready and would be ruined if he were out another minute. But when she saw that he had remembered the lights and decorations, she threw her arms around his neck and kissed him. "Our first Christmas," she told him. "It's going to be our best Christmas."

And it was. Peter had a hard time convincing his father that he could make it up the driveway and into their apartment until he reminded Tom that the apartment was once a garage and that all they had to navigate was the sill. Tom could do that by balancing on his good leg and letting Peter fit the wheelchair through the door. In the end, Tom and Nancy Chello came to their apartment and even managed to get along with the Carlsons. They ate together at two card tables set with a single large old bedspread that doubled for a table cloth. Tom Chello drank some of the red wine he brought and Harry Carlson had four cans of Narragansett beer and both got progressively louder as the evening went on. But Peter could see that they were doing well enough with each other. He and Alice served the dinner. He had helped getting the turkey ready, rubbing it with butter, mixing the dressing, and doing the stuffing. The only touchy moment came when the question was raised as to who should carve. Mr. Carlson rose at once when the bird was presented to the table and headed to it rubbing his hands. But Peter picked up the carving knife and began slicing just as Alice brought the plates to catch the first piece. Peter knew that a man carved the turkey in his own home.

It all worked out, and everyone seemed suitably sentimental about their marriage, and the wonder of the season, and the blessings that everyone in the family enjoyed. The Carlsons called their other daughter, Sherry, and talked with her children and husband and the only sour note was muffled by his parents, who had wanted him to come to midnight mass on Christmas Eve, but Alice was Church of Christ Congregational, so it was not to be. Instead, he and Alice went with her parents to Ricky Coddle's morning service on Christmas day. Peter's mother satisfied herself by saying that at least he was in some church on the most important day of the year.

CHAPTER TWELVE
New Year's Eve 1971

The Great Muldoon planned a New Year's party at his renovated house. His guests could get there if it did not snow, and no snow was predicted for another week. The hitch was that Steve Clements had his ferry in dry dock and the Great Muldoon had to buy a Boston Whaler for his own transportation and decided that it would have to do for his guests as well. No one in Quarrytown had ever heard of anyone giving a party on one of the islands in the middle of winter, much less on New Year's Eve.

Muldoon called Peter the day after Christmas and asked him to come out to discuss some details of his plans. Alice wanted to know if she and Peter were invited to the party, and when Peter told her they were, she was much less reluctant to let him go. She was concentrating on getting a reasonable brochure ready, and it occurred to her, she said, that it wouldn't be a bad idea to have it there on a table by the Great Muldoon's door for people to see. Those were the folks who had enough money, she said, to use his talents in the winter time.

"The place is a barn," Muldoon said. Peter was dressed in a heavy pea jacket and watch cap. He had taken his own skiff out to the island and, with the gray overcast, the air was frigid. "So I need some more wood for the stove. I'm glad you told me to keep that damned stove in place. I see now why they got it." Peter took his hat off and Muldoon signaled him to take off his coat, and he felt the heat from the stove. It wasn't really such a barn after all. Muldoon's blood must have been thin.

"All that insulation." Muldoon handed him a glass. It was bourbon on ice. "Drink up." He took a healthy swig and turned to the rest of the room. "But by God it looks like a show place now. I'm so glad I didn't bother with that glass idea. Told your father to scrap it. Not a good idea at all. He understood, I think." As he spoke the telephone rang. "Yes, but not now," he said into it. "No. I said later. Right." He put the telephone down. "Look, I'm going to need some help and I thought you'd be the fellow for that."

"Sure."

"I need someone to ferry over the guests. I thought I'd have them all assemble at the Café over there and then bring them out here. Then there's a couple of folks from the islands."

"Miss Wainwright's the only one actually staying on the islands in the winter."

"Yes, I invited her, too."

Peter wondered how well they knew each other.

"It's not going to be a big crew. I have a list. There's twenty-two. Including you and your father."

"I was wondering if my mother is invited."

"Oh, yeah. Sure."

"And my wife, Alice?"

"Okay. So it'll be twenty-four."

"And we'll need Buddy Dooley and his wife."

"The guy you work with?"

"I need him to help put dad in the boat."

The Great Muldoon seemed reluctant, but after a second, he said, "Okay, that won't be many in here. Plenty of room. You can use my new boat. Maybe four or five trips. How's that sound?"

"Okay."

"Pay you a hundred bucks. Okay?" Peter nodded and they shook hands. "Deal."

Alice had seen the Great Muldoon on television and thought he was wonderful. The thought of actually meeting him in his own house was almost too much for her. "How does he behave? Will he talk to me?"

"Sure, he'll talk to you. He's just a guy."

"He's a lot more than just a guy," she said in surprise. "He's the Great Muldoon. You see him on TV."

"Right."

Peter's father asked, "You're going to ferry everybody out there?"

"He's paying me."

"I know, but do you need it that bad?"

"Actually, I do. Alice is worried about what we're going to do this winter."

"We'll get by. We always do."

"Yes, but this year we've got to plan for the baby."

"Plan?" His tone was skeptical. "I'm not even sure I'm going to go to this thing out there. How the hell am I going to get out there? Besides, I like to stay home on New Years."

"Mom's invited too. And Alice. So's Buddy and Linda, so we can get you in and out of the boat."

"Oh. Well."

"So it will be fun. The place really looks good. And he loves the south wall now. He thinks it was your idea to change it to glass and his idea to change it back."

"That fits. I don't know. I'm not sure I want to go. Who's going to be there?"

"Friends of his. He's got a list. I didn't see it."

The early part of New Years Eve day was bright, sunny, almost warm. Peter ferried out some of the supplies and the caterers in the afternoon. The Great Muldoon's guests were standing on the town dock after it had turned dark. Some of them were shivering. Only the few locals were prepared for the trip out to Extra Island. People huddled together cursing the cold, cursing the spray whenever the boat crashed on a wave.

Peter took Alice and his parents over in the third group with Buddy and Linda. Buddy had already had a few drinks and brought a funny hat with him. Linda seemed to be sulking, but like Alice she wanted to meet The Great Muldoon. On his way back to the dock to pick up the few latecomers, he veered over toward Crown Island and found Marie in her library waiting for him. When he saw her, he felt his breath catch and sensed a familiar dull ache in his breast. Her eyes were liquid and her skin fresh and radiant in the warm library light. He wanted to touch her, to hold her again, but a sense of guilt and propriety held him back.

"Peter, I hoped I would see you at Christmas."

"I wanted to see you, too. But I couldn't. Alice needed me. I just couldn't get away."

"But I have a present for you."

Peter had no present for her. He stood there until she smiled and touched his cheek.

"Don't look so shocked." She leaned up and kissed him. "You are such a sweet man. I hope you're happy. Did you have a good Christmas?"

"We all had dinner together with our parents at our apartment. It was nice."

"I had a quiet Christmas right here. It was such a beautiful day. I listened to Rachmaninoff's *Vespers* and Bach's *Christmas Oratorio*."

"You were alone?"

"With my thoughts. You needn't worry. I'm used to being here with my thoughts. Does Alice treat you well?"

"Sure."

"And your father is less worried?"

"He's already at the party. You'll see him."

"That will be nice. I'll try not to frighten him. Should I give you your present now, or later?"

"Later. We can't take it in the boat."

"Then, you'll come by and we can talk?"

"Yes."

"When? I'll be here, so any day will be fine."

"I guess Monday. Would Monday be okay?"

She smiled at him and they went down the walkway to

the Great Muldoon's new Whaler. The guests standing on the town dock were huddled in loud conversation. They held packages of drink and house warming presents and, following Peter's instructions, loaded the boat properly and held on as he turned and moved them out toward the brightly lighted island whose music, now Bob Dylan's raspy plaintiveness, boomed out across the water. Marie stood next to Peter with her back to the windshield and her hair flowing around her face. In the dark, she was even more alluring and romantic than he'd anticipated. She seemed happy, cheered by the jaunt across the water. "You know I did this as a child," she said. "We had a small Chris-Craft then, and I sometimes took it out at night to visit friends on the islands."

"Not in the winter?"

"No, not in the winter, but in late fall. When it was chilly. My mother didn't think it was a problem, but my father once gave me a terrible talking-to. He knew how dangerous the waters are out here. But she didn't."

"If you know the waters, though."

"Well, I did, you see. I grew up here just like you."

"Not quite. You were away at school."

"Some of the time, though, I was right here."

"Are we there yet?" one of the passengers said as a joke. "What the hell is Muldoon doing out here anyway?"

"He's built a bank on the island and has gorgons guarding it," another guest said.

"This could be *The Murder on Granite Island.* You'll see. If Vincent Price is here, we all turn right around and get back to the mainland."

"Not me. If Vincent Price is here I'll change into my costume from *Virgins in Bombay.*"

"You change into that, and you'll freeze your ass off."

"You change into that and I'll take your photo for my porno files."

Everyone laughed and Peter pulled them up to the

wooden dock and let everyone off. Marie hesitated on the dock while he tied the boat off. "You should go up with them," he said quietly. "I'll be there in a minute."

Marie looked at him, then nodded. She turned and walked toward the lights and the music. Peter watched her and when she was in the house, he sat on an old wooden bench the Jensens had used when they waited for the ferry. He was surprised how difficult Marie made this for him. She couldn't know how he felt, how his heart raced when he was near her. She seemed so good. And so patient. Looking at her there in the house before she got into the boat, he felt the pain of a terrible loss. If there had been some way he could have made Marie his own, some way he could have given himself to her and stayed with her on Crown Island–he would have done it. He would have given up whatever he had on the mainland in order to live with her on Crown Island.

He might have stayed sitting there a while longer considering what had gone from him, but when the cold got to him, he began to shiver. He rose and went into the house.

People admired everything, from the wood stove to the lights outside. The Great Muldoon had a large decorated tree in one corner of the main room. The gift-wrapped presents beneath it looked like props. There was plenty of food and drink on the tables against the west wall. Alice came to him when he stepped inside.

"Where were you?" She had had a couple of drinks and already seemed unsteady.

"That's the last group," he said. "I was tying up the Whaler."

"Constance Faynell just came in." He didn't react. "From *Once Again?*" He didn't know what she meant. "On TV. It's one of the best soap operas. She's right over there."

Peter looked across the room at a shapely young woman who gave the Great Muldoon a kiss. She was the woman who threatened to put on her costume from Bombay.

"You didn't introduce me to Mr. Muldoon," Alice said. "Neither did your father."

Tom Chello was at the far end of the room near the stove holding a can of beer. Peter's mother stood beside Tom looking a bit nonplused at the company. She may have known who Constance Faynell was too. "Come on," Peter said. "I'll introduce you."

They walked over to where Muldoon still held Constance Faynell's hand. When they got close Muldoon looked at him and in a loud voice said, "For God's sake, man, take off your coat. You built it tight as an oven in here. Don't make it look like the fire's gone out."

Everyone laughed and Peter struggled out of his coat and let it fall as he reached for Muldoon's outstretched hand. "This is my wife, Alice."

"What a beautiful gal," he said. Alice's face lighted. "You've got a talented fellow here. Do you know Constance?"

"Absolutely," Alice said, reaching for Constance's outstretched hand.

"Charmed," Constance said. "You did the remodeling?" she asked Peter.

"Well, some of it. Our firm." He nodded in his father's direction.

"Ah yes," Muldoon said, "and this is the fellow who made sure I didn't glass that wall over there, the one that would have made us freeze our asses off in weather like this."

"I didn't really . . . ."

"That's his father over there." Tom Chello moved his free hand in recognition. "This is a hell of a team," Muldoon said.

"You do nice work," Constance said. "You don't do any work in Chappaqua, do you?"

"No, I'm sorry."

"You shouldn't say no so fast," Muldoon said. "Could be a big job."

"I'm thinking about a total overhaul. I've got a Simon Braithwaite house built in 1921. It could use a genius like you."

"Thanks," Peter said.

"Hey, Tom and Buddy," Muldoon said, signaling him over.

Tom Chello wheeled over to him and waited while Muldoon got everyone quieted down. Buddy was kneeling, talking with one of the young men and got up and came over next to Tom.

"These are the fellows who took this wreck and made it my showplace. I want you to give them a big hand. Tom and Peter Chello. Chello & Son. And Buddy Dooley, artists of the old school."

Tom Chello looked faintly embarrassed as everyone clapped. Buddy brightened and clapped along with them. He was obviously a little drunk, but happy.

A few people mouthed compliments. Some just said "Happy New Year."

When the compliments subsided, Alice spoke up. She held up a handful of brochures and put them on the table with the drinks. "If anyone needs a brochure for Chello & Son," she said. "They're right here." Peter felt embarrassed, but he said nothing as she put them down and fanned them out. They were fold-over brochures on shiny white paper with two black and white photos. Alice had written the copy and made it sound as if Peter were a master carpenter-designer with a considerable reputation. He almost hoped that no one would look at them, but when Alice moved away from the table, a couple of people, including Constance Faynell, picked up a brochure and looked at it. Some, he noticed, tucked it in their inside pocket. His father took one and stared at it. This was his first look at the finished product. Peter tried to read his father's expression, but he wasn't sure what to make of it.

While he watched, the Great Muldoon turned from him and his father and looked over at Marie. Constance Faynell moved away to talk to another woman who looked like an actress. Muldoon walked over to Marie, bringing her a glass of champagne. She had been talking with two smartly dressed men but turned and smiled at Muldoon as he approached. Peter's eyes were riveted on her when Alice took his arm.

"This might get us some business," Alice said.

Peter's father growled quietly as he took a hit from his beer. "That's not even fifteen minutes of fame, is it?" he said to Peter. He wheeled himself back to Peter's mother, who had stood there alone smiling, but who was clearly uncomfortable. Peter and Alice waited for a moment, then slowly edged over to his parents.

"Mr. Muldoon is really nice," Alice said. "He was very complimentary."

"It was nice of him to ask us," Nancy Chello said. "I never expected to see so many famous people here in Quarrytown. That's Miss Wainwright over there, isn't it?"

"Yes."

"You should introduce us."

"I will if I get a chance."

"Don't bother," his father said. "You can see she's all tied up. They all know each other. We're going to go."

"We only just got here," his mother said.

"We've been here almost two hours," Tom Chello said. "I don't think I can take another hour of the Great Muldoon. Ask yourself, who's talked to us since we've been here?"

"Mr. Muldoon, for one."

"Mr. Muldoon is all. And he's finished. So, we are too." Tom Chello took Peter's arm and looked over at Buddy and Linda. "You ready to ferry us back?"

"You wanna go, Tom?" Buddy asked. Tom nodded. "Ready?" Buddy asked Linda.

"We gonna go?" Linda asked. "I was just gettin' warmed up." Peter could see that Linda had been drinking too.

"We can go over to Tony Grillo's now. That's gonna go

on all night," Buddy said.

Linda shrugged. She, like Tom and Nancy, had not been talking to any of the Muldoon crowd. She wasn't the social butterfly that Buddy was. So, she went over to a corner and pulled out their coats and said, "Yeah, let's take a fast boat and cut out."

"I'll get the Whaler," Peter said. He looked at Alice. "I wish they'd stay a little longer."

"We don't have to go, too, do we?"

"No. I'll come right back."

Peter and Buddy steered Tom down the dark path and got him settled in the Whaler next to his mother where they would get the least spray and aimed the boat to the town dock. Neither of his parents spoke through the brief ride. "Don't get a cold," his mother said when she was up on the dock. "And make sure you get home at a decent hour."

Peter helped get his father into the van. "You can get dad out and into the house?" he asked Buddy. "Shit yes," he said. "I done it before. He's fine."

"Be careful out there," Tom said to him. "Bunch of drunks."

Peter grinned at him. It was the pot and the kettle talking.

"Don't worry about us," Tom said. "See you later. Happy New Year."

Peter steered back over the water and aimed at Muldoon's lights. He was afraid that no one would have talked to Alice while he was gone and that she would be standing alone looking irritated and lost. But when he got back to the party, Alice was dancing with a tall young man who, he later learned, just landed a character role on *Blow Out!* An actress casually explained that Chip Revere was an investigator who teamed up with the Great Muldoon on a number of the "cases" on the show. Peter did not recognize him, but he realized at once from his California good looks that he had to be an actor.

The lights were low, the music was loud, and a good many people danced. The Great Muldoon danced with Marie while Peter got his jacket off and stepped over to get a can of beer. Because he was driving the Whaler he allotted himself one beer for the evening. He didn't want to chance an accident in the darkness.

Chip Revere gave Alice another glass of champagne and seemed to be talking ardently about something and, when Peter turned with his opened beer can to look at Marie, Constance Faynell stood before him. "You do dance, don't you?" she said, taking his hand. Tony Bennett crooned a love song.

"Sure." They took a few steps and Constance pressed herself against him.

"You've got the largest hands," she said softly. She pressed his left hand as if it were an object for sale. "And I meant it when I said you do wonderful work. I have one of your brochures."

"Thanks."

"This is my first time here. Is it lovely in the summer?"

"All year round. Each season is beautiful."

"But it's so cold. People must cling to one another in this weather. And with all that water around us. The way you navigated us out here in the dark was terrific."

"I grew up here. I've been doing this since I was a kid."

"Miles tells me you work with stone."

"Quarrytown stone. It's very beautiful."

"You'll have to show me some time."

Peter felt her breasts against him. She was a startling, beautiful woman and he hardly knew what to make of her.

"Have you seen me in *Once Again*?"

"Actually I haven't. It must come on when I'm at work."

"Oh, that's a terrible thing to say. I was hoping you'd seen me. You seem to be very strong." As she said that she leaned into him for support.

Peter saw Alice across the room laughing at something

Chip Revere said as he twirled her around. Most of the other people in the room were dancing, too. Marie was dancing with a short man in a dark blue suit. He may have been famous, but Peter did not recognize him as anything but a slim, balding man with horn rim glasses.

Miles Muldoon held a glass of whisky in one hand and the fingers of a busty redhead in the other while she turned under his arm and giggled as she wound up back next to his body. The Great Muldoon was behaving much more like his character, O'Reilly, in his TV show. He was courtly and elegant with the women in the room.

Constance Faynell must have been a little drunk when she looked up at him under lidded eyes and quietly asked him if he would like to fuck her. At first he was shocked, but then he started to laugh and looked away.

"What?" she asked.

"It's a great question," he said.

"What do you mean?"

"There's no right answer to a question like that."

"Of course there is," she said, clinging to him as he turned her to the rhythms of the music. "It's yes. Just a simple, fucking yes."

"I don't think so."

"What, because you're married to that little groupie over there hanging on Chip? How boring."

"It's not boring."

"Marriage is boring. God. I thought you had a little life in you. I need a drink." She pulled herself away and moved to the bar and fixed herself a drink. "I suppose you don't drink, either."

"Not tonight."

"It's fucking New Year's Eve. And you don't drink?"

"I have to pilot the boat back when people leave."

"Nobody's going to leave. It's too late. Where would they go?"

"Home, I guess."

Peter watched a man across the room fill Alice's glass with more champagne. She sat on a large leather easy chair near the twinkling Christmas tree with Chip leaning over, talking intimately. She did not notice Peter at all. Another young man, someone called Carson, stood near her, chiming in with pieces of conversation. Alice was a little drunk and having a good time.

"Show me the upstairs, at least," she said. "The least you can do. She won't miss you."

Constance took his hand and they went up the back kitchen stairs to the second level. Muldoon had a workout room above the kitchen, then four bedrooms. The daylight views were spectacular, and this evening the lights from shore radiated sharply along the surfaces of the water. Even in the dark they could see the working boats of lobster men riding at their moorings.

"It's nice," she said. She pulled him from room to room and commented on the furniture, which she did not like, and the views, which she did. "You did all this?" she said, pointing to the walls and the warm painted surfaces.

"Some of it."

"You do good work," she said, matter of factly. "What's this go to?" She had opened a door off the master bedroom. A set of stairs lay behind it.

"It used to be a widow's walk. But it's been enclosed. So it's an observatory now."

She pulled his hand, but he didn't move. "Be a gentleman, for Christ sake," she said. "Take me to the observatory. I want to see it all."

He took her up the stairs to a space large enough for five or possibly six people. He and Buddy had built benches under the windows and the Great Muldoon had found cushions that fit them perfectly. The space was square with windows on all sides. The view was impressive. The horizon had a lush glow from Elm City and the moon had risen over Mother's Island so that it was a clear, crisp evening in all directions.

He sat on the bench and Constance turned and faced him. She still had a drink in one hand and Peter was afraid it might spill, but somehow, turning and even gesturing, she managed to keep the champagne intact. She took a drink and put the glass on a windowsill. She turned and bent down to kiss him. Her lips were full and warm and her tongue darted into his mouth. Her fragrance was intoxicating and subtle. He kissed her back. Before he could say anything, she stood up and pulled the top of her dress apart. "Look what the cold's doing to my nipples."

Her breasts were large and beautiful and her nipples stood upright, taut, and rigid. They were right in front of his face.

"For God's sake, warm them up," she said smiling at him. She lifted her breasts toward him and he held them as she moved slightly from side to side.

Peter kissed each in turn and felt himself growing hard. In a moment he found himself eagerly touching her and felt her hands in his lap. She opened his trousers and pulled out his penis and lowered herself to kiss it and take it in her mouth.

Outside he heard the sound of people who had gathered far below on the lawn. The observatory was dark so they could not see him and Constance, but he could see the shadows near the water. The first large firecracker went off and they heard the Great Muldoon's cheer. He was setting off fireworks for the new year. A spate of cherry bombs exploded rapidly and the entire group cheered. Peter's hands were on Constance's neck and he felt himself coming and wanted to shout, but he held back. A roman candle shot in the air over the water and wheezed into the surf. More cherry bombs exploded, one after another.

When Constance was done, she rose. "You haven't been fucked in a month," she said. "Either that or you pack a hell of a load. How was it?" she said with a smile on her face. She slipped herself back into her dress. "Tell the truth."

"It was great," he said, telling the truth.

"You're funny. Look me up in Chappaqua. Miles will give you my number." She turned and went down the stairs and Peter got up and tried to get himself back in order.

When he got downstairs everyone was out in front of the house. The music was blaring a tune by Janis Joplin and the house was empty. The front door was open. Another cherry bomb drew loud cheers from the crowd. Peter looked out the door but did not see Alice, although he saw Chip Revere and after a moment saw Constance, who had slipped into a man's overcoat on her way out. The Great Muldoon laughed and sermonized on the superb new year they were all going to have. People cheered his words and he punctuated his speech by throwing a cherry bomb into the water.

"Are you having a good time?" Marie emerged from the bathroom and surprised him. "Did the starlet seduce you?" She seemed more amused than irritated.

"Constance?"

"She's supposed to be notorious, you know."

"I never heard of her before."

"She set her sights on you the moment you walked in. I'm sure you saw that."

"Was it that obvious?"

Marie laughed. "I need some champagne. Would you pour me a glass?"

Cheers outside followed another burst. Peter gave her a glass of champagne and hoped nothing in his expression would give him away. Seeing Marie looking so marvelous made him feel even more guilty than he would have if Alice were standing before him.

"Do you know the Great Muldoon well?" he asked her.

Marie brushed his sleeve and smiled. "I met him a while ago in New York. He says we're neighbors and should get to know one another better. He's rather charming in his way, isn't he?"

The cheering outside grew louder. People were shouting "Happy New Year!" The Great Muldoon threw several large cherry bombs out over the water. Their report was magnified and shocking.

"Happy New Year," Marie said, giving him a kiss. He held back only an instant, then kissed her ardently with his arms around her in a long embrace.

"I love you," he said softly in her ear.

"I love you, too," she said fondling his hair. She picked up her champagne glass and held it out before her. "Here's to love and to the New Year." She drank from her glass and then walked out onto the lawn with the other revelers, who were now singing "Auld Lang Syne."Peter looked around the main floor and caught sight of his reflection in one of the windows. In the bathroom he washed his face and hands and sprayed the room with Lysol to take the fragrance of both women from his clothes and hair. The strange thing was that whatever he had done, he did not regret it. He only wished it had been Marie in the observatory instead of Constance.

When he came out, people were coming in slowly, still singing, heading for the bar to replenish their drinks. Constance came in with red cheeks. Peter saw her erect nipples when she slipped off the dark overcoat. She poured a drink and smiled at him while the rest of the crowd came in.

"You look a lot better, now. And if you come to Chappaqua I can make you even happier. I've got lots of work for you, sweetie."

"Peter. There you are," Muldoon said, clearly drunk and cheerful. "My good man, these unfortunates need your services back to the dreaded mainland." He pointed to two couples clutching their coats about them. They looked flushed and anxious. "What a good time," they said, shaking the Great Muldoon's hand. "We'll see you on the coast next month."

Peter helped them out and down the slippery ladder to the float. The women were unsteady, and the men were no help.

They chattered away about the incredible spot the Great Muldoon had found, how terrific a host he was, and how lucky Peter was to have him in the neighborhood. Peter got them settled in the boat and gave them careful instructions not to stand up and not to move around, and then pulled out.

He took them back slowly to keep them from falling overboard. Back at the dock it only took a few minutes to get them settled and positioned relative to the Café and their car, which they were taking back to New York. They all thanked him lavishly. Each of the women gave him a kiss and the men shook his hand and wished him a happy New Year and Peter hoped they were not so drunk that they would be stopped by the state police at the intersection to the highway.

It was not as cold now. The trip back to the island left him a few minutes to think about Constance Faynell and her beautiful breasts swaying before his eyes. He had promised fidelity to Alice and now he'd been married only a short time and already he had failed his own pledges to himself. He knew he should feel guilty, but somehow as he approached the island he realized that what he felt was desire.

When he returned, people sat around listening to John Denver's rustic harmonies, talking and drinking. The Great Muldoon was curled on a sofa with Constance lying across his lap looking up at him, holding her glass erect. Chip Revere was in a chair with his legs stretched out in front of him. All the fireworks were gone, the lights were low, the music soft. Marie sat in the only lighted corner looking at a book. Muldoon signaled to him.

When Peter came to him Constance looked at him knowingly and smiled. Muldoon reached into his shirt pocket and took out a hundred dollar bill and handed it to him. "Thanks. I think everyone else is staying, so you can take your skiff back and I'll ferry everyone over in the Whaler tomorrow. Thanks again."

Peter thanked him and went over to Marie. "Would you

like a lift back to Crown Island?"

She looked at him for a moment and he thought that she was going to refuse him. He couldn't have let her stay in the Great Muldoon's house with this group. If she said no he wasn't sure what he might do. But she held his eyes with hers and nodded slightly. "I'm ready," she said.

Peter looked around for Alice, but she was not there. He went upstairs to the first bedroom, which was empty, then to the second in which a couple snored lightly on top of the covers. In the master bedroom Alice was stretched across the bed on her stomach. She had fallen asleep or passed out. He couldn't tell which. He knelt down and talked softly into her ear. "Alice. Time to go. We're leaving. Can you hear me?"

When she started groaning, he felt much better. Her silence frightened him for a moment. He got up and looked around for her coat. He found it and at the same time found the young man named Carson on the floor with a pillow under his head sound asleep.

He bundled Alice downstairs despite her resistance and unawareness of her surroundings. She said she wanted to stay, but she was incoherent and very drunk. She leaned against him as they managed the narrow staircase. Peter headed for the kitchen door so that no one else would see quite how bad she was. Marie followed them, then came abreast of Alice when they were outside and helped him steady her. They barely got her into Peter's skiff. The low tide helped in the maneuvering. "I think she will be all right," Marie said when they started off.

Alice echoed her with "okay, okay." But they had not gone far before Alice became sick and vomited. Peter had to pull up and help her. "Are you okay?" Alice coughed and rolled into the bottom of the skiff. Her coat came undone and Peter tried to button it up against the cold.

"I'll watch her," Marie said. "We should take her home right away. She could hurt herself otherwise."

Peter heard more fireworks near the dock on Granite

Street. Some wags were still at it. He had hoped there would be no one to see them arrive. He tied up at the town dock and with Marie's help he got Alice into his truck. He hated the thought of Marie's having to climb into his pickup with Alice in the condition she was in. The smell of vomit was all over her. Alice was totally unaware of herself or where she was.

Luckily, the Carlsons were asleep. He and Marie got Alice through the door to their apartment and placed her on their bed. Peter took off Alice's coat, cleaned her up, rolled her on her side, and pulled the covers up over her.

"I think she'll be all right now," Peter said. "I'll take you home."

It was past three a.m. when Peter pulled away from the dock. The street lamp glared down at them, but the town was quiet. The Great Muldoon's lights were still visible on Extra Island. The moon had set and the water was unusually calm.

"That was awful," Peter said.

"She over indulged."

"She can't drink very much. I'm sorry you had to see it." Peter skimmed around Kidd's Island and listened to the echo of his Evinrude. Marie stood near him holding on to the windshield as he steered the boat clear of Tufte's rocks, visible in the gloom because the tide had fallen sharply.

"Can I come in for a minute and warm up?" he asked, when they reached Crown Island.

"Yes, I want you to. I'll make us some coffee."

"That was an extraordinary scene," she said when they were inside.

"With all the ferrying I hardly know what kind of scene it was."

"I thought Constance Faynell was going to undress right in front of you. But I don't think your wife noticed at all. She was with that sandy haired fellow most of the evening."

"Are all those people actors?"

"Yes, as far as I can tell. Then there was the writer, Stan

Kislocky, who I talked to. Miles Muldoon invited me because he said we were neighbors and that because we were staying on the islands in the winter we were a special breed."

"I thought you knew him well."

"Because we were dancing?"

"I suppose. I wish I had danced with you."

"Instead of Constance?"

"Instead of anyone. But I was afraid to ask you."

"Are you still afraid?"

"No. If I had it to do over again I would have asked you to dance."

She came to him and held her hand up waiting for him and when he took it she brought him close and began singing softly in his ear, and they moved their feet almost silently across the floor. He felt the softness of her cheek against his face. Her subtle French perfume reminded him of their afternoons and their rare evenings together. He felt his knees weaken when he thought of how they had made love only a few months ago, how he wished then that he could be with Marie always.

Peter kissed her in a long embrace. "Are we doomed?" he asked.

"No, my sweet, we are blessed."

He kissed her again. "Then make us both happy."

CHAPTER THIRTEEN
Spring, 1972

Alice's student teaching busied her throughout the winter while the brochures she placed in the Café and the local libraries secured several extensive interior remodeling jobs for Chello & Son. Because of Alice's strategy, the pressure to survive through the cold months was off.

When Peter went back to Crown Island several days after Muldoon's party, he found Marie working in her new library on her next book. Her Christmas present to him was the Random House *Complete Greek and Roman Plays* in a boxed set. For her, he had found a small antique brooch with the head of a male Roman figure that she pronounced beautiful. "It almost looks like you," she said.

They made love that afternoon and while he knew this was not what he originally planned when he married Alice, he knew he still loved Marie and would find ways to get himself free to go out to Crown Island as often as he could.

The winter was mild, and for many days the light was beautiful and the sky an intense winter blue. Winter in Quarrytown had in many ways been his favorite season. When he was young he skated on ponds and sledded on the hills in the woods behind the church. When the harbor froze, which was very rare, he cut holes in the ice and fished. He enjoyed going out on the water on beautiful days. And being on Crown Island with Marie was very heaven. They read and talked and made love throughout the winter. He had taken to various deceptions to get out to the island. He stored his skiff out of sight at the Peck's, a small private marina in Burnford, not far from the Nickel Plate Saloon and the playing field. When he said he was going out for a beer with one of the guys, Alice was deep in her work, and almost glad to get him out of the way. He was able to get free for a few hours every so often at night. During the day, when Alice was teaching, he made sure his father was on the job with Buddy and Len, and then he would supervise Beady and Packy on their jobs and excuse himself to go back and check on his father. But he went, instead, for his skiff and spent an afternoon with Marie. No one knew him at the Peck's and no one from the harbor could see him coming down from Maples Point toward Crown Island. And with very few boats out that time of year—except for the fishing rigs that he carefully avoided—he was sure that no one had taken any interest in his comings and goings. Even in Quarrytown he could be anonymous.

He felt a sense of guilt every so often, but when he was with Marie the guilt melted away.

"I tried to be faithful," he said to Marie one late March afternoon. When he was in her arms he felt a sense of joy in the midst of a fear that it was doomed to end.

"Yes, and I wanted you to be faithful. But I also wanted you to be happy."

"Are you disappointed in me?"

"Oh, Peter. How could I be disappointed in you? When you began work on my pathway I hadn't been able to write for months. You were my muse. You brought me back to myself."

"I don't know what to say."

"But you needn't say anything. I just want you to know what you mean to me and what you did for me, and still do."

"You make me feel alive, too. I think of you. . . ." He stopped. For a moment he did not know how to say anything. "I was so afraid when you came back from France. And I missed you more than you can imagine when you went away. You opened worlds for me. You still do."

Was it possible to love more than one woman? Whom could he ask? Buddy or Packy would have thought him mad even to worry over such a triviality. Peter's life had been constructed around the expectation of marrying Alice. Now, with her being so pregnant she had trouble moving around, Peter knew he had come to love her and would love the child that she would bear.

"You'll have to do dinner," Alice told him when he came back from a commercial job in Franklin, working with Packy Caserto and Len Moore, who had joined Chello & Son full time after working on his own. Tom Chello's hip was getting better, but the cold weather made it extremely painful for him to move, and, with the jobs they were getting, they needed the help. Because of Alice's brochures, they landed a job constructing a cinder block Chrysler agency on Route 1, using specifications that were clear enough, but certainly not aesthetic or interesting.

"How do you feel?" he asked Alice.

"Weak right now. It's been a long day and I've been on my feet." She sat on the couch watching the TV news. She turned it down and all he saw were dancing figures advertising some kind of toilet cleaner. "It's going to be soon, I think. I feel like it could happen any minute."

Peter filled a pot with water and took down the linguini and marinara sauce. "You want a salad?" She did. "And bread?"

"I shouldn't, but yes. And butter."

Alice had put on more weight than the doctor recommended. She had morning sickness once in the third month, but since they were married, the only time Alice had been really sick was on New Year's Day, most of which she spent in bed. They had never talked about New Year's Eve. He wondered if something could have happened with her and Carson as had happened between him and Constance Faynell.

He still had not seen Constance in *Once Again*, but he had seen both Chip and Carson in an episode of *Blow Out!* That New Year's Eve–so much of it–had seemed unreal to him. But the most important part of that night was his time with Marie. They, neither of them, had expected to make love then, or perhaps ever again. But when he brought her home and held her, he knew he did not want to let her go. For a short while life was profoundly uncomplicated and their feelings for each other so simple that it was almost confounding to think that any problem existed at all.

"The school's been good about this pregnancy," Alice said. "They've made sure I have a chair no matter where I am, but I still have to stand if I'm going to teach well. Fourth graders are very active, and they don't realize what difficulties I have just getting around."

"Just be careful," Peter said, sounding a little like his mother. "Don't over do it."

"Easy for you," Alice said sharply. "I feel like a blimp most of the time. I looked at myself in the mirror and I could hardly believe I could get that big and not explode right there in front of my eyes. I've never seen anyone that big. How can you love me when I'm that gross?"

"You're not gross."

"You're just saying that."

After dinner, Alice turned on the TV and made up her lesson plans while watching old *Honeymooners* episodes. Peter had a small workshop area in the garage and took his books out there. He was beginning Plutarch's life of Caesar and was amazed at Caesar's crucifixion of the pirates who were his former captors. But all the more astonishing was Plutarch's ability to tell story after story about all these famous Greeks and Romans. The thought that men so long ago could do such wondrous things as Plutarch says they did made Peter question whether such things could be done today.

One night, reading by the light of his trouble lamp, he heard Alice cry out. He ran into the living room to find her on the floor in pain.

"Something's happening," she said, struggling to get up.

"Careful. Let me help you."

Peter knew she had another month to go, but he did not argue. He helped her up, got some towels and a pillow and brought her out to the pickup. They drove into Elm City and to the hospital emergency room. They had insurance through the company account and the nurse took Alice, in great pain, upstairs while he filled out the paperwork.

"Where is she going?"

"Maternity ward. Labor unit. You can go up in a moment."

Peter took the elevator to the third floor and looked around. At the nurse's station he asked for Alice and no one knew where she was. "Wait a minute," a nurse said. "I'll call downstairs." Peter began to get worried.

After another twenty minutes a nurse came to him and told him she was in an operating room. Something, the nurse said, went wrong and Alice's doctor had been called in and he ordered surgery.

"Surgery? What is it?" Peter felt a sense of panic for the first time.

"As soon as I know," she said. "I'll be sure to tell you. Your wife is all right, but you are going to have to wait until the doctor comes out."

Peter paced up and down the hallway. Everything seemed just fine a short time ago. What could have gone wrong? Their doctor said everything was happening just as it should. Why was there such a sudden change?

No one could tell him anything. His imagination ran wild, but he tried to tell himself that it was just precautionary because of an early delivery. He asked the nurses if it was normal for a baby to come a month early and they reassured him that it did happen and that it was not a terrible thing. He tried to be calm. He sat and read yesterday's newspaper, but without remembering a word. He picked up a copy of *Time* magazine, but he could not think straight. He thumbed through it looking at the photographs.

By the time the doctor finally came down the hall, Peter was exhausted and fearful. "Is Alice all right?" he said, jumping up.

The doctor nodded, but indicated that he needed to sit down. "Your wife is fine, but we lost the baby."

"How? Why? We did everything right. She was fine. How could we lose the baby?"

"The birthcord strangled the baby and that was why your wife suffered so much pain. Sometimes in the seventh month we have this situation. You can't predict it, but sometimes it happens. I did not think it would happen in your case. But the fact is your child was dead before we began to operate."

Peter put his head in his hands. The doctor touched his shoulder. "Your wife has to stay here for a few days. She's completely out now. I think it would be best if you came back in the morning."

"No. I want to see her now."

"She's not alert."

"That doesn't matter. I need to see her."

Finally the doctor gave way. "Certainly. I understand. Just give us a few more minutes and I'll send out an OR nurse and she'll bring you to the recovery area."

They had both hoped and prayed that their child would be normal, that if it were a boy he would be strong, but gentle, and if it were a girl she would be pretty and curious. Alice made a list of family names that she thought would be good for a girl, and Peter had a list of names for a boy.

He was permitted to see Alice for five minutes. She was still unconscious, although when he squeezed her hand she squeezed back. She was bluish, drained, and weak looking. He held her hand and called her name, but she did not respond. The nurses explained that she needed her rest and after a short time, he left the hospital.

"We lost her," Alice said when he came into the room the next morning. She was sitting up with her breakfast in front of her.

"They wouldn't let me stay."

"I know."

"We can have another baby," he said after a pause.

Alice did not look at him. "I don't know. I don't know that I could stand this again."

"We don't have to decide now."

"We don't have to decide at all," she said. "They say that if I get pregnant again I may have to stay in bed for the last three months. Can you believe that?"

"You can get maternity leave, can't you?"

"When I have a real job. I don't know how they will handle it, though." She began crying. "It was a girl that we lost. A sweet little girl." She sobbed loudly.

"Alice, please." She looked suddenly small and weak and dependent. He wanted to reassure her, to hold her, but the way she was positioned in the hospital bed all he could do was lean over and touch his head to hers.

"I want to give her her name," Alice said, still crying. "I want her to be Leslie Alice and I want her to be buried in the church plot. I don't want to lose her entirely."

Peter kissed her and told her he was proud of her. He wanted his child to have an identity and to think of her as part of a family that would have been. It was very important.

The next week at home was painful. Alice could not get out of bed the first three days, and when she could get out of bed she could get no further than the couch. Susan Carlson essentially took over their lives. She did the nursing, the cooking, the laundry, and the cleaning, and when Peter came home from the job he felt almost as if he were an impediment to both of them. Peter tried to be understanding. Losing a baby was terrible, but it was overwhelmingly terrible to a mother who had nurtured the child within her own body for months. He kept telling himself that Alice would soon be back to her old self, but it did not seem that she was making much progress.

Susan Carlson did not eat dinners with them. She fixed dinner, then went back to her own kitchen and fixed dinner for herself and her husband, who came infrequently to talk with Alice or with Peter. He was filled with platitudes, but Peter understood. This was not a situation Harry had ever dealt with before and he hardly knew what to say to either of them.

Peter managed to get to Crown Island while Alice was in the hospital, but he stayed only a short time. He was expected on the job site and he knew that he would be missed. He explained to Marie how things had happened, how their little girl died. Marie did what she could to console him. They talked about children and about the pain of loss, and Marie agreed that they should probably not see one another for a while.

"I don't want to make you unhappy," she said. "And you mustn't think this is your fault."

Peter did not think it was his fault, but he nonetheless had the nagging suspicion that the gods were tormenting him for his behavior. Would things have been different if he had stayed only with Alice?

Saying goodbye to Marie was difficult. She had helped him feel better, but then he wasn't sure he wanted to leave.

By the second week, Peter was fixing their dinner and they sat at the table usually without talking. They began to turn the TV on and eat their dinner watching early evening re-runs or the last minutes of the national news. Alice rarely dressed. She stayed in her bathrobe and after dinner moved to the couch and either drifted off or watched more television. She was not happy with the way the apartment looked or the way it smelled. Peter got the Carlsons' vacuum cleaner and went over the entire apartment despite Alice's occasional pleas with him to turn it down so she could hear what someone was saying on the TV. He made the apartment neat and happy looking. He did not want Alice to feel any of this was her fault, but there was little he could say to her that helped.

"If you tell me what you want for dinners, I can get it," he said. "Some of your favorites, lamb chops, or macaroni and cheese. Just let me know."

She looked at him as if he were a stranger.

After the end of the third week, Alice seemed to come back from a distant place. She was able to do things in the kitchen and one evening when he came home she was fully dressed and had done her hair and put on makeup. She was not talking as much as usual, so he knew she was still feeling down, but at least she was making an effort.

He fixed them a swordfish dinner with mashed potatoes and they left the television set off. "You look better," he said.

"Did I look awful?"

"No, but you were pale. You look much more like you're back to normal."

"I want to go back to school. The year is almost over and I need to have everything finished if I'm going to get my degree."

When they had coffee and fruit cocktail for dessert, Peter thought he could bring up something that had been a question in his mind. "When Dr. Birkstein tried to explain to me what happened he emphasized that it was nothing you or I did that caused this. It was a freak, something completely uncontrollable. But he said something that I didn't understand."

Alice put her coffee down.

"He said that this kind of thing happens in the seventh month sometimes. I didn't tell him we were in the eighth month because I figured he just lost track of the time. But he's been your doctor from the first. What was he talking about?"

"We weren't pregnant," she said flatly.

"Which means?"

"When we got married. I thought I was pregnant, but I wasn't."

"You mean, you got pregnant after we married?"

"Jesus," she said. "Can't you count?"

"Sure, I can count. So we didn't need to get married?"

"No, we didn't *need* to get married. So now you want a divorce? Is that it? Now that we've lost Leslie Alice?" She got up and went into the bedroom and slammed the door.

Peter sat there stunned. Why had he put it that way? He sat with his head in his hands. He couldn't leave the apartment and he couldn't stand in front of the bedroom door and cry out to her that he needed to talk. He really didn't need to talk. He needed to think. Was it possible that Alice knew she was not pregnant when they got married? Was this the situation he'd heard about from guys he had worked with who always knew somebody who knew somebody who had been suckered into marriage in the classic fashion?

Now he felt as depressed as Alice had seemed a day or so ago. It was not so much that they had gotten married, but that they thought they were under pressure to get married. Somehow, the pressure removed the force of free will and substituted the force of obligation.

If Peter had never met Marie, he might never have had any of these feelings. Everyone knew that Alice and he were made for each other, that they would marry as soon as the opportunity permitted them—which, in all practicality then meant when Alice finished college and was ready to teach. That was the primary given in his life until the day his father's accident brought him home from the University and sent him to Crown Island.

As he thought about the way in which his life had shaped itself, he heard sobbing beyond the bedroom door. He listened for a few moments, then rose and touched the handle, expecting it to be locked, but it was open. Alice lay there with a small hand towel near her face. She was flushed and frightened looking.

"I didn't mean it to sound that way," he said, hoping somehow to help her pull herself together. She didn't respond except to try to hold back her tears. Her eyes were closed and the towel clutched to her lips. He felt pinned to the spot and did not know what else to say. He finally moved to the bed and sat beside her. He put his hand on the back of her neck and rubbed her lightly. He wanted her to stop crying. He wanted her to go back to the way she was before they got married. He wanted her to feel better about life. He wanted to feel better about it himself.

Three days later, his father wanted to go out fishing with him. Peter was surprised and looked at Tom wondering how he was going to manage a fishing expedition. But Tom was beginning to get around in the house with a walker and he said he thought he could manage if they took Peter's skiff. All he needed was a chair that was bolted down, and that part was easy. Peter got his father to the dock and with a little help from a bystander they got Tom into the skiff and settled in his chair.

They had an ice cooler with some cans of Budweiser and they had positioned the boat out by the Coast Guard buoy, which rang a soft bell as it tilted in the mild swells. Tom Chello tried to be light-hearted and pretended that everything was fine with Peter and Alice. Peter could see how hard he worked at it.

"I don't know," Tom said, "but I don't like porgies. But then, not everyone likes blues."

"I guess not," Peter said.

"But there are a lot of blues out here. Make good eating."

"I suppose. I'd rather catch a sea-bass."

"Later. Much later. You might catch a blue now, though. If you were really lucky. Of course, if we're really lucky we'll catch something more than seaweed."

Peter knew neither of them truly expected to catch fish. When his father took him fishing it was usually to get something off his chest. Or to let Peter get something said that needed saying. One way or the other, fishing was a metaphor for communication. They used nylon filament instead of copper cable.

"So you probably figure you were blind-sided," Tom said. "That it?"

Peter sat quietly looking at his float.

"You don't figure you're the first fellow that's happened to, do you?"

"It isn't that." His father was making an effort to reach him. "I guess it's losing the baby. That's the big thing. I wanted her to live. I kept seeing her in my dreams, holding her on my knee, singing songs to her. I had no idea if it was going to be a boy or a girl, but in my dreams she was a girl, and beautiful."

"You lost your first one, but you can have more," Tom said. He pulled in a small flat porgie and put it into the large basket he'd placed in the bow of the boat. The fish snapped around noisily for a few minutes, then eventually stopped. "What's Alice say to trying again?"

"She's not saying. She doesn't seem very interested in the prospect right now."

"Okay. I can understand that."

"I'm not rushing her. Anything but. I just want her to be careful not to get too depressed. She's back in the classroom now and that is good. She has to keep her concentration, so that's also a very good thing for her. We don't talk much, though."

Tom cast his line again. He settled himself and stared into the dark waters. "Maybe it's better not to do too much talking right now. Until she perks up. Lose a baby . . . . It's probably a lot tougher than we think."

"Yeah, and I said the wrong thing."

"What, that you wouldn't have gotten married?"

"We probably would have gotten married. But not then."

"So what's a few months?"

Peter thought about that. "I don't know," he said off-handedly, just to punctuate the interchange. He really did not know, but somehow he thought it might have made a difference. Time was always the crucial dimension in life. If he had not thought Alice was pregnant he would not have married when he did. That much was obvious. He even thought Alice would agree with that. But it was also true that they would have married when Alice got her degree, so maybe his father was right. A few months one way or the other could hardly have made that much difference.

However, it was difficult for Peter to reconstruct that time, though it was such a short while ago. If he had had his wishes at the beginning of September, he would have gone back to the University.

Then there was Marie. He remembered waiting each afternoon for the sound of typing to stop and for her voice to call him in at the end of his own workday so they could talk, have their tea, and sometimes take the stairs up to her soft bed where he realized fantasies he'd had all morning. He imagined the feel of her skin against his body and the brilliance of her hair brushing his face.

As he thought about Marie, a large bluefish struck his line and almost pulled him into the water.

Alice did not talk to him for several days. She wandered around the apartment dressed, but in slippers, pausing only to sit in front of the TV. Peter ate alone and supposed that Alice did, too. He went into the garage and read in the evenings. He thought that he had tried to communicate with Alice, but no matter what he said she ignored him. He even held her once by the arms, but she shook him off and wouldn't look in his eyes.

Finally, he decided he had to leave. It was impossible to stay in the apartment with someone who seemed to be in an angry stupor. For a brief moment he stood on the town pier and looked out toward Crown Island. But it was not right to think of going to Marie in this situation. It would not have been fair to her, and it would have truly solved nothing.

Instead, he asked Packy Caserto if he could stay with him for a week or so. Packy had a fold-out couch and looked at him as if he were crazy, but he said yes.

Peter took only a few clothes and some books. Packy lived up above the Café in a garret-like place with drafty windows and paper-thin walls. They were still working together in Franklin at the Chrysler agency, so it was easy to make the arrangement and for Peter to stay there and not have to say anything to his parents. He needed to give Alice some space. He didn't think she wanted them to separate or divorce, but with the way she had been depressed and unhappy, he was not entirely sure what she wanted. A few days, maybe a week, would tell the tale. Packy, meanwhile, kept quiet, which impressed Peter. No one liked to ride him more than Packy did, but for once Packy was virtually silent.

Peter decided not to go to Crown Island at all. He wanted to think things through alone, trying to see as clearly as he could what he ought to do. He was afraid Alice might go into a deeper depression that would damage them both.

At the end of the week, Mr. Carlson pulled up behind Peter's pickup in a new silver Malibu with dealer plates. He got out of the car and stood at the construction site while Peter balanced on a scaffold installing a neon-lighted Chrysler sign with Packy and Len. When they got it in place Peter climbed down and walked over to him.

"How is it going?"

"I guess it's okay," Peter said, looking back at the sign.

"Working for the competition, eh?" Harry said, looking up at the sign.

"I guess. But you know there's no real competition for a good Chevy."

"Right."

"How's Alice?" Peter asked.

"That's what I came over for. She wants you to come home. We all want you to come home. You kids must have had a terrible fight."

"No, no fight. We didn't have a fight at all. It's hard to explain."

"Then it should be easier to get back together. You two have a lot to live for."

He wasn't sure how to respond to this cliché. Living in Packy's place had not been wonderful. He kept in his room and stayed away from Crown Island. He had told her about losing their child, but he couldn't burden Marie any further with his problems. He thought to call Alice, but he stopped himself. Now, standing with Harry Carlson, he wasn't entirely sure why he had left Alice alone in the apartment or what he expected to result from having done so. His life seemed in disorder. He wasn't sure what to do.

"Why don't you come to our place for dinner tonight. Around six. I think it'd make her real happy. Sure make me happy. What do you say?"

Peter thought about it.

Harry turned to see what Peter was doing. "Sometimes," he said, "you gotta take some extra steps. Like when something bad happens to you, which it did. I figure you both took it pretty hard, and I can understand that. But a marriage is something you gotta work at and keep working at. At least that's the way I see it. Too many people these days don't take it seriously and they wind up splitting when what they really ought to do is work harder and keep it together. Especially if there's kids involved."

Peter began to wonder if Harry Carlson was talking about his own experience or just delivering the commonplaces of magazine psychology. He and his wife seemed pretty well matched to each other, but Peter never noticed any special closeness, no tenderness or deep communication. They seemed like old people who stayed where they were and who could just as easily be apart as together. Sometimes Peter felt that way about his own parents, too. People just got used to each other and after a while it was impossible to imagine things being any different from what they were.

"I wish there *were* kids involved," Peter said.

"Yeah, well, maybe there will be." He turned and got into the Malibu and looked up at Peter. "I'll tell them to set your place at the table. You take it easy there." He left assuming Peter would be there, and, watching the Malibu enter into the traffic stream, Peter decided that he ought to do what Harry

Carlson asked him to do.

Packy and Len had heard most of the conversation. They were adjusting the sign and making the final hookups to the fuse box, and when Peter came back up to the scaffold there was nothing left for him to do.

"Going home is good," Len said.

Peter put his things into the pickup and drove back to Haycock Street and pulled up to the garage. It was still light out and several crows foraged on the grass next to the house. As he came up the steps to the door he realized he didn't know if he should knock or just use his key. Alice was inside with the light on and music on the radio. He decided to knock. It took several minutes for Alice to turn the music off and come to the door.

"Hi."

"Hi."

She looked at him as if she expected him to say much more. She seemed calmer, more herself.

"I"m sorry," he said. "I think we should talk."

"I know. Did you miss me?"

"Yes, I did," but even as he said the words he knew that he did not so much miss her as he fretted over his behavior and worried about her health. The idea of either of them missing the other seemed almost irrelevant, given the way they had ignored one another.

"Are you going to give me a kiss?"

"Sure." Peter put his arms around her and kissed her. She put her head on his shoulder and held him the way she had done since they were high school sweethearts. She pressed her hand on his back and held tight. There was hope for them after all.

Dinner had a few awkward moments, but most of them were smoothed out by Mr. Carlson, who told a joke or two and made some comments about the car trade, telling them which cars were stolen most often and what the thieves did with them. Peter couldn't believe that anyone was really interested in knowing such information, but at least it took their minds off the events of the past week.

Alice and Peter slept in the same bed that night after kissing and holding one another. Their lives were far from returning to normal, but Peter felt better about their chances. Alice had gotten back to the classroom and began to focus on what she had to do to finish her degree. Her students made life more bearable and made her think more of the future.

Alice's evening conference with the parents of her students fell on the following Thursday. Peter called Marie to tell her he was coming and took his skiff out to Crown Island. The cut was filled with boats at anchor, some rafted together with parties under way. Late afternoon sailors dotted the Sound and the breeze moved them along at a quick pace. When Peter pulled his skiff up on the sand, he heard music coming from the house.

"We'll try not to talk about the loss of children this evening," Marie said. "All it produces is pain."

"I never saw my daughter," he said, as if he had not heard her. "They took her away and I never saw her."

"I never saw my husband again, either. We had a memorial service, and my daughters are buried here, but Paul was left in the sea."

"It's an absence," he said. "We live with absences."

"In some ways the essence of my life is absence. There are so many who might be here, so many I wish I could see and talk with."

Marie had made them a cold dinner starting with a cold potato soup. Peter listened to the music as they ate.

"I spent last week at a friend's place. Things got so bad I had to leave. I think I made Alice even more depressed than she already was. Everything I did got on her nerves. She was almost catatonic. I really didn't know what else to do."

"Do you think you did the right thing? How does it feel now?"

"I think it is a little better. Alice is teaching again, and that's a lot better, really."

"But how about you?"

"I'm okay. We're finishing a job and I think I'll get some more work from it. People call us now and hire us. It's not like before when we had to scrounge for work."

Marie brought them a salad and a pot of tea. She had laid out some goat cheese and a plate of tomatoes in a vinegar sauce. "I'm glad you went back," she said. "I would have counseled you to give Alice some time and then go home. She needs you much more than you can know."

"I don't think I would have gotten married if I had known the truth."

"You say that now, but remember how long you had planned your marriage. You might not have married at that moment, but you would have married eventually."

"If I had my choices I would have stayed here with you."

"So we could be hermits together? I don't think hermits live together."

"We wouldn't be hermits out here."

"You think not? That's what people on the mainland call me, I'm told. The hermit of Crown Island. That's because I like to live here in the winter, which is simply not done by the islanders."

"It's too cold, too risky for most of them. They don't have houses like yours. Even the Great Muldoon is taking some serious risks out here in the winter. He doesn't know it, but if he stays here long enough he'll figure it out soon. No, we wouldn't be hermits. We would be lovers."

"On a romantic island. That's very lovely, and very sweet, but my dearest Peter, we would probably lose the romance in a year and end by despising each other."

"You don't really mean that, do you? How could I ever despise you? Do you really think you would despise me?"

She laughed. "Oh, my dear Peter, don't worry so much. I said that because it's what I fear, not because I think it's what

I'd do. I told you that we cannot treat our love as an ordinary thing. But you need to know and understand that I need to live as I must live if I am to continue writing and if my imagination is not to grow stagnant."

"So you wouldn't have wanted me. Is that what you mean?"

"If you mean would I have wanted you to abandon Alice and come live with me, I would not have wanted that. In fact, I don't want that. I love you as you are and I especially want you to live a full life and not attenuate any portion of it by a choice that would limit you. And choosing me for a life partner would limit you."

"More than choosing Alice?"

"More than choosing someone your own age, someone with as much to learn about life as you. Learning together is a precious part of life. I wouldn't take that from you."

Peter shook his head. "I don't know. Since I dropped out of the University I don't get the feeling I have so many of life's choices. I get the feeling that the choices are being made for me, and the one choice I would make I can not make. My choice of a wife was made for me, and not just because of a false pregnancy. It was made a long time ago and I never noticed that any other choices existed until I met you, until we began reading together, and until we made love. It was only then, that I saw something other than what had been my future until that time. I saw something different."

"And hasn't it been different?"

"Yes. Yes, it has. You've opened worlds for me. The people Plutarch talks about were so much different from me. They weren't stone workers or carpenters. They were great poets and statesmen. Two thousand years ago they lived lives that were so much richer, so much bigger than the life I'm living now."

"And larger than mine as well."

"Yes, but your life is not as small as mine. My life is

limited to here. You write and people everywhere can read your work."

"I write in words and you write in stone."

"Shakespeare says the words last longer."

"He may be right, but I have the sense from watching you that you derive much more pleasure from working with stone than I do from working with words, and I'm not at all sure that your work won't outlast mine."

"I don't want my work to outlast yours. What I want is to figure out how to live a life that's got significance to it. When I sit in my apartment with Alice, or when I'm in the garage making a tool or a fitting or just reading, I know just how small the life I lead really is. And I feel my life getting smaller still."

"We all feel that way."

"You can't feel that way. You can leave here and go live in France or England or Italy, or anywhere, and people would not only know you, they would come from great distances to talk to you and seek you out because what you write means so much to them."

"Is that supposed to be a formula for a significant life?"

"It's obvious that your life is significant to those who read your work and who want to see you and know you. No one would come from anywhere to see me."

"If they knew you as I do . . . ."

"But they don't," he said, raising his voice slightly. He could feel his face flush. "Until I put out a brochure nobody ever called me. I had to wait around for jobs."

"But now people call."

"Yes, now some do. But they aren't calling for me. They're calling for someone who can make them something they want, or fix someplace they need to live in. It's a service they want, not a person. I know that much and I don't kid myself. When I'm most significant is when I'm mending a seawall or fixing a house against a storm, or remodeling a kitchen. People then think I'm pretty significant, and maybe I am. But it doesn't last, not like you do. My value pales out when we get the work done."

"Don't you think it works that way for most people?"

He was not sure that was true. He was not sure it was true about Marie. "I think I'm looking for a different kind of significance. I'm not even sure I know what it is. But I think it has to do not with what I do in life so much as what I am in life. You, for example, are a lot closer to being what you do–people call you a writer because you write."

"And don't people call you a carpenter because of what you do?"

He nodded. But he knew there was a difference. "With the right chances I wouldn't necessarily have to be a carpenter or even a stone worker. It was circumstance that made me what I am. I was born here in Quarrytown. My father was a stonemason and a carpenter. His father was a stonemason. Another couple of generations and maybe my name would become Peter Stonemason the way people get named in Europe. That's what I mean. It's not me, not the inward part of me that makes me what people see in me. It's the circumstance that I live with that shapes my destiny. Didn't Shakespeare say something like that?"

"Maybe he did. Or someone even more modern."

"But the Greeks saw it differently. If we were Greek you would be a Queen and I would be a shepherd, or maybe a slave. And that would keep us apart forever. And maybe we would even be satisfied with that."

"But you are not satisfied."

"No. I think you taught me that. I used to be satisfied I think, at least for a time. But now things are different."

"You have a grand view of things. I'm not sure I would know how to move closer to your vision myself. And what frightens me is that your vision does not seem to include Alice. Don't you think that it should?"

"When I thought we were going to have a child, I think it did. It was more with me than just honoring Alice because she was pregnant. I fantasized about being a father, raising a child who I could help change from what I was. It meant a great deal to me. I feel very empty now without that."

Marie sat quietly for a few moments, then she rose and began to clear the dishes. When he offered to help, she said no and told him to sit and have his tea. She placed the dishes in the dishwasher and cleaned out the pots on the stove and then washed and wiped her hands. Peter could see her only partially, but he could hear her as she ran water and opened and closed cabinets. When she came back to the table she sat across from him and touched his hand.

"I think I've hurt you, Peter."

"No."

"I'm not sure you'll understand what I mean. But I know that I've hurt you in a way that someday you'll come to see. Will you let me play therapist for a moment?"

Peter did not know what she meant.

"What you need to do, Peter, is go home and spend time with Alice. I don't want you to see me for a while."

"What?"

"I mean it. I want you to spend your time with Alice. I want you to try to have another child."

Peter felt a burrowing ache in his chest. He was not sure he could do what Marie asked.

"Both of you are in shock right now and it's going to take you a long time to get back to normal. But I think you can. I think it will happen slowly and I think you will find yourself a happy man when things go back to the way they were."

"I've got to see you," he said. He tried not to sound desperate, but he held himself together sometimes just by thinking of the promise of an afternoon with Marie, the hope of a conversation that would elevate and clarify his thoughts.

"No," she said. "I want to see you as much as you want to see me, but I don't think we should be together for a while, perhaps several months." She rose and came around the table to him. She leaned and kissed him, then held his face close to her body.

Peter's heart sank. The thought of not seeing her for months almost paralyzed him. He had depended on her. Even when she was away, he imagined their time together and sometimes imagined their conversations. "Not see you for months?"

"It will be more difficult at first. But it will help. I honestly think it will help."

"I don't think it would help. It won't help me."

"I think it will. And I have to be away for a while, so it won't be that difficult."

"You're going away again?"

"Yes, my sweet, I"m the kind of person who goes away. I come back. But I go away."

"Where are you going?"

"First to London. Then to Los Angeles."

"Are they making a picture of your book?"

"Yes. I didn't want to talk about it, but Marcel Ravenel is directing it and he wants me to be there in the planning stages."

"Will they film it here do you think?"

"I won't let them. We'll find another island, one that will still permit me some private life. I have no idea where."

"So you'll be away how long?"

"I can't say right now. Perhaps through the summer. It's not entirely in my hands at this point."

"My God," he said, almost involuntarily.

"Is it that bad?"

"No, no, I didn't mean it that way. For you it's wonderful." He sat quietly for a moment.

"You'll see this will be for the best. It will." She touched his hand. "I'll be back, but not for a while. I've thought about this. And you know I love you."

Peter guided his skiff toward the town dock feeling pain

and emptiness. Darkness had fallen and his way back to his mooring was lighted by the red/green running lights on the boats coming out from the harbor and those going in. He thought now that he should never have come out to Crown Island this evening. Despite her words and her tenderness, he felt rejected as he had never felt rejected before.

CHAPTER FOURTEEN
October 1976

Stanley Chello was born July 9, 1975, during the first summer heat wave. They had planned his arrival to allow Alice the dignity of her last two bed-ridden months of pregnancy to fall at a time when she was not in school or in planning for September's beginning. He was a big boy, nine pounds six ounces and nineteen inches long. Alice designed an announcement and Peter had it printed and sent it to their friends. Stanley, everyone said, looked like him. He thought that Stanley looked a bit like Harry Carlson, who was now working in Elm City selling Volkswagens. Harry tried, unsuccessfully, to get Alice and Peter to replace her Malibu with a Volkswagen, but they wouldn't have it.

Alice was completely entranced by Stanley. She doted on him, and Peter admitted that he was quite the perfect child. He was alert, smiling almost all the time, and quick to sense when someone wanted his attention. His vision was clear, straight on, and sometimes remarkably intense, as if he understood much of what went on around him.

When Alice was in the hospital, Peter had to run out and buy a crib and a bed and a stroller all at once. Alice had not let them buy any baby things until after Stanley was born. Peter understood exactly why she felt that way, and he never said a word to her about her decision. When their first baby died, Alice gave all the children's toys and furniture to the Salvation Army. Nothing Peter said could change her mind, so he said nothing.

In a way he agreed with her. Stanley represented a new start, a new being in his own right, and Alice was correct in being careful.

Peter credited Alice's drive with changing his business. Alice refashioned Chello & Son's brochure after she went back to teaching and created a Yellow Pages ad that attracted the attention of several larger construction companies who needed their expertise in stone. The result was that he became not just an owner of a local construction company, but was able to take on some important projects in cities farther inland, as far north as Glastonbury, as far east as Pomfret, as far west as Bridgeport, as well as in Elm City. They had three trucks now marked prominently: "Chello & Son Construction Co. Stone Work."

Tom Chello held back at first because he realized he could not do the work that he once could. But Peter and Alice convinced him that he could rely on the basic crews that had already been working for him, especially if he was willing to use Beady, Packy, Buddy, and Len as managers on their own projects. They could hire local workmen and pay a decent wage and still keep the firm local in feel. Besides, the obvious success of Alice's advertising was difficult for Tom Chello to fault. If he was truly reluctant about their expanding the company, he did not say much about it.

Marie Wainwright had closed her house shortly after Peter had left on that April evening in 1972, and appeared to him again only in the occasional notices he found in the Quarrytown Herald gossip column. In April of 1974, sitting in the Quarrytown Café reading the house copy of the New York Times, Peter saw that she married Eustace apRoberts, a British journalist who disapproved of her writing novels that people wanted to make movies of–or so the article said. The Times said apRoberts was celebrated for his reportage on the war in Vietnam, much of which had been gathered into a book highly critical of the United States's involvement. Now he was covering events in Indonesia over his byline. After that, Peter read the Times in the Café, looking for mention of Marie or her husband. The positive review of her latest book, *A Perfect Love*, appeared in January, 1975. The film version was just out now in October.

Quarrytowners naturally read the book and talked about it, wondering who among them could have appeared in disguise among its pages. The local gossip column implied that quite a few people ought to be more careful of what they said, or else they would show up in the pages of her future novels.

When Alice saw Peter reading Marie's book, she quipped that if he weren't careful he might find himself mentioned in it. Her comment made him start, but he read the book in three nights. Alice had no time, she said, now that she was five months pregnant and up to her neck with schoolwork, to read a novel, even if it was written by someone from Quarrytown. Alice did not read anything that she did not have to read, which meant that she read very little. Her sense of curiosity was very different from his, and there was no point in his trying to interest her in anything he read. It took him a while, longer even than he thought it might, for him to accept that there was no one in Quarrytown with whom he could talk about what he read.

Every so often he recalled his pleasant conversations with Professor Steadman and realized how luxurious it had been when he was young to be able to discuss books with him. His reading had become something of a family joke among the Carlsons, who visited their grandson regularly. Alice and her parents often played with Stanley while Peter read.

Peter put his other books aside when *A Perfect Love* was published. He buried himself in the book and saw immediately that he was Carpenter Halliwell. Carpenter was a mysterious figure in the novel, a young man who had returned from a war emotionally scarred and almost silent. He was hired to restore a great old Victorian mansion on a sanctuary, High Gull Island, off the coast of Maine. The man who hired him, Charles Macclesfield, was a recluse whose daughter spent her evenings in the ballroom playing Bach on the piano and her mornings out on the rocks painting emotional portraits of the sea crashing on the shingle. She was cloistered on High Gull Island partly of her own choice, and partly to care for her father, whose health made him fragile despite a will of iron. In the novel, Carpenter Halliwell rebuilt the house to make it whole again, to make it filled with light and filled with possibilities.

Charles Macclesfield's daughter, Alexandra, expressed a considerable distrust of Halliwell, who was approximately her age, until her father fell in the garden of a massive stroke and had to be put to bed. Halliwell, a former army medic, found Macclesfield in time to save his life. The doctors gave Alexandra little hope but told her she would need help if her father was to have any chance at all. It was then that she asked Halliwell to stay on the island to help nurse her father. While working side by side, she saw how tender and important to her Halliwell was. His knowledge helped keep Charles Macclesfield alive for another six months longer than the doctors expected.

The most emotional moments in the novel involved the way in which Alexandra and Carpenter, while working together to keep her father comfortable, discovered their mutual love of music. Alexandra played the piano and Carpenter played the cello–a cello he had fashioned himself while working on the island and living in the cottage Charles Macclesfield once used as his personal workshop. They played Beethoven and Mozart together and at one point in the novel, Alexandra stopped in the middle of an emotional passage when Carpenter rose to kiss her in a passionate embrace. While they kissed and made love in the large ballroom of the mansion, Charles Macclesfield died calling Alexandra's name in the deep recesses of the upper floor, too far for them to hear him.

Halliwell decided to leave the island after Macclesfield's death, but Alexandra melted at the thought and persuaded him to stay. "If you love anything about me," Alexandra said, "You will not leave me alone here."

Halliwell did not leave her alone, but took her from the island and to the mainland to begin a new life.

Peter found himself deeply moved not only by the novel

itself but by the memory of his days on Crown Island and the fantasies he had built around the hopes that he and Marie would somehow have a romantic life of their own together. Even after he was married, and he discovered that he and Marie could still have a profound relationship as lovers, he fantasized about his place in Marie's life. She had told him that she did not want to marry again–although now he knew she did remarry–and he tried to be happy for her. What he wanted most was the simple intercourse of thought and feeling that came with talking with Marie about what they both loved most, books.

After reading her novel, Peter felt as if he had lost part of himself. Alice thought his reaction was a result of his not liking the book. Alice had heard from a teacher at her school that it was not a great book, but she also heard from local people that it was a best-seller and that it would be made into a film.

When the film came to Burnford, he and Alice were among the first to see it. Alice was struck by the emotional pull the actor who portrayed Carpenter Halliwell embodied. She said she couldn't see how any girl on an island could have resisted him as long as Alexandra had. She also felt that Alexandra Macclesfield was cold and distant and behaved "much too superior" most of the time.

The film version portrayed the love-making scene as something almost close to a rape. Carpenter Halliwell lost control of himself during the middle of one of their musical interludes. Alexandra protested that she was a virgin and had never loved a man, nor ever knew a man, well enough to have a sexual relationship. The power of Halliwell's large and inviting body, tempered by the romantic music they had been playing, Brahms, finally overcame her protests and she gave herself blissfully to a love that "was unlike any love she could have ever imagined," while the strains of Brahms rose in the background of the action.

The landscape of the island seemed in many ways false to Peter, and the work that Halliwell did on the Macclesfield

Mansion seemed to him to be amateurish. But he was touched by a scene in which Carpenter Halliwell discussed the way in which he would restore the fieldstone cottage that perched on the edge of a cliff and presented some of the great views of the mainland and the ocean below. Some of Peter's own words showed up in the novel, and he was surprised to hear them again in the film. The actor, someone he had never seen in a film before, was a strong young man with a clear expression. He seemed to understand stone, although in very few other ways was he anything like himself. In the novel, Peter could see himself clearly as Carpenter Halliwell. In the film, that became impossible.

In the aftermath of the film, Peter found himself in a mood close to depression. Alice was totally involved with Stanley when she came home from school. Alice's mother came over in the day time to care for Stanley while both of them worked. Before Stanley was born, Peter and Alice used her inheritance to buy a Quarrytown house near the top of Haycock Road. It was originally built for a lobsterman whose family had been in Quarrytown for generations. Archie Biondello had never had children and his brothers told people that when Archie died of stomach cancer the house would be available. Harry Carlson brought the news in one night while he was still working at the Chevy dealer. He just sold both brothers matching Chevy Caprice Classics, probably with money from Archie's insurance.

Peter's parents gave them some extra money for the down payment and Peter got them a mortgage at a reasonable rate. It was tight, but they managed it and when Chello & Son started to improve, the mortgage was no problem

The house needed work. Archie was alone in it for more than sixteen years, with no skills at housekeeping. Alice was astonished at the way he kept garbage in many of the rooms. Archie's brothers sold the house "intact," as they put it. They took nothing out of it, which meant they did not clean out the garbage or get rid of the impossible furniture. It took Peter two months working on his own–two months in which he could not read Herodotus or any other book–to get the house to the point where they could repaint the interior and then address the problems of the sagging and flaking clapboard exterior. The roof, at least, was all right. The roof beam had a dip to it, something like an old swayback mare, but at least it was sound. Once they got the first floor rooms painted in Alice's colors, she began to see the potential of the place. It was high up on the street, and, from the second floor in the winter months, they saw Long Island Sound and had good views of Mother's Island, Parker's Island, Kidd's Island and even Extra Island. They were further removed from the Elm City train track lines, which intersected the main part of Quarrytown, dividing it into the upstreet and downstreet neighborhoods that had long since lost their ancient class distinction. Not only did Peter and Alice have much more room, they also had more peace and quiet.

Their garage was small and unheated, useless for the kind of work Peter did in his father's old garage, but the house itself had a water-tight basement and Peter was quick to set up some of his power tools so he could do some finish work when he needed. The appliances in the kitchen were antique and much as he did not want her to do it, Alice went to Sears and replaced them.

Peter's business absorbed him enough that there were times when he did not think of Marie. But those first weeks after he left Crown Island were dark and frightening for him. Even Alice recognized signs of depression and told him to buck up and pull himself together. She said she thought that his moods were a result of having lost their baby. She had somehow worked it through and told him that he was suffering a belated shock. The term came from a magazine she had been reading.

He could not talk with Alice in those first few weeks. She was busy with her work, and his quiet moods were less obvious when the Carlsons came to dine with them, which they did for a while in an effort to help them over their sorrow. Harry

Carlson was filled with his usual clichés and Susan Carlson smiled knowingly and nodded when he talked. She sometimes reinforced his advice with advice of her own, and while Peter knew they were both well-meaning he found himself annoyed at their simple-mindedness. Everything they said seemed pre-digested pap and it took a great deal for him not to leap up from the table and leave them all alone.

In those weeks Peter found himself less hurt by Marie than he was angry at her. Marie had turned him away from her and he thought that she must have seen him in the same relation to herself as he saw the Carlsons. She was so far ahead of him in everything that mattered to them both. She was sophisticated, educated, thoughtful and more aware of the world than he might ever be, no matter how hard he tried.

Alice was lost in the problems of fourth grade and would be forever left there. Peter stopped reading for more than a month. What was the point? What would he do with his reading? With whom could he talk? Reading suddenly seemed painful.

Chello & Son had gotten a job working on a shopping mall in Guildford on the Boston Post Road. Peter had a limited role in the project, hired on by the general contractor to oversee the stone work and some of the interior finish. He tried to throw himself into the project in such a way as to take him out of himself. He wanted to forget Marie and forget his ambition to go back to the University and the pain of seeing his world contract into the narrowness of Quarrytown. Packy Caserto recognized Peter's moods and avoided making the kind of jokes he was known for, the jibes, the ball-busting humor that Buddy Dooley, Len Moore and others just loved. Tom Chello was back with the crew, although he needed his cane all the time and much of the time he needed a chair to sit on. The doctors were right. Tom had a limp that was permanent, and he also had pain that was permanent. He was robbed of some of his strength and most of his endurance, although he maintained his knowledge of how the jobs they contracted for ought to be handled. He was still a good manager, even when he was frustrated by his inability to do much of the work he supervised.

Peter and Packy ate their lunch at the diner on Route 1 and talked about the way the Connecticut Shoreline was changing, the influx of new people, the way the summer people treated the locals as if they were servants. It was much the same kind of conversation that Peter sometimes had with his father. All the old timers hated the way the shoreline was changing.

Things seemed to settle down–but not exactly return to normal. Peter thought that things would never be normal for him, but he recognized that he could not maintain his level of disappointment forever. He began to understand what Marie meant when she told him she had hurt him. It was not because she had left him, but because she had shown him a world that he could never belong to. She had opened a door that would close before he could pass through to another world. Eventually, Peter understood that his mourning was not for the loss of Marie, but for the loss of a life he might have had if he had discovered how to grasp it.

"You've got to stop this," Alice told him severely. "You put the diaper on wrong and the pin came loose. Look, it's stabbed him. That's why he was crying. Why can't you learn to do it right?" Her impatience startled him.

"I thought I did it right."

"For God's sake, watch me. Just watch me and try to learn." Alice lifted Stanley up and slid a new diaper under his bottom. She folded it between his legs and showed Peter how to attach the pins so that if they opened they would not stab Stanley's side. "Like this," she said, as if she were addressing one of her pupils. "That's all there is to it. I've showed you how to do it several times now, and I want you to learn and put a stop to this. Look at him. He's got two welts from the pins you put in."

"I'm sorry," Peter said.

"Yes, well, let's see some improvement." She finished

with Stanley and slipped him into his pajamas. "Do you think you can put him to bed properly?"

Peter did not answer. He took Stanley and held him next to his shoulder and patted him lightly on the back. Holding Stanley like that made things better for him. It made it possible for him to absorb the hostility and irritation that inflamed Alice. He took Stanley to his room and put him in his crib and then sat and read aloud some simple poems while Stanley stirred, played with a rattle, chewed on some colorful plastic disks and cooed up at Peter. Somehow Peter had the feeling that Stanley loved him. He had no idea if the concept was even possible–could a year-old infant feel the emotion love? He seemed to, and that was probably enough. Peter read each evening to Stanley even though he knew Stanley could not understand what he was reading. What Peter wanted most for Stanley was that he would love books the way he did and that he would have a chance as he grew up to become a person in his own right. It was what, he thought, all parents wanted for their children. Even if Stanley had to leave Quarrytown to become a full person.

Buddy Dooley was the first to notice a change. "You feeling better?"

"Yeah, I suppose."

"I see you with your book again."

Peter had brought a paperback copy of *The Odyssey* with his lunch. "Oh, yeah. I figured my brain was turning to mush watching TV. Getting back in shape."

"Funny. I thought it was weird the way you used to read while the rest of us bullshit away the lunch hour. But I kinda respect it. You know? Shows something. Ambition maybe. What's the book?"

Peter showed him the cover.

"Over my head," he said. "But maybe I'll get a book to read, too."

So far as Peter knew, Buddy never got himself a book to read on the job at lunch. Maybe he read when he was home alone, but Peter doubted it. The important thing was that Buddy made an effort to reach him, to help him over a bad spell. Buddy was a good guy and always a good friend.

On a Saturday morning late in October, Peter took Stanley in his stroller down to the strand in front of the Congregational church. The sand was marred with a few discarded bottles, odd pieces of styrofoam, and anomalous black smutches. Even though it was a mild day, no one came to the beach and no one cleaned it up. He walked along the asphalted path toward the town dock and nodded hello to other people out for a nice Indian Summer stroll.

The leaves were luminous along the water's edge. Busloads of people from the city, gray-headed tourists, came into town to see the water and the radiant oak and maple leaves. They passed him in groups and sometimes paused to admire Stanley, who held out his plastic toys for them to comment on.

On the town dock Peter stood looking out at Kidd's Island and Mother's Island. The tide was in and mild swells caused the *Lost Penny* to tug at its mooring. Steve Clements leaned next to the telephone pole smoking a stubby cigar. His hat said "Captain," and he watched as people made their way down the gangplank into his ferry.

"We got royalty in town," Clements said. He didn't take the cigar out of his mouth.

"Like what?" Peter asked.

"Like that English guy Miss Wainwright married."

"What do you mean?"

"They went out to Crown Island last night. I took them out myself."

"Now?"

"Yeah. They want me to take them back tomorrow. I didn't think I'd run tomorrow, but the weather's pretty good, so I said sure. I don't think they wanted anyone to know they're in town."

Peter held the stroller handle tight. "Can you drop me

-166-

off there and pick me up on the way back?" He said it before he thought about the words.

"You know them?"

"Kinda. I'd just want to say hello."

"You mean good bye. They won't be back for a while according to the Brit. He's a fancy chap, the way he talks. How'd you meet him?"

"I didn't. You remember, I worked for Miss Wainwright. I thought I'd bring Stanley out to say hello."

Clements looked at Stanley. "I don't have a life preserver small enough for him."

"When was the last time you sank?"

"Very funny. I just have to tell you that. I got a life preserver for you. You could double up if we get torpedoed. Why don't you go down and see if there's a seat left."

Peter went down the gangplank holding the folded stroller in one arm and Stanley in the other. He put the stroller in the cabin where Clements manned the boat and broadcast his regular lecture on the history of the Granite Islands. All the people on the boat were from the buses that showed up on these grand Saturday mornings. Peter waited for Clements to get going and wondered just what he was going to say when he got to Crown Island.

When they reached Crown Island, Clements dropped him off. "You got about 23 minutes," he said. "I'll be back. If you're not here waiting I'll toot twice. If you aren't in sight after three minutes I'm back to the dock. Okay?"

"Sure." Peter got the stroller up on the pathway and put Stanley in it. He reached in to see if his diaper was still dry. Miraculously, it was. Stanley seemed to enjoy the boat ride and he definitely enjoyed the fuss all the old ladies made over him on the way out to the island.

He pushed the stroller up the hill to the house and saw that the shutters were closed on the upper floors and on the library windows. He went up the steps with Stanley in his arms and knocked on the door. A minute later a short moustached man in shirtsleeves, wearing a dark blue half-apron, like a blacksmith, came to the door and looked at him. "Hello? Did we order a baby?"

"I'm Peter Chello."

"ApRoberts here." He held out his hand. He had a silver tankard in his other hand. "Who 's this diminutive chap?"

"This is Stanley."

"Hello there, Stanley," he said, touching him under the chin. "What business have you got here, Stanley?"

"I know Miss Wainwright. I did some work on the house."

"Was she expecting you?"

"No, no. I just hopped the ferry. Steve Clements told me you were here."

"Good Lord, I told him to keep it mum. What do you have to do to get some privacy?"

"I'm sorry. I didn't mean to disturb you."

"Well, we're disturbed, and that's an end on it. So come on in. I'll announce you." ApRoberts held the door while Peter pushed the stroller inside, then he turned and looked up the long staircase. "Darling," he said, in a voice that was not loud, but which carried through the house. "You have company. An infant has arrived via the last ferry. And with him a fellow straight out of Puvis de Chavannes." He looked again at Peter. "A summery child of the earth."

Marie stood at the head of the stairs. She wore a lavender pants-suit and a dark silk scarf about her neck. She looked very different. "Peter," she said. "Is that you?"

Peter waved familiarly, pushing the stroller with his other hand. Stanley rattled his teething ring at her and made several noises that approximated a greeting. "Hello," Peter said, wishing he had something more interesting to say.

"And is this your son?" Marie said, coming down the stairs. "He's lovely. He looks so much like you." She took

Stanley from Peter's arms and held him close. "You're such a lovely boy," she said to him. "Yes." Stanley was blissed out.

"Does he have a nickname?" apRoberts asked.

"Just Stanley."

"Ah, like the steamer no doubt. Does he gush periodically and blow it off like a whale? I would think he would. A big fellow, too. Going to be a muscular one."

"Peter is an old friend," Marie said. "He built that wavy walkway, as you called it, up from the water, and he designed and built my library. You said you loved it."

"Oh yes," apRoberts said. He gestured vaguely with the silver tankard. "Yes, a splendid piece of work. Very cozy."

"You're closing up the house," Peter said.

"Yes," apRoberts said. "I was looking for the muslin throws, but it turns out there are none. Strange. One always relinquishes oneself to the morbidity of dust. I told Marie to hire someone to do it for us, but she insisted we come. We were in New York, so I suppose it isn't the end of the world, is it?"

"Where are you going?" Peter asked.

"Back to France," Marie said. "We have a home in Vence. That's down near the coast, near Nice."

"I don't know where that is."

"Well, you must discover it one day, before it's totally ruined," apRoberts said.

"Can you stay for some tea?" Marie asked.

"Everything's packed away, my dear," apRoberts said. "That's what I've been doing down here. Sealed tight, don't you know? I've even drained the water. We have enough for tonight and tomorrow morning. You know I've never done this kind of thing before. You could probably show us a few tricks," he said to Peter.

"I couldn't stay anyhow," Peter said. "Steve Clements will be back for me in another fifteen minutes or so. He said he'd strand us here if I didn't appear at the dock."

"Well, then," said apRoberts. "We can't have that, can

we? Stranded on Crown Island, my God, what Defoe would have done with that–or perhaps has done with that. Have you read Defoe?"

"I think so."

"Oh, you would know, you would know. What a rascal he was, consorting with Molls, wasn't he?"

Marie put her free hand on apRobert's arm and held him back. "Why don't you put that tankard in the kitchen, darling, and finish up. I'll walk Peter down to the dock and wait for the ferry's return."

"Ah, *The Return of the Ferry*, another lovely title. We generate two or three a day around here. Very literary, isn't it. This island. Romantic. But rather crude, too, I should say."

Marie held Stanley in her arms and moved toward the door. Peter saw that she was leaving apRoberts behind and he followed her. ApRoberts said a cautionary farewell and returned to the kitchen.

"You're going to live in France?" Peter asked as they went out on the verandah. He looked around for the Adirondack chairs, but they were gone, stored away.

"For a while, yes. I've always been happy there."

"How long have you known your husband?"

"I'm sure you're surprised. I never thought I would marry again. I've known him for more than a year. I met him in Provence with some friends at dinner. He's a writer, you know."

"I read about him in the papers. He seems weird."

"He's very sweet. He's not weird, Peter. He's British."

"Are you happy?"

"I was going to ask you that question."

"Yes, but are you happy with him?"

"I think I am," she said after a pause. She kissed Stanley on the forehead and held him out to look at. "What a lovely child you have, Peter. What a wonderful prospect for you."

"I know it's impossible, but I wish I were going to France with you."

"Don't talk that way, Peter."

"I loved you. I still love you."

"I loved you as well, Peter. Very much. But not so much that I would rob you of this," she said, turning Stanley toward him. Stanley smiled at him and waved his teething ring.

Peter held out his hands for Stanley and held him close.

"Will I ever see you again?"

She took his hand. "Of course. Of course you will. Do you think I would ever forget you? No more than you would ever forget me."

They walked down the pathway. The chrysanthemums, yellow, white, and pink were in bloom on both sides of the walkway. The leaves in the young maples were turning red and the sky was bright with sunshine. "I won't be away forever," Marie said. "I'm just beginning a new book. But for now we need to be in Europe. I have a new life, Peter. And so do you. We both have lives that need our attention. And you have Stanley as well as your wife. I think you'll see it's for the best. At least, I pray that it is for the best." She stood with him at the pier head. They both looked out toward Long Island, visible in a low haze far away.

"I'll never really believe that," Peter said. "What I believe is that we need to make the best of things, but not that it is all for the best. Change can't be avoided. You made me see that. Change is what life is. But it is not always for the best. Those that dare sometimes succeed and sometimes fail. But I don't think you can say that those who do not dare either succeed or fail in anything. They simply are. They simply stay where they are. I think we dared a great deal. I don't want to think that we failed."

"Neither of us failed, Peter. Don't say that. Don't ever let Stanley hear you say that. He deserves much better. Much better."

They stood silent for a few moments until *The Lost Penny* came into view around Parker Island and headed toward their dock. "I don't want to say goodbye," Peter said. "There was so much more I did want to say. So much I saved up, and I don't know how to say it."

"That's the good thing about us, Peter. You don't have to say it. I think I understand. I want you to know that I wish you great happiness. And great love in your life. You deserve that. And please think well of me." She put her arms around him and kissed him. Then she kissed Stanley and turned and went back up the walkway. Peter watched her until he heard the ferry scrape against the wood palings.

"What was that all about?" Steve Clements said, surprised.

"Just a goodbye kiss," Peter said. "Saying goodbye to the help."

CHAPTER FIFTEEN
May 1986

Peter studied the plan for the circular Temple at Tivoli in the fourth book of Vitruvius' *Ten Books of Architecture* late one May evening in 1986 when Alice came home from her PTA meeting. She had to discuss several problem children with parents, two of whom were high school friends, Sarah and Tony Pellegrino.

"You're still up," she said. "I stayed for some coffee afterward. I'm a little wired. How's Stanley?"

"Asleep, I think. He did his homework and then stayed up reading for a while."

"He's got your disease. He should get out and play more."

"He plays plenty. How did they take it?"

"I don't know. It gets harder every year. The Pellegrino kid is nasty in class and sometimes violent out of class, but Sarah thinks he's perfect. They want him to be a fighter, according to Tony. And then the Winstanleys think Martin is a genius, but I can't get him to finish any of his homework. Nobody seems able to face the truth about their kids."

Alice touched the cover of his book. "You read that a long time ago, didn't you? I don't know why you read that old stuff. Why don't you ever read something new, like Patricia Cornwell. They tell me she's really good."

Peter didn't answer. Alice left the room as she spoke and Peter closed the door now that she was home and turned out his light.

Marie Wainwright had returned to Crown Island twice since that day when he felt so awkward leaving without the satisfaction of the kind of talk he'd hoped for. She had lived on the island alone for a month in the summer of 1982, during the Reagan Recession. Peter Chello Construction had a bad year that year and Peter was working in Simsbury on a project to build a lifetime care facility for the elderly. The way the plans called for space and finish details, he knew it was for the rich elderly, people who could afford high class health care and expensive services. The commute was a problem, but he was grateful to have the work.

In March of 1982, while Peter was away on the job, Tom Chello died out at the quarry, watching some stone being loaded on a skid. He grabbed his chest and reached out for support, but, according to the quarrymaster, Tom Chello was probably dead before he hit the ground.

Marie Wainwright sent him a note of condolence. It was simply written in green ink on a piece of heavy card stationery. He saw that it had her maiden name on it, the name she used for all her books. All it said was that she thought his father would have been proud of him and that she knew how terrible it was to lose a parent. She also hoped he would hold up under the strain and that she thought fondly of him. He did not show the note to Alice.

At the funeral, Peter's mother was so shaken that she said she didn't think she could live in the little house on Toth Street by herself.

"But it's a good place, Mom."

"I know, your father always said it would be fine for me after he went. I never paid any attention to that kind of talk. He was always saying what I should do after he went."

Peter helped her go through his father's papers looking for insurance policies and some indication of what he wanted done with his things. The Connecticut General Life Insurance covered him for $7500. Aetna wrote another policy for $11,500. He had a term policy for $50,000 that had lapsed. At first Peter thought it was in force, but a phone call told him otherwise. At the bottom of his father's "document drawer" was a paid up policy from Traveler's for $20,000. Peter also found the deed to the house with that policy. So his mother would be all right. She had a mortgage-free house, $39,000 in insurance, his father's social security, and their savings, some $9200. She also had an interest in the trucks and equipment that he would honor.

Surprisingly, his father had purchased a plot in the Quarrytown Cemetery for both him and Peter's mother. The deed was with the deed to the house and it had been purchased in 1971 for $400. Peter never knew a thing about his father's wishes until he saw that deed. Fortunately, he found it while the wake was still in progress and he reached the funeral director in time to make the arrangements.

After the funeral, Peter explained what his mother needed to do to get things organized, and told her he'd drop in every day for a while, until she got herself stabilized.

"I don't think I'll ever be stabilized," she said, with her handkerchief to her eyes.

For a while, Peter's mother was confused and uncertain how to proceed. She sat in the house as if she were waiting for Tom Chello to come home, and when Peter showed up after work, she seemed to treat him as if he were his father. Peter at first came alone, but he soon learned to bring Stanley as a kind of buffer.

Stanley was in fifth grade and brought pictures and stories for his grandmother to see, and dutifully she tacked them up on the refrigerator and on the wall behind the kitchen table. After a while, the place looked like the corkboard in his classroom. Nancy Chello began to drop hints that it would be nice if they could all be under the same roof. After several weeks Peter raised the issue with Alice.

Alice was absolute. "No. I don't think I could stand it," she said.

"My mom's not that bad."

"Don't you see the way I need to work? I can't have her

in here chattering while I'm doing lesson plans or correcting papers."

"She doesn't talk that much."

"To you she doesn't. She's always talking with me about cooking this and cooking that. She'd be shocked if she knew you were doing some of the cooking."

"My dad cooked plenty."

"I can't have it."

"We have the guest room with its own bath."

"Peter. If you want to ruin a marriage, this is the fastest way. I've seen it. It never works. It's like what they say about lighthouses."

Stanley looked up. "What do they say?"

"I'll explain later," Peter said. "You're just saying you won't even think about it?"

"I'm saying I've thought plenty about it. Long before this. For God's sake, Peter, would you want my parents, either of them, in the same house for years? Think about it. And you don't have to work the way I do, either. You get your work done and then you're free when you get home. I'm not."

Peter thought about it. Alice was right in one way. He could never have stood having Harry Carlson in his house day in and day out. It was trying enough to deal with him in his own home on holidays.

Peter's first reaction was suppressed anger when Alice said "No" so absolutely, without even a discussion. In actual fact, he was not at all sure that they should have his mother with them, either. But at least he thought it was worth talking about. He felt his mother's fears and he understood her hopes. She just did not want to be alone. Who did at her age? As far as Peter himself was concerned, though, the thought of being alone for a while was attractive. He loved Stanley and had somehow found ways to appease Alice, although he never dreamed he made her truly happy. She was wrapped up in her classroom and at times seemed not to notice he was in the house. When they did talk it was very often about the issues current in the Lower School, which was relatively new and very open in its plan. That was good and bad, Alice told him again and again. He had been to the school with her to see various concerts and presentations, but he never felt very comfortable in the place.

Peter never told his mother about his talks with Alice. They had Nancy Chello over to dinner several times in the first weeks after his father's death, and in a few months Peter saw that his mother was beginning to go out with women friends, all of whom were also widows. They supported each other in a touching way. And by the middle of summer, his mother was involved in day trips and events at the Senior Center to such an extent that she was often not at home when he stopped by.

In the late spring of 1986, sitting on the end of the dock in the evening, as Peter sometimes did–almost in his father's stead–he thought of Marie Wainwright out there on Crown Island writing another book. She had come back in April as a divorced woman, according to the local paper. She had left Eustace apRoberts in France after a bitter divorce that hit gossip columns in London and New York. Peter knew none of the details, but he thought about her now living again on Crown Island and wondered whether he would go to see her.

The years had dimmed his feelings for her. She was no longer the mysterious beauty of thirty-four, and Peter was no longer a youth with ideals that he thought were realizable. His life had taken the shape it was destined to find, and he made his peace with his place in the world.

Quarrytown was not a bad fate. Many people with strings of degrees behind their names and quantities of money to support them had moved into Quarrytown, just as Tom Chello predicted, and had driven real estate to unheard of heights. They thought Quarrytown was exceptional, and Peter knew they were right. What he hoped was that Stanley would find a place in the world that would include Quarrytown if at all possible. But he did not want Stanley's life totally delimited by its moral and social boundaries.

On May Day, Peter decided that it was time for them to talk once again. He telephoned Marie and asked if he could visit. Her response was one of surprise, but also delight. "Of course, of course, Peter. I've thought of you so often. How are you?"

"I'm fine," he said. "I'll come alone this time."

"You mean I won't see how big that lovely child is?"

"He's a giant. He's playing Little League Baseball these days. Our neighbor takes him to the games. I usually bring him back. He's quite a handful."

Peter took his father's skiff, a newer Boston Whaler, out to the island that afternoon. The air was cool and the clouds overhead implied that they might get a shower. The rains in April had come late and the tulips along the walkway were brilliant. Marie waved to him from the porch. She looked a bit tired and her hair had become almost totally gray. As he walked toward her he felt some of the old pangs that had disturbed him so when he was a young man.

Marie Wainwright was no longer the young, beautiful woman he had first met and loved. Her figure was a little thicker, her complexion a bit sallow, and age was claiming them both. But still, her smile warmed him, and her radiance was such that he saw even now how easily he might fall once more under her spell. She had been a beautiful young woman, and now she was certainly a beautiful older woman.

When he reached her on the porch she held out a hand and he took it in both of his. "You look lovely," he said.

"Sadder, and wiser," she said. "Certainly not lovely. But you're kind."

"I was sorry to hear of your divorce."

"It was long in coming. I hope you never have to go through one yourself."

"I can't say I liked your husband."

"I saw that when you met. He was in particularly nasty form that day. We were under a great deal of strain. I tried to write about it all in *Here in the Sunrise.* Have you read it?"

"Of course. A romantic marriage in the south of France. It sounded exciting and very interesting."

"For a while it was. But he hated the novel. I didn't show it to him until it was in print, and I'm very glad of that. My editor, Sybil Forstner, whom you once met, insisted that I send the pages directly to her. She had a premonition, I think. Eustace was intolerable and blamed me for all kinds of awful things. His own work, you know, suffered. He said it was because of our marriage, because of the compromises I forced him to make. As far as I could see, he made few if any compromises. He went where he wanted when he wanted. I think I had little effect on the scope of his life."

"Have you given up on France?"

"For the time being, yes. I've been happy being home. The island is so calm, so peaceful, so much a centering experience. And you?"

"Fine. I've been fine."

"I was sorry to hear about your father. Is your mother well?"

"I think so. It was tough on her. Very tough. It was all so sudden. Stanley sees her a lot, more than I do, really. I think it helps. Alice's folks are getting on, too. But she's okay. She's deep in her teaching."

"You bought a house."

"Yes. A long time ago, now. I've fixed it up and we have a view of the islands from the top floor. Have you ever thought of us?"

"Us? Yes, I suppose I have. I worried a great deal about us."

"How do you mean?"

"My selfishness is what I mean. How much I needed you and how little I thought about what you needed. You came to me when I was at such a low point. I'm not at all sure you can understand what I mean. You were so young."

"Right now, I'm as old as you were when we first met. I think I'm beginning to understand what you mean. We reach certain points in our lives when things look different, when we need different people to rely on, to be with. My life would be much fuller if I had had you in it all these years."

Marie smiled at him and touched his hair. "I love your curls," she said. "They always made me think of the Roman statuary, all those dynamic men with their Empire haircuts. You still have so much of your youth about you, almost a sense of innocence."

He laughed. "Not innocence. And not much youth, either."

They went into the house and into the library. Things were much as he remembered them. Now a computer stood on the desk where her IBM Selectric once sat. A pile of galley proof sat nearby and he knew that another book was coming out.

"A new book. What's it called?"

"*Looking Out to Sea.*"

"Is it sad?"

"In some ways, I suppose. But I think it ends well. What are you reading these days?"

"Right now I'm reading Vitruvius."

"Vitruvius? I've never read him myself."

"He's in my line of work, you know. I think he's pretty remarkable. I've learned a lot from him. A lot about how to look at buildings that I didn't know before. He's made me think about design in ways I wish I had learned when I was a kid. Amazing stuff. I want to read more of that kind of thing."

"Good for you. Have you given up the idea of going back to the University?"

Peter was surprised by her question. "I'm a little old for that now."

"I don't think so," she said. "You would certainly get much more out of it now than you would have when you were young. You haven't given up the dream, have you?"

"It just seems so far out of reach. We're saving for Stanley, although I think he'll get a baseball scholarship. He's a better player than I was and he's a lot smarter. He's a really bright kid. But to tell the truth, I can't see how I could ever really go back. It seems so long ago. So far away."

"I hope you will change your mind some day, Peter. You've left something unfinished, and you know that is never a good thing."

Peter had given the idea of the University a thought now and then. He knew that he could probably take up Dean Coulton's promise of letting him return, but he was not sure Dean Coulton was still alive. Professor Steadman had died four years ago. Things would have changed enormously.

Marie let the subject drop. Peter sat on the leather couch and Marie sat in her old reading chair. They talked for several hours, some about books, some about her life in France. Peter told her how he had renamed his company Peter Chello Construction and how he had expanded the business. He feared at one point that he might be sounding vain, the way he went on about the kinds of projects he got to work on.

"You must be very proud," Marie said. "Having done that all yourself."

Peter shook his head. "It wasn't all myself. It was Alice, really. She has the knack for organization that I don't have. She got me to advertise. You may remember that brochure she put on the table at the Great Muldoon's New Year's party. Well, that was the start of it. People found out about Chello & Son and we had to start hiring people instead of being hired. That was how it all began."

"So your fate, then, has not been all bad."

He thought about that. Was it fate, or was it something else. "I think I've outgrown fate," he finally said. "It seemed so important when I was younger, when I thought there was a chance that you and I could be together. When we were reading so much wonderful literature."

"Oh, it's so strange. As I get older, I think more and more about fate. My view is almost the opposite of yours, I think. The world has acted on me in different ways from you. You seem to have acted upon the world and made it do your will."

"In the smallest way. But you act upon the world. Think of your books. Thousands of people are affected by your books. Their lives may be changed because of them."

"Too grand, too grand a view, I'm afraid. My books please some and displease others. I hear from them. I can see by what they say how little my work really affects them, no matter what they tell me. At the best, all I do is make them feel better about what they decide to go ahead and do anyway."

"Do you think that's true of the Greeks?"

"No. I doubt that anyone ever wrote them fan letters or told them how much their work changed their lives. But I do think that their work does change lives. My work is so limited in comparison."

"Yet you write."

"Yet, I'm compelled. I cannot stay emotionally healthy if I don't write. You know that. I've told you that before. My job is to entertain, to provoke, perhaps, and possibly, in some cases to enrich a life."

"The way you enriched mine."

"That's good of you to say. Very good of you. I so worried that I had done you damage. If I have enriched your life, then you have enriched mine. You gave me moments of happiness."

She stopped and seemed to hold back her emotions. "I have not had so many since."

Peter left the island with less a sense of loss than he felt when he set out. Marie was still the lovely and thoughtful woman she had always been, but he himself was a different man from the twenty year-old who had first planned the walkway that took her daily down to the water for her views of the Sound. He saw his obligations not as weights or cumbrances, but as connections with people he loved and who loved him. When he tied up the skiff, he got in his truck and drove to St. Paul's Lane and caught the last several innings of Stanley's game. He sat in the stands quietly while some of the parents yelled at their children. Stanley saw Peter and tipped his cap as if he were Lou Gehrig. Peter laid his finger at the side of his nose as if he were giving him a signal to hit and run.

CHAPTER SIXTEEN
September 1997

Stanley began law school at Georgetown in the first week of September, 1997. Peter saw him off at the train station in Elm City. Stanley talked about coming home for holidays, but it was pretty clear that Stanley would soon marry his sweetheart, Kathleen DeVille, a girl from Baltimore that he met at Brown. She would certainly have something to say about his visits home.

In college Kathleen's friends called her "Caddy" just to make her bristle. She was a free-spirited woman working with Children's Aid in Washington. Despite Alice's smoldering, mostly silent, protests it was also clear that she and Stanley were going to be living in the same apartment once Stanley got to Washington. Peter thought that was a reasonable way to go, but Alice talked about values, restraint, and propriety.

In 1985, only three years after Tom, Nancy Chello died in the Hospice in Burnford following a brief period of wasting disease. His mother had grown quieter and quieter until she could not speak at all. When Peter visited her in her own home, with the health-care provider in the next room, he found that her silence made him feel a sense of guilt that had no clear origin and no specific object. It was a general guilt he felt for the difference between their lives, for the fact that there was so little that they could talk about beyond their conversations about his father.

Nancy Chello had lived for Tom Chello, despite her independent streak, and despite her complaints and demands while he lived. When he was gone, she made remarkable efforts to shape a new life and seemed to thrive on a new level, but it was not long before she began to turn down offers of day trips, to stop answering the phone when friends called, and to seem to become, if this were at all possible, smaller and more diminutive each time Peter and Stanley visited her. What none of them knew, was that an occult tumor had taken over her body and her life.

Harry Carlson died in 1992 in the new Infiniti showroom in Franklin. He and two other salesmen were playing craps by throwing dice into the open trunk of a Q45 when he suddenly crumpled and fell on the floor dead. It was his heart, although he had had a checkup only the month before and the doctor told him he had the heart of a first-baseman. Susan Carlson followed him in less than a month.

Alice was overwhelmed emotionally and physically. Her parents died when she was involved in complex planning for a curriculum overhaul for the fourth grade. Peter helped her through it all as best he could, but she was overwhelmed and he ended up making all the funeral arrangements. Alice's older sister, Sherry, came in from Boston to help clean out the Carlsons' house and put it on the market. For a few days, Alice could not face the idea of selling the house and insisted that she and Peter should live there. But Sherry took charge and told her that the house needed to be sold now, while people were still interested in moving into Quarrytown. Peter knew that Alice wanted to save the house for Stanley, but he also knew that Stanley, if he came back to Quarrytown, would want a house very different from that cramped, old-fashioned place.

Throughout this time, Marie Wainwright occasionally came and went from Crown Island. Peter saw very little of her, but when he did see her he began by wondering what he would talk with her about, and then usually ended by listening to her in much the way he did when he was young. Marie had been in a great many interesting cities. Venice, Rome, Trieste, Verona, Florence, Paris, St. Paul de Vence, and London were most in her conversation. She showed him photographs of Venice. He knew that one day he would have to go and see buildings built on pilings in a lagoon.

Marie published *The Searching Soul* in 1992. Its settings included those cities and several others and the novel was clearly–at least in Peter's mind–a study of the kind of life Marie tried to live after leaving her husband. It was in many ways a sad book, and Peter saw how painful much of Marie's life had been. The loneliness that pervaded the book was so obviously what Marie must have experienced through these years that Peter felt a tinge of sadness. He wished there were something he could have done for her to help relieve it. But these were years when his business needed him almost as much as Stanley and Alice needed him. He had become a major player in building and construction in the Quarrytown area. When people wanted something interesting built in stone, Peter Chello was the man they called.

Life changed for Peter when Stanley left home for Washington. Both of them knew that Stanley would never live with them again. Stanley was beginning a new life, one that would take him far away and which would make it more and more difficult for them to communicate with the ease and depth that had marked Stanley's growing up, when Stanley hung on every word Peter spoke, when he deferred to every instruction, every word of advice. Since he had gone to college, all that changed.

Stanley had grown so much intellectually that Peter could see that there were times when Stanley seemed to be merely tolerant of his conversation. They had differing views on politics and religion, on work and commitment, on love, and on many other important issues. It was, Peter thought, the price he had paid for not getting his own college degree all those years ago. He was incredibly proud of Stanley, while at the same time he knew that Stanley was in a world that he could only imagine, but never truly be part of.

Peter loved Stanley from the very first moment he saw

him, and he loved every moment of his growing up. They went fishing and camping together. They played ball together. When Stanley was in high school he worked alongside Peter in the summers just as Peter had done with his own father, and at that time he began to understand how his father had grown to rely on him, how he must have had the same feelings of pride and delight in having his own son by his side. The difference now was that Stanley was off on a different path, one that led far away from Quarrytown. If Stanley had wished to stay, Peter would have been conflicted. His wishes for Stanley's future were totally different from Tom Chello's wishes for Peter. But now that Stanley was leaving, and even as he was proud of Stanley's decisions, Peter had a sinking feeling, a sense that he had lost something that could never be replaced in his life.

Alice had not wanted Stanley to go to Washington at all. There were other law schools, she told him, but his interest in international law took him where he felt he would get the best degree. Peter did not argue, but Alice did. "You've got to tell him to study closer to home," she said one evening. "You've got to be firm with him."

"He's twenty-two. I'm not going to be able to tell him that. He'll laugh at me."

"You never take my side," she said.

"What side? There's no side. I don't want him to go, either. But I can't tell him to give up his dream."

"You've never taken a firm stand when it comes to Stanley."

"That's not true. And it's not really to the point."

"Oh, now I'm not satisfying your sense of what the point is? Is that it? You're trying to tell me I'm not able to understand what's important here?"

"No. It's not that. Stanley knows that I am serious when I tell him what I think is true. And right now, I think he's got to follow his dream."

"And that girl's going to snag him. You mark my words."

"I think he loves her."

"He's too young to know who he loves."

"We were that young."

"But we stayed and helped our parents."

"Is that what's bothering you? That he won't be here to help us in our sunset years."

"Don't make it sound like a joke. It's not a joke. Look at your mother. What would have happened to her if we weren't there? Just think about it. We took care of her and made sure she was in her own home for as long as possible. Longer, probably, than she should have been there if you ask me."

"We did the right thing by her."

"Of course. Do you really think Stanley will come back here after law school?"

"No."

"And that's okay with you?"

"You know, it's Stanley that you should be talking about. Not us. We've had our opportunities. Stanley has to have his now. And Stanley's going to take his chances and make something of himself whether we like it or not. That's the way he is."

"That's the way you let him grow up."

Peter was about to answer, but he decided that nothing would be accomplished. Alice was angry and nothing would make her less irritated or any easier to get along with.

With Stanley away in school, when Peter had time to read, he had sometimes taken to commanding a large leather chair in the University Library general reading room. Most of the readers were graduate students or undergraduates, but few of them seemed ever to take notice of him. He thought of himself as an invisible scholar.

When he could take time from his job, and visit the library, he kept an entry in a notebook on each of the books he read. Recently he was reading in the history of architecture and studying the work of Mansart, Wren, Perrault, and others, all of whom amazed him. He examined the elevations of the buildings they built, read their own testimonies on architecture, and examined the plans that were available in order to see just how they solved the problems they were presented.

He made a special study of the Italian architects and found the work of Andrea Palladio to be very close to his heart. But he also loved the work of Bramante and Bernini and when he had time, he made drawings of their work. He had begun keeping a sketcher's notebook along with the ordinary notebook he kept for his reading.

He had not thought to visit Marie Wainwright right after Stanley left for college, but one rainy Thursday afternoon he decided to take his father's Whaler out to the island and see if he could reconnect with her. While Stanley was growing up, there was little room in his life for Crown Island, and Marie made arrangements with other workmen in the brief periods she spent on the island. Now, the local paper had told him she was back from a long time spent in London. When he called her, he was afraid she might not want to see him.

"Why would you think that?" she said. "I think we've reached an age when old friends are all the more precious, don't you think?"

"For me there is one friend who will always be precious."

"Yes, I feel that way, too."

"Are you staying for a while now that you're back from England?"

"I think I am. London is wonderful, but Crown Island is in my genes. I do some of my best writing here in the library you built for me. Are you still proud of it?"

"Even more. Yes. I am very proud of it. The light is so rich and perfect in it. Sometimes I go to the University Library to read, and the light is awful. I don't know how they could make a general reading room that is so vast and yet so poorly lighted."

"What are you reading these days?"

Peter described the plan he set out for himself.

"Admirable," she said. "I'm a desultory reader. But there are pleasures in that, too."

"I am going to start reading about Frank Lloyd Wright soon. I realize there are so many great modern architects and I can actually go and see some of their buildings close by. I don't think I'll ever see the great houses of Palladio or the inside of St. Peter's. Or St. Paul's. You've been in St. Paul's, haven't you?"

"Yes, and St. Peter's as well. But I was there to admire and be astonished. I would not have had your eye or your feel for the stone itself. For you it must be like seeing a structure carved out of the living rock. For me, it's just another wonderful space and a powerful expression of imagination. You'll feel that way when you go to Chartres or Salisbury Cathedral. Such noble buildings."

"I don't think I have much chance of seeing them. Alice likes to stay home."

"You should go alone."

"Maybe so. Do you go alone?"

"Sometimes. People often take me when I'm abroad. I suppose I enjoy it most when I am with friends. Going alone is fine when you know you could go again with a friend."

"Our son Stanley just left two weeks ago for Georgetown Law School."

"Congratulations to him."

"I miss him. I really don't think he'll ever be back with us again."

"A sense of loss," she said. "I understand fully what that is. But at least you will see him again."

"I'm sorry," he said. "I wasn't thinking when I said that."

"I know. It's all right. I've lost so much. Sometimes it's difficult. Maybe it's why I wander away so often. I've thought about it. People shouldn't wander the way I do."

"You wander and I stay here."

"You're like the center around which I go. Did we read

Donne's poem together?"

"Yes, and I didn't understand it at first."

"Do you like the rain?" she asked, looking out the window.

"Yes. Immensely. I know it sounds odd, but I like to watch the rain fall into the water, and I like the smell of the rain in the fall and in the spring. It comforts me."

And he realized how comforted he felt now in the library where they sat, warm and dry, looking out through rain-streaked windows. The world was more complex than he had ever thought it might be before he met Marie. In that early time he saw things much more simply, much more limited to the world of his father and the world of Quarrytown. Life had a simple shape and he understood it implicitly. Now, things seemed much more difficult and unlikely.

"There was a time when I thought you and I should be together always. I'm not entirely sure even now that I was wrong about that. But at the time when we first knew we loved each other, I saw the world as a simple place. Our love seemed to be the most important thing in the world and I was sure that we were destined to be together always. I don't know whether you have any idea how I suffered when we broke it off."

"You were a married man, Peter. You and Alice deserved a life. I had already had my chances. You deserved yours."

"But I wouldn't have married if I'd known the truth, and when I wanted us to go off together I don't think now that I would have hurt anyone as much as I feared I might. It's so strange. I was so worried about my obligations to other people. I had no concept of my obligations to myself."

"Obligations are always to others. Obligations to oneself are nothing other than selfish desires. You had so few selfish desires."

"We were the strangest of lovers, then. You had even fewer selfish desires. You gave me up."

"No. It was because I sensed so much selfishness in

myself. I wrote about that in my last book, when I finally faced myself and thought to do something about it. One thing about my writing is that it clarifies my own life. Few people would know it, but my books are like mirrors I hold up to myself. I'm sure you see that."

"Only sometimes. Most of the time your books put me in a world so real that I'm part of it. Books affect me that way. Ever since we began reading together."

Peter and Marie talked as they had years before. But even as they spoke, Peter saw that their differences, both in age and culture, had widened more than he expected. When he was twenty he thought that the years between them could be made irrelevant, but now that he was forty-five and Marie was sixty-four, he saw that he was wrong. And he saw, too, that, despite his constant reading and his love of books, the differences between them were not to be surmounted just by a strong personal effort on his part. He and Marie had grown more different than alike.

He had come to the island feeling the loss of his son. When he left the island he had another sense of loss, a loss of opportunity. Circumstances created the foundations for the choices one made, and they sometimes contributed to the symmetry of decision and desire. The mystery, he thought, as he pulled his skiff back to the town dock, was that somewhere between decision and desire the question of happiness was resolved.

Although he was not an unhappy man, Peter could never say honestly that his life had been continually happy. He always wondered what life would have been like if he and Marie had been closer in age, closer in upbringing, and closer in education. Those differences were virtually Greek in their force in his life. Changes in any one of them would have helped him be closer to Marie, but the only way he could have had the life he thought he wanted was for changes to exist in all of them. Marie and he were alike primarily in terms of sensibility. At one time, Peter thought that would be enough. He was wrong.

On the other hand, the disparity in sensibility between Alice and Peter was greater than either ever admitted. Her degree virtually ended her education, while he kept reading and learning.

In the final analysis, Quarrytown had destined Peter and Alice for one another. When he left Crown Island, Peter took a last look at Marie, standing there with her scarf protecting her from the rain. She did not raise her hand or move her head. He turned back toward the harbor to weave his way through the last of the season's moored boats wondering what his destiny might have been if he had managed somehow to stay on Crown Island when he was young.

CHAPTER SEVENTEEN
August 1998

Marie wandered away again shortly after Peter left her in the fall of 1997. She published her last book, *The Mention of You*, in early August, 1998. As with her last two books, she had her publisher send him a copy. When Alice said she thought it was strange for a woman they hardly knew to send him copies of her books, he reminded her that Miss Wainwright had promised to send him copies of all her books when he first worked for her. It was a thoughtful courtesy, he told Alice.

"You know there's always been talk of you and Marie Wainwright," she said.

Peter was surprised, but he could tell from her lack of curiosity that she didn't think it likely that Marie Wainwright could take a real interest in him. The social gulf was really too great to countenance such a possibility. "People talk a lot of nonsense," he said.

"I'm just saying. And you've got to admit it's a little weird that she keeps up with you with her books."

"Remember, she wrote most of them in the library I built for her. She's just grateful is all. Besides, the publisher just does that automatically. It's not as if she signs the books or anything."

"Well, people talk, you know."

"Let them."

In the past, Peter did not always hide his feelings for Marie as well as he wanted to. Alice rarely mentioned her, although she once complained that Marie Wainwright thought she was too good for her. In the Café or on Granite Street Marie treated Alice politely, but never spent time talking when she met her in the post office, as some other islanders sometimes did. Alice once said that Marie Wainwright seemed to have few if any friends, and that explained why she was always running off to distant places at the drop of a hat.

When *The Mention of You* arrived, Alice took it into her bedroom before Peter got a chance to look at it. She read it for two nights and gave it over to Peter with a shrug. "I don't get this one at all," she said. "It just seems to go on and on and nothing ever happens. How can you write a book where nothing ever happens and expect people to read it?"

"Some great books are that way."

"I'm not sure this is a great book."

Peter took the book and saw that Alice had not got past page thirty. Just as Marie had told him, this was a mirror she held up to herself and in which Peter began to see her clearly. The novel was set in L'Aussac, a small French village in which two Americans lived separate lives until a third, a black actor, arrived and took the largest available house to rent. It looked out over the Mediterranean and sat at the top of a long, hilly gravel road. His name was Elias Cantrell and he had become a household name in the United States, but in France he could walk through his small town unremarked except for the figure he cut as he strode out, with a walking stick as tall as he, wearing a red fedora with a long red feather. He enjoyed, as he said in one scene, all the drama he could create.

Eventually, he found Verena Moreno, well known as a daring pilot of small planes, in the café in the tiny plaza. She, in turn, introduced him to the other local American, a young poet named Halstatt Stone. Cantrell immediately christened him Prince Hal and read his poems aloud one evening in the smallest restaurant in the village, first in English, then, after a moment's hesitation, in an impromptu translation in French. Although the audience was under ten people, Cantrell made Prince Hal an instant success. The proprietor brought a bottle of her best vintage to their table and Cantrell insisted that she put a bottle on every table and put the cost on his bill. But Halstatt's sense of success was fleeting because Cantrell made Verena Moreno his mistress when Halstatt was too insecure to tell her he loved her. Before Cantrell came to the town, Halstatt had fallen in love, but he felt much too young for her and hesitated in his attentions.

While Cantrell and Verena traveled to Paris and Lyon, Halstatt suffered a depression that left him unable to write poetry. Instead he began a long philosophical work that centered on the theme of love and the agony of rejection. When Cantrell returned to Hollywood to make another film, Verena thought of going with him, but she stayed in L'Aussac writing her memoirs. When Halstatt killed himself in imitation of Sylvia Plath, the manuscript he left behind was largely unintelligible except for a long passage–presented to the reader in *The Mention of You*–that talked about the lost opportunities of a would-be lover and a would-be man. Verena, reading the manuscript, realized that he was talking about her and instead of waiting for his return, booked a passage on a flight to Cairo where she felt Cantrell would never find her and where she could start a new life that made more sense than anything she might have with an actor whose greatest love was for himself.

When Peter finished the novel, he thought Marie must have seen Hallstatt Stone as a version of himself. He was no poet, but he remembered Marie's once saying that the walkway he had built for her was like a poem. And Elias Cantrell could only have been the Great Muldoon.

Did she have an affair with Muldoon? The thought tormented him. In so many ways, Cantrell was like Muldoon. He always spoke and moved in a fashion that was larger than life. And Peter knew that Muldoon was attracted to her. He saw it that New Year's evening in 1972. Was it possible that they had traveled together? Marie had called herself a wanderer, but so was Muldoon a wanderer. The winter that Marie had lived on Crown Island, Muldoon had spent part of his time there as well.

And Muldoon had his own boat, so he could have gone to Crown Island any time. Could it be? *The Mention of You* told him it was. He thought of his father's certainty that the islanders were a people apart, that they cleaved to one another. But Muldoon was hardly an islander. He owned an island, but he had not been an islander for generations like Marie Wainwright.

Marie returned to Crown Island in the summer of 1998 to stay. She moved away from Europe like Verena Moreno, perhaps to start a new life. Peter took his boat out to the island on a breezy, but hot August afternoon. When he came up the walkway Marie was standing on the verandah watching him.

"I was hoping you'd come," she said.

"You're here to stay is what the gossip column says."

"Yes, I think they are right. I've reached a certain age, and home has reached a certain value in my life. The island is more beautiful than it was even in my imagination. You have no idea how the imagination transforms the places that are far away and important to you. But even my imagination only shadowed the reality of the island. In some ways, I think, I should never have left."

"You plan to stay year 'round again?"

"Yes, I think so. Winters have been mild, haven't they?"

"Winters, yes. But the hurricane seasons have been strong."

"The shutters work. This old house has been through them all. I'm not worried."

They went into the kitchen and sat at the table where they had once sipped tea and read the classics. "I read your new book, *The Mention of You*."

"Did you like it?"

"Yes. I did. But I thought of what you said the last time we talked, when you told me your books were mirrors you held up to yourself."

Marie's graying hair was wrapped up behind her head. Her eyes studied him and he could see the intelligent face grow interested. Her expression reminded him of the way she sometimes had looked at him when they began to read the love poems of Ovid.

"And you were looking for signs of me in the book?"

"Yes. I was. Did you have an affair with the Great Muldoon?"

"Peter. How can you ask that?"

"He was like your character Cantrell. He was just like him. I just haven't been able to get it out of my head."

"Peter, that was years ago."

She was admitting it. Peter had tormented himself with the thought that it might be true, and now she was telling him that it was.

"Marie. He's so gross."

"It was long ago, as I said. And why should I not have an affair with him or anyone else? You can't be jealous of him or anyone, can you? We haven't been lovers for years, Peter. How can you be jealous of what I do?"

Peter shook his head lamely. "I don't know. I can't get the idea . . . . I can't imagine that you'd want him. He's loud and insensitive, and really dumb in a lot of ways."

"He was smarter than you think."

"I know I don't have a right to tell you what to do."

"No, you don't. But now you're trying to tell me not about what I will do or am doing, but what I've done. Peter, you can't do that. Miles Muldoon was very romantic. And, yes, he was showy and dramatic, too. But when I gave you up, I had nothing. Do you remember that time? Not the New Year's party, but much later. When you had your son."

"Before you got married."

"Yes

"He came here in his boat and we became friends. Only for a time, and I realized that he was not a person of real dimension. But you've got to see that he wanted me and I wanted someone too. And Peter. He told me about you and

Constance Faynell."

"What could he have told you?"

"He told me what you did not tell me. About how she took you upstairs to the widow's walk observatory. About how she tried to seduce you and partly succeeded. And that was the night we made love ourselves, and you never told me."

"That was stupid. So stupid. I never meant for it to happen, and I agonized over it. God, that was so wrong in every way. That woman was so meaningless to me. I don't know what she wanted."

"She wanted you, Peter. She wanted you just as I wanted you. Do you remember how beautiful you were at that age. How could she have not wanted you? For her it was a conquest."

"Was I a conquest for you? Is that what I was?"

She smiled at him and touched his hand. "You were my loveliest conquest, Peter. And my most terrifying conquest because you conquered me much more than I conquered you."

Peter thought for a moment about himself as he now was. How strange to think of himself as a conquest at any age, but now he could hardly imagine the idea.

"Didn't I warn you about her?"

"Yes, yes. Alice was with that fellow. I don't remember his name. I was feeling so awful that night. I thought my life was ruined."

"Your life was only beginning. That's what you didn't understand. It was my life that had been ruined, and more than once. Losing you was only one more instance."

"But how could you sleep with that man, Marie? How could you do it? He was so vulgar. Or not vulgar, just ridiculous. The way he showed off and the way he fawned over all those people. God."

"You're judging me, Peter. You think you're judging Miles Muldoon, but you're judging me. Do you think that's fair? Have I judged you?"

Peter knew she was right. "No, no. You haven't. But

sometimes I felt judged, because I left the University."

"It was something you had to do. But it's true. I've often thought you might want to go back to the University and take up where you left off."

"But you were educating me."

"That's not the same."

"I was reading great books. I kept reading books. I've always read books because of you. You got me going and I have not stopped yet."

"Yes, that's a wonderful thing. You and I were lovers in several ways. We loved each other and we loved the literature we read together. But as lovers of what we read, we were not antagonists of that literature."

"I'm not sure I know what you mean."

"We accepted what we read instead of contesting it and coming to a new understanding. That's one of the many things that were missing for you and that's why I thought you might want to go back and acquire a real education."

"Then you're saying I've still not got it, not a real education. Is that right?"

"That's for you to decide, Peter. I don't want you judging me and I resolve not to judge you. That will be up to you to judge for yourself. Only you can know whether your education is complete."

"No education can be complete, can it?"

"No. We read because we know there is more to understand, more to feel, more to learn."

"Is that also why you write."

"Yes, in a way it is one of the most important reasons why I write. But what I'm educating when I write is my soul, my inner self, my emotional life. Does that make sense to you?"

"I'm not sure."

"For me it's true."

"Did Muldoon help you with your inner life?"

"Peter, that's cruel. I've told you I needed him at a time

when I was myself vulnerable. And, yes, in his way he did. He hurt me in ways that I think I ultimately deserved, but before that he was very much what I needed. I think I used him as much as he thought he used me." Marie watched Peter's expression. "Yes," she said, "I was capable of using someone, even a lover. I've told you that before. One thing I worried about was my using you when you were too young to understand what real love meant."

Peter was stung. "I knew what real love meant." He thought back to his early days on Crown Island and the way he often spent the mornings fantasizing about Marie, imagining her coming to him and taking him into her arms and holding him tenderly. They were fantasies long before they became realities, but in some ways Marie was right in saying he did not know what love meant, not really. He knew what fantasies were. And he knew what obligation was. His relationship with Alice was based on an intense and complex web of obligation. But his relationship with Marie was totally different. He felt no sense of obligation, no need to satisfy something outside himself. Instead, he felt a welling of emotion that bound him to Marie in mind and body. When he and Marie became lovers he found himself so helplessly a part of her world, so much in need of her touch and her attention that he was like a man possessed. Loving Marie was unlike anything he had experienced or imagined. He was utterly unprepared for it, but once he had it he was unprepared to lose it. The thought that the Great Muldoon had possessed any part of Marie in the way he had, tormented Peter. It seemed to him a betrayal of the worst kind, and yet the pain he felt even now, so long after their romance had become something other than what it was, told him just how shocking love could be, how deep it reached in his life even though his life was in fact removed so far from Crown Island that it was, in the very sense his father had tried to tell him so long ago, a foreign territory.

"You discovered what love meant when you had your

son."

"I discovered it when we touched each other the first time. It was like nothing I'd ever experienced, like nothing that I thought I could ever feel. You were like a goddess to me."

"And now Miles Muldoon has made me human in your eyes?"

He shook his head. He didn't want to think of it that way.

"If he did, then bless him. I should be human in your eyes. You were like a young god walking into my life that morning so long ago. You could never see it, but in the Greek world it was normal for a god to walk out of the water into the sunshine of a young woman's life, and you did exactly that. So now, Peter, we are both humans at last. How does it feel?"

Peter placed both hands over his face and held them there. He knew that she was right. Marie was always right. Maybe this day would help him make better sense of his life. But no matter what she said, or how right she was, Peter knew he was not yet ready to accept things on the terms Marie set out, even though it meant that he could forgive himself for his own stupidities and his own missteps. One of the painful things he knew about himself was that he could forgive Marie much more easily than he could ever forgive himself. Marie's life was so clearly different in scope from his, so much more marked by the depth of her thought and understanding of the forces in the world around them that he felt the limits of his own life closing in on him again. He had no right to judge Marie. What right did he have to feel such deep pangs of jealousy? The Great Muldoon was long gone from Extra Island and long gone from the world of television. He was at best a shooting star. Yet, Peter felt the pain in his heart when he thought of Marie in his arms, in his bed.

"I would have stayed with you," Peter said.

"You would not have had your son."

"You would not have had your loneliness."

"I'm not at all sure of that. You could not have cured all my troubles, you know. Some of them were my own to work out, and painful or not, I think I worked them out as best I could. And I hope I hurt you less than I would have if we had ignored the world and stayed together."

"Oh, God," Peter said.

CHAPTER EIGHTEEN
Fall 2001

Her obituary in the *Times* made much of Marie's father, Senator Aldridge Wainwright, and the several tragedies in Marie's life. It also described her novels and discussed the likelihood of their enduring reputation. Marie had died of sudden heart failure and the newspaper said she had been living on borrowed time according to the specialists who had treated her. The photograph showed her standing outside her home on Crown Island. Her expression was serious, but her beauty was clear and apparent. She was standing on the walkway he had constructed for her.

Marie was buried in the last week of July in Quarrytown Cemetery in the Wainwright plot. The local Firehouse Bagpipe Brigade played in front of Channel 8 television crews and some locals responded to the demand for interviews to make the evening news more interesting. Buddy Dooley predicted that the television crews would be out in force on Crown island. Late on the day Peter brought Marie's Jasper home, the crews took the ferry out one after the other and set up in front of the house and performed their eulogies. A professor from the University commented on Marie's novels and tried to say something about her place among distinguished women in the literature of New England. None of what the professor said made much sense to Peter.

Peter had been careful to stay away from anyone with a camera. Most people in Quarrytown knew he was a friend of Marie Wainwright, but he could not discuss his feelings with anyone, especially someone who would broadcast them to the world. He set up a sleeping basket for Jasper in the garage. Alice denied Stanley's plea for a cocker spaniel when he was young and having a dog in the house now might cause trouble, but Peter did what he knew he had to do.

"How long do we have to keep it?" Alice said when she realized he was not going to take it back to the island.

"I don't know," Peter said. "As long as it takes."

"As long as it takes to what? Drive me crazy? You know how I am about dogs."

"Jasper's a good dog. He's not going to get into trouble. All he wants is some peace and quiet."

"I can't figure out what it is between you and that woman."

"That woman is dead. She's a ghost. There's nothing between us. I just want to be sure the dog isn't put down just because he's homeless. Marie loved him."

Alice looked at Peter as if something was dawning on her, but she held herself back. "Keep him in the garage," she said. "Just keep him away from the furniture. He sheds. I don't have time to deal with dog hairs all over my house."

By the middle of September they had gotten used to Jasper. He ingratiated himself with Alice, finally, and took a place in their evening lives when Alice and Peter watched television or when Peter sat in the small living room reading. Jasper had been Marie's dog, and now he attached himself to Alice. It was a clear gesture, one that broke Alice's resistance and allayed her resentment. She responded as anyone might to a creature who seemed to love her.

The letter came from Ellington and Edwards on Thursday, September 13th. It was a thick letter looking very official. Peter had seen such lawyers' letters in regard to various projects he had worked on, but this one was not addressed to his company. It was addressed to him.

What it told him left him in shock. Marie Wainwright had left him a bequest in her will, and Staunton Ellington wanted him to come to his offices to hear the reading of the will on Monday, October 15th. The reading was to take place at one p.m.

"I can't go with you," Alice said. "What do you think it's all about? Why wouldn't Mr. Ellington just tell you rather than keep it a dark secret? And what in the world was going on in that woman's mind to leave something to you in her will? How well did you know her?"

"I worked for her. We got close after a while. We got talking about books. I've told you all about that. We would sometimes read to each other. Books were important to both of us."

"You never read anything to me."

"I offered to. But you were always busy."

"I had to keep up. I had too much to do. But you must have been very close if she thought you wanted something from Crown Island. You know, I've heard things in the hairdresser's from time to time. They say she had a lover here in Quarrytown and had one for a number of years. They say he shows up in her books."

She looked at him as if she were waiting for him to admit that he was that man. For a few moments he thought he should tell her the truth. He didn't feel the need to lie anymore and he didn't want to cover it over. He had been discreet out of consideration for Marie, not for himself. He always thought it was Marie's reputation that would be hurt, not his.

"You were having an affair with her, weren't you? That's why she sent you those books and that's why you went out to work on the island so much. When we were first married. You were out there everyday, sometimes very late. Did you think I didn't notice?"

"She changed my life," Peter said. "I don't think you'd understand that."

"I'm your wife. Peter. You think I wouldn't understand? How could I not understand?"

"She needed me."

"Oh, God. Peter. How lame that sounds. How goddam lame that is. Needed you? And you needed her, I bet? Even though you had a wife and a son. You thought you needed her?"

"I did need her. I didn't know it at the time, but I needed her to help me see what I didn't know and what I didn't understand."

"Were you sleeping with her?"

Peter couldn't look at Alice at first. He studied the carpet. "The answer is yes."

"The answer is yes? The answer is yes? My God in heaven. Is that all you can say? You've been sleeping with another woman for how many years? And all you can say is the answer is yes?" Alice fell into a chair by the dining room window. "How long have we been married? Thirty years. I haven't so much as looked at another man in all those years. And all this time you've been in love with another woman." Alice looked shattered. Her eyes were red and the tears welled from them. She splayed her hands out on the table top and stared at them.

"It's not been all this time."

"What does that mean?"

"It was before we got married. Then for a while afterward, but we stopped. It stopped. She got married and wandered away to Europe. We were friends after that. Only friends. She felt bad about all this, too."

"Oh, that's great. She felt bad. How do you think I feel? After holding our marriage together after we lost our child? How do you think I feel?"

"Would you have done things differently if you had known then?"

"Yes," she said, looking up at him. "Yes, I would have done things differently. I almost left you when we lost our daughter. You have no idea how I felt. And I can see why. You were too busy elsewhere at the time."

"That's not true. I felt just as bad as you."

"Impossible. You couldn't even fathom how I felt. I never knew a person could feel so bad about life. And if it weren't for Stanley, I would have left you. If I didn't have work–if I didn't have my teaching . . . ." She looked up at him.

"Marie's dead. There has never been anyone else in my life. I don't know what to say. But I do know that I needed her when she was in my life. She's held up a lamp for me in ways that were crucial to me. She made me a different kind of person than I was."

"Now, I realize exactly what you mean, because after we were married there were many times when I wondered where the man I thought I married had gone. You were totally different, totally unreachable at times. You don't even realize how much you were different. You always had your nose in a book, and you never seemed to like the things we used to do before when we were dating. I thought you might have been going through a change of some kind and that you'd soon become the man I had planned so long to marry. But your change was not a phase, the way I thought it would be. That's why I wanted to leave you. I didn't recognize you. I couldn't talk with you."

"I loved you in a different way than the way I loved Marie."

"Oh, God, don't talk to me about love. She was using you. You don't see it, though, do you? She was out there a lonely widow and then you came along and took off your shirt and she fell for you the way rich women fall for their gardeners or chauffeurs. She's like all the rich snobs out on the islands. They look on us like we're their servants."

"It wasn't like that."

"I'll bet it wasn't. Maybe it was worse. So what did she give you that was so important, that I couldn't give you?"

"Don't put it that way."

"What way can I put it? Is there a good way to put it? Is there something wrong with the way I put it, now? Just tell me. What was it that was so important?"

"She taught me how to live. That's what she taught me. It was something nobody else ever gave me a clue about. Not a clue. We talked about Greek and Roman literature on the surface, but below the surface we were talking about the way we ought to conduct our life. My life. Fate. Up to that point all I had been doing is what I was told to do. What my father needed me to do when he got hurt, when I had to drop out of the University. I did what was expected of me. I don't think you can understand that."

"Don't tell me what I can or cannot understand. What I understand is that you've been living a lie for years and I should have known it. Tell me one thing."

He looked at her.

"Why didn't you just run off with her if she was so important to your life? Why didn't you do the honest thing and stop making a mockery of our marriage?"

"I wanted to."

"Oh, my God. You wanted to?"

"Yes. She wouldn't do it. There were too many years between us. I was too young, she was too old. Now I think she was right, but then I couldn't see it. I thought we could get past that difference."

"That was when you left me? When you went to Packy Caserto's to stay? Is that what happened then? I never could understand that move on your part. Why didn't you stay away?"

"For one thing, she wouldn't have me. She wouldn't let me stay. And for another thing, I still thought we could make it all work somehow. I don't know. I was crazy, I think. I tried to make it work, and who knows? I was young."

Alice glared at him. She took her things from the dining room table and moved through the hallway and up the stairs. He listened to the determined violence of her feet on the landing, then the slamming of the door to her bedroom. He was not sure whether or not she was crying in her room, or if she were on the telephone to her sister or a friend, or maybe just lying on the bed staring at the ceiling. Her anger was immense, but he knew she would soon have to calm down, and soon they would have to talk again. Somehow, instead of feeling terrible, he began to feel much better, much more relieved.

Alice was right in one way. He had been living a lie for a long time and now that it was out and she knew the truth–or as much of the truth as he knew himself–he felt a sense of enormous relief. The world was on balance now. Marie Wainwright, the lovely, generous woman he loved for so long, was now gone and his guilt went with her. If he had not told Alice, he would have felt the sad pressure of guilt that had plagued him over the years. He had done something that Alice knew was wrong, but that he knew was right. Alice was going to have to deal with its complexities now, and he was not entirely sure she could.

They did not talk for three days. Alice took refuge in school and went up to her room after she had her own dinner. In the evenings when she had to leave for meetings, she stayed out until they were over. Peter came home from his own work as late as he could. He cooked his own meals in the kitchen when Alice was not home. He read in his own bedroom as much as he could. But not every night. Some nights he was so emotionally torn that the words swam in front of his eyes. He wanted to talk with Alice, but he had no idea what he would say. He simply thought it was essential that they say something. He did not expect her to forgive him, and he half expected that she would have told him to move out. But she said nothing to him. Their house was large enough that they could live in it virtually independently and not have to see each other or speak to one another. He remembered once when Alice was in high school how she had given the silent treatment to one of her classmates, her boyfriend before she began to go out with Peter. Alice had been a forceful personality as a young woman. She could impart her rage from transcontinental distances even then. Now it was Peter's turn.

The weekend was the most difficult time for both of

them. The Saturday was a bright, hot day with people sitting on the beach with their children, looking out at the islands, welcoming the boaters. Peter drove alone in his pickup truck to see how happy people were living. Alice stayed home. He gave her as much room as he could. He had lunch in Franklin and roamed through the one good bookstore in the area looking for something that would take his mind off his pain. Most of the great books he saw were explorations of pain very different from his. He leafed through a recent biography of Frank Lloyd Wright. Peter studied the designs Wright sketched in advance of executing some of the interesting personal homes he prided himself in making. They were homes that Peter saw had a kind of physical poetry embedded in them. They resonated and sounded in a visual manner that was as explicit for him as the sound of music. Wright understood stone just as he understood space.

On the last Sunday in September, Peter spent the morning at the church in Quarrytown looking out at the islands. Ricky Coddle, standing in his sermonic robes, spoke about the struggle to free oneself from guilt and Peter thought that he must have been speaking directly to him. How had it come that he should have dropped into church just then, when his own deepest concerns were on the lips of the minister whose son had once asked him for a job in the building trade?

Ricky was unaware of his troubles with Alice. Or could Alice have told him? He couldn't imagine it. Instead, Peter thought that guilt must have been a regular problem in Quarrytown and that it was appropriate for the minister to talk about self-forgiveness every three months or so, when the pressure built up and it was time to let off the moral and ecclesiastical steam.

Alice did not come to church. He did not think she would. Ricky Coddle spoke with him at the door, but said nothing that indicated he thought the sermon was more appropriate for him than for anyone else. "Are the blues running?" Ricky asked.

"Sure. You're not out there?"

Ricky shook his head sadly. "Too much to do. Always too much for me to do around this time of year. Drives me crazy. Of course, folks bring me the odd fish now and then as an offering. I'm pretty sure they think it's symbolic, like those fishy things you see on the backs of Volvos. Maybe they think a nice fish will be a protection against accidents, so I don't fall down the cellar stairs back of the church."

"You ever fall down those stairs?"

"Not yet. Maybe you can check them one of these days. Make sure I never do."

"You worried about that?"

"When you got stairs, you got to be careful," Ricky said. Peter smelled cigarettes on his breath and wondered what kind of guilt Ricky Coddle worried about. "You coming to church regularly now?"

"No. Just want to keep you guessing, Ricky." Peter turned and walked down the cement path to the street. Several people gathered there in conversation, but most people went across the street toward the water and got into their cars. Some of them had newspapers under their arms and were heading home for a nice Sunday, reading about the world.

Peter felt a little better. Ricky Coddle was a curious man. He rarely said five words when you met him on the street, but when you got him in church he waxed thoughtful, philosophical, and spoke at length without reference to notes or books. He believed the things he said, and, though the church was essentially Congregational, Ricky attracted a number of Catholics and Jews from Quarrytown, all of whom came to hear his good natured sermons. As far as Ricky was concerned, guilt was always with us, like the bacteria living inside our bodies. The trick was not to let it become an infection, a wholesale attack on our system.

Alice was at home most of the day, busy in her room.

When she came out of it, she timed herself against Peter's own movements. So they spent the day without seeing one another.

On Monday the 15th, in the morning, Peter checked in on a new local project. It was a house down on the far eastern end of Termite Falls Road, almost all the way to Guildford. The owners were a young couple from New York City who wanted their house faced with Quarrytown stone rather than the vinyl that was being used in most of the new houses they were building at the developments in Bobcat Springs and The Newlands. Vinyl siding was unacceptable to Peter, but no one else seemed much to mind. They hardly noticed. He was especially glad that the house on Termite Falls Road was going to be distinguished with stone.

When he pulled up outside the Ellington and Edwards office after lunch, he was a few minutes late and the secretary signaled to him to go right into the conference room where he heard some voices. He was shocked when he saw Alice in the room talking with Staunton Ellington.

"Hi," she said, as if nothing had happened.

"Hi. You're not in school."

"I thought this might be more important."

"It is more important," Staunton said. He came to the door and shook Peter's hand. "Wow," Staunton said, looking down at his own hand. "What a grip."

"From working with stone. Sorry."

"No, it's okay. I thought I had a big hand." He gestured to the two women already seated. "You know Buffie Callaway and Molly Parady?"

"I've seen you both," he said, shaking hands more carefully. "Hi." Buffie Callaway lived on Spyglass Promenade. She was a large woman with lemon colored hair. Molly Parady was in her seventies. He had seen both women on Granite Street and elsewhere in town, but had never had conversations with either. They were the governors of the Quarrytown Land Conservancy. He had read about them occasionally in the paper.

Staunton Ellington walked to the far side of the table and pointed to a chair next to Alice. Peter sat down while Staunton stood and shoveled a few files back and forth in front of him until he found the one he wanted. Staunton Ellington was a thin man with a gray striped suit and dark suspenders just visible under his jacket. He wore a narrow silk tie almost the same color as his suit. A gold tie pin held it in place.

"Is this going to take very long?" Peter asked.

"I don't know. Maybe. All depends. Let's see." He found another folder and opened it. "Ah. Here it is. We had a correspondence with you when my father had the firm, didn't we?"

"Did we?"

"Sure. Just curious about it. Had to do with some building you did for a client. As far as I can tell, anyway. Is that right?"

Peter waited while Ellington thumbed through the file.

"Sure, here it is. I guess that was taken care of." He read the paper before him. "You did some building for Marie, too, didn't you?"

"Some repairs. And an addition."

"Yes. She was very pleased with your work." Ellington reached behind him and poured a glass of water. He offered it to Alice, Buffie, Molly, then Peter, and when they turned it down he drank it off himself. "Well, we have some interesting things to discuss today. Do you have any idea what Marie Wainwright intended in her will? Peter, did she ever discuss it with you?"

"No."

"Did she ever discuss anything with you?"

"Nothing that had anything to do with her property. No. When we talked, it was usually about literature or art. That was our common ground."

Alice looked at him, then averted her eyes.

"And, Buffie, have you talked with Marie about the arrangement she had with the Quarrytown Land Conservancy?"

He examined the papers in front of him. "Since 1986, when Marie got divorced?"

"I've not talked with her for some time. I can't remember when."

"We had an arrangement that was supposed to be in effect starting in 1971, I believe," Molly Parady said. "But you must know about that because your father was the lawyer making the arrangements. I saw Marie after her divorce, but we didn't have much time for a conversation. She was living on the island very much like Garbo. I was really worried that she might be suffering depression."

"So you've not had any talks with the Conservancy about Crown Island?"

"We maintained the flower beds this month, and sent men out to keep the house in order. We didn't want it to be damaged or lure people to vandalize it."

"Well," Ellington said thoughtfully. "We may have something of a problem here, but then again there may be no problem at all. Peter, back in 1971 Marie Wainwright had some serious discussions about giving her property, which is essentially all of Crown Island, to the Quarrytown Conservancy. She intended to have the property remain much as it is as a tribute to her parents, and I imagine her lost family, too. I'm not entirely clear about that. The arrangements were made then by my father. I was away at school at the time. I don't even remember any discussions of the subject in our family. Not that my father would breach confidentiality. That's not what I mean, but something like this would have been big news and I wouldn't have been surprised to hear my father talk about it. Crown Island is a pretty important place in this town, after all."

"I know. And it's a beautiful place as well."

"Quite beautiful, yes. So this will come as something of a surprise."

Ellington held his pen at a sharp angle and leaned back thoughtfully as if wondering if he should impart the news or hold back. His expression became suddenly distant, as if he were musing on the past. He moved one of the files in front of him and looked down at it for a long moment.

"Marie Wainwright has left the property to you."

"What?" Alice said, shocked. "You mean she's left the island to us?"

"Well, technically, no. She has left the island, the house and all appurtenances, as well as a considerable sum from which the interest will pay upkeep and maintenance to your husband."

Alice studied him. "You mean only to Peter, not to us jointly?"

"Essentially, that's what I am saying. Now, I know this is all a technicality and that you will both want to decide what to do with the property, but as I said, it is Peter's decision alone that will count in a court of law. It is his property now."

Molly Parady was stunned. "How is this possible? She made it very clear that we were to take the property and maintain it as it currently is to memorialize her parents."

"But that arrangement was changed when Marie got married. You know that. We talked about it in this office. I was just starting out with the firm."

"But she got divorced," Buffie said. "We assumed then that the original agreement was back in effect, that she would leave Crown Island to the Conservancy."

"Marie was clear with me on that," Staunton said. "I have gone over her papers and I have made sure that there is no later document that might invalidate this will–and believe me I have been thorough–so we must honor her wishes as she established them here. She has left a sum of $35,000 to the Conservancy in any event. But Crown Island goes to Peter Chello."

"Don't I have a say in this?" Peter asked.

"How do you mean? You always have a say in anything pertaining to you."

"I mean, is this then automatically mine, or do I have a

right of refusal?"

"What? What do you mean a 'right of refusal'? In a will, property is transferred from the deceased to the intended recipient. You can sell the property or give it away, but legally it is yours. Which reminds me that you should immediately take out liability insurance just in case some crazy kid beaches his boat on the island and kills himself in the process. You don't want to take chances."

"Wait, I don't own anything yet. There has to be a transfer of deed before I actually own it."

"Yes, of course. But that's all a formality."

"You said there was money to maintain the property?" Alice was following the discussion carefully.

"Yes, the amount at this moment is . . .," he put on his glasses again to study the file before him, "approximately three million four hundred sixty-two thousand and change. But that will be somewhat altered by the time you take possession."

"I don't understand," Alice said.

"Well, with the transfer of the island you also will have the transfer of Miss Wainwright's royalties, which will, as far as I can tell, continue for some time, perhaps for your lifetime."

"Three million?" Alice said.

"Of course, that would have been quite a bit more before the divorce. I'm sure you know that. Mr. apRoberts was given a substantial settlement and that reduced the size of the estate by more than half. Actually, much more, really. Mr. apRoberts had a very good London solicitor. We had a remarkable fight on our hands. I was just joining the firm at that time, but I did take part in some of the discussions because my father wanted me to see how lawyers behave when they play hardball."

"I'm not sure I want any of it," Peter said.

"Peter!" Alice was shaken. "Don't say anything now."

"Yes, your wife is correct. You really shouldn't do anything more than listen to what I have to say before you make any response. No action on your part is necessary at this time. I have some issues to take care of in State Court in Elm City. We have time, in other words. And there's more."

"More? What more could there be?" Peter hardly knew how to respond. When he read the letter saying that he needed to talk with Ellington and Edwards, Peter thought that Marie might have left him some of her books, or perhaps a painting. They had spent hours talking about the beautiful Childe Hassam that hung beside her bed. It was a scene from Old Lyme near the Lieutenant River where a woman sat in the high grasses. She bore a striking resemblance to Marie because the woman was her father's mother. But he never expected that Marie would have left him the entire island. What would he do with Crown Island? How could he ever take up residence there now that Marie was gone? What was Marie thinking when she decided to make such a bequest? Suddenly, Crown Island seemed a burden to him.

"What do you mean, there's more?" Alice asked.

"Yes," Buffie Callaway said. "There must be more."

"Well," Staunton continued, "the money in the portfolio right now is mostly invested in conservative instruments, and I recommend that you keep it that way. The terms of the will insist that the money be used for only a narrow range of purposes. One, of course, concerns the upkeep of the property. There is a liberal arrangement in the structure of the investments, which have yielded approximately 7.63% annually. The interest on three hundred thousand of that money is allocated for repairs, garden maintenance, and related expenses to keep the house in proper shape. There is a conservator arrangement with our firm. I am to hire annually an inspector to review the property and make recommendations. Should our firm be dissolved, that responsibility devolves onto the Elm City Bank and Trust company, by whom the funds are managed. Do you follow me on that point?"

Peter nodded.

"Then, the most interesting detail. For a limited period of time Miss Wainwright intended that funds from her investments service you directly, Peter."

"Service me?"

"Well, I may use the wrong language. I don't exactly mean 'service' in any technical sense. But Marie Wainwright felt very strongly that you lost a great opportunity when you dropped out of the University. Her bequest to you has conditions attached, although I would say they are painless conditions."

"She wants me to return to the University?"

"In essence, yes. Now, I don't think you should bristle at that thought. Marie Wainwright was one of the most generous women I have ever known. We became friends in these later years after my father died and I began to work on her behalf. I found her sensible and intelligent to a degree that deeply impressed me. I would not just call her an intelligent woman. I would call her a wise woman. A woman who understood the meaning of wisdom. As few of us do," he added.

"What is the condition?" Alice asked.

"Well, it's a bit unusual. Miss Wainwright was a very patient woman. She did not expect things to happen instantly, and I certainly believe she did not want to coerce anyone into anything. But what the terms of the bequest insist upon is that the property be transferred to you with this one caveat. Well, actually, two caveats. The first is that you are restrained from developing any of the land on the island that does not already contain a building. As you may know, Aldridge Wainwright once applied to the town for the right to develop the island and was granted that privilege, but for some reason he held off. That's the first thing. The second is that if, after ten years you have not satisfied the requirements for a degree at the University, Crown Island and its appurtenances, including the Wainwright House in excellent condition will become the property of the Quarrytown Conservancy, to be managed by them as a memorial to be used for the public good as the Conservancy sees fit." Mr. Ellington smiled warmly at Buffie and Molly. "So, you see that she has been more than generous on every count."

"This is final?" Molly asked. "There is no question about this?"

"It was Marie Wainwright's specific wish. She was absolutely certain on this point. But you see that the Conservancy still has an interest in the property on condition that Mr. Chello not complete the degree in the allotted time."

"Who is responsible for monitoring him? Must we do that?"

"Our offices will take care of that, or if our offices are closed, Elm City Bank. Mr. Chello must present his degree transcript to our office some time before the ten years are out."

"I hope," Buffie said slowly, "that the Chellos will honor Miss Wainwright's memory and keep the Island as pristine as it has always been." Her tone made her disappointment and skepticism clear. She seemed shocked at the disposition of the Island.

Peter was still overwhelmed by what Ellington told him.

"Is there some way we can inspect the property?" Alice asked.

"Well, of course. You can go out to the island whenever you wish. I don't have a key to the front door, though. I'm not sure that Miss Wainwright ever locked it. There must be a key somewhere, but if so it's probably in a desk drawer somewhere out there."

"Did Marie have any other relatives that you know of?" Molly Parady asked.

"None that I know of, and none that would figure in this settlement. I quizzed Miss Wainwright very carefully when she drew up this will. It replaced a former will that had been in effect from her marriage to the year of her divorce, when she drew this will up. You know, this is really astonishing to me. If you'll permit me, Peter. You must have made an amazing impression on Marie Wainwright."

"She made an impression on me, is more the point," Peter said.

"Yes, but it's not every day that someone who is not related by blood comes into such a remarkable property. These islands, you know, have been passed down through the generations very cautiously. Some go back six or seven generations, to before the Civil War. Kidd's Island, for example, has property that goes back to the surveying techniques George Washington used. You can see it in the deeds and statements of ownership in Town Hall. It's remarkable. So my point is that you must have meant a great deal to her."

"We were friends for a long time," Peter said.

"Can we go out to the island?" Alice asked again.

"Oh, certainly," Ellington said. "But first I've got to ask you, Peter, to sign a couple of these forms indicating that I have read you the will and that you understand the nature of the bequests that are involved in everything here."

"They don't commit me to anything?"

"No, but they're important legally."

Peter signed the forms and saw the expectant look on Alice's face. He wasn't sure what was on her mind.

Ellington looked toward Buffie Callaway. "On behalf of the Conservancy, and to protect its interests, you'll want to sign this." He passed a document in triplicate toward her and she signed it with a flourish.

"I think," Buffie began, "that what we would most like to do is make sure you know our long term interest in Crown Island. We made some plans that Marie Wainwright approved. She approved of them heartily. We want to help you."

"Help? How?"

"Well, for one thing, by offering you a detailed understanding of Miss Wainwright's wishes. I would assume you would want to honor her wishes in the use of the property."

"She seems to have left that up to me."

"Perhaps, but if you do not get a degree at the University within ten years the island reverts back to the Conservancy according to the same terms Miss Wainwright originally laid out.

I'm correct about that, am I not?"

"Yes."

"Well, then, it is in our best interests to work together. It's one way we can respect Miss Wainwright's wishes, and honor the family that maintained the island for so long."

Staunton Ellington stepped forward after taking the document from Buffie and placing it in a large folder. He looked at Peter. "Now, I'll be in touch with you again later in the week, Peter. And I wouldn't be surprised if you hear from some of the other people at the Conservancy. They will maintain an active interest in Crown Island. If you have any difficulties there, I would like you to call me. I want everything to go as smoothly as possible."

Peter nodded and put on his cap. Alice was at the door waiting for him. As they went out, she held onto his arm.

"I'd like to go out to the island," Alice said, as they went down the front steps.

"Now?"

"Yes. I want to see it during the day and this is the best time. Will you take me?"

Peter did not want to go to the island, nor did he want to take Alice out there. He looked around for Alice's car, but saw only his own pickup. He had left Jasper inside, sitting in the driver's seat. "Where's your car?"

"I had Matty Ross drive me from school. I thought we should have only one car. Will you take me out there, or do I need to get Steve Clements?"

"You don't have to get Steve Clements. Why do you want to go to the island?"

"Why would you think? I want to see what you have inherited. The price was very high, so I want to see what you paid for."

"I didn't pay for anything. I don't even want the thing."

"Peter, if we are going to keep this marriage together, we need to work together. I've done some thinking. There was a time when I would have left you over this, and gladly. I would have given you your freedom any time you asked for it in those years when you and Marie Wainwright were making love behind my back. But I decided something. I decided that she's now a ghost, and there is no point in being jealous of a ghost, or of harboring any hard feelings toward a ghost. I don't know whether I can forgive you for what you've done, but we've had a life together. There's Stanley, and our parents, God rest their souls. And there's the work we did to make the business what it is. All that is important, and we did it together. Do you think what we did together is worth keeping together?"

Peter turned the corner down Granite Street toward the town dock. "Yes," he said. "I thought so even when you weren't talking to me."

They rode in silence. Peter found an open spot and looked out over the water. Jasper headed to the end of the dock. The surfaces of the water reflected the sun in large clots of light as the wind whipped up some small whitecaps. Trees on the nearest islands bent slightly and their dark leaves drifted off over the water.

"We're going to get wet," he said. He had tied the Whaler near the fireboat and they had to climb down a wooden ladder from the pier house where his father had spent so many evenings talking with his friends. "You up for this?"

Alice nodded. She had a light blue sweater that came up to her throat. The wind was brisk and the light strong, but she indicated with her hand that she'd be fine. Peter maneuvered to the nearest float, where Jasper waited for him. As he pulled alongside, Jasper jumped into the skiff and headed for the prow. Peter took the boat out over the water past Mother's Island and on a straight line toward Kidd's Island. The water was rough and the boat hauled and tossed on the surface, fighting against the tide and the wind together. Instead of moving swiftly out toward the cut leading to Crown Island, the boat struggled against the water and moved slowly past the empty buoys and around the rocks until they began to see the island ahead of them. The afternoon sun reflected from one of the highest windows in Marie's house for a moment as they turned toward the pier. Peter pulled in and hitched his boat to the large iron ring and helped Alice out. Jasper ran up to the house. Alice stopped and looked at the stone steps, then mounted and stopped again to look at the granite walkway leading up to the house.

"This is what you did for her all those years ago?"

"Yes."

"It looks almost new."

"It's the way I had the granite finished. I didn't want it to weather badly."

"The stones are tight together."

"The drainage. I wanted it that way."

"A good job," she said. Peter had educated her over the years so that she could tell quality work when she saw it. She walked up to the steps of the house and looked at the second floor windows. "This is the library?" she said, pointing to the structure on the right that he had built. She knew the general layout of the house because Peter told her about it when he was doing the construction. She had also seen the house many times from the water over the years, so none of it was surprising to her. However, until now, she had never set foot on the island. In a way there was nothing new in that because unless she was a hired hand or an invited guest, Alice could live all her life in Quarrytown without ever visiting any of the islands. They were like the king's preserves, off limits to most people. And Crown Island had been the most regal of all.

Alice turned and looked back at the walkway. The wind drove the leaves across the front of the house. "That garden must be beautiful in the spring. Look at the way she's put in the plantings to follow the walkway. Is the door open?"

"Yes." Peter went up on the verandah and held the door open. The wind was strong enough to force him to hold on to it. Alice walked into the foyer and looked up the grand stairway and slowly turned around as she admired the hall.

"This was a hotel once, wasn't it?"

"Years ago. Never had that many bed rooms, though. Probably no more than six or seven. But you can't tell, really, from the way the place is now. Could have been more. This living room was the original lounge. It's got that big fireplace and the beams."

Alice wandered into the library. She walked around the walls looking at the books and paused when she came to Marie's novels. "Look at them," she said. "There are some here I haven't heard of." She sat down on the large leather couch in the middle of the room. "This is a nice room. I think I'd use it as a sitting room. We could use some of the shelves for decorative plates or knick-knacks, things that are nice to see."

"It's a library."

"I know. I'm just saying. The living room is big. I don't know what I'd do with it. But the furniture is much too out of date. I'd want to refurnish it, maybe get a decorator to help me. It's a real challenge. You wouldn't know about that kind of thing. It doesn't have anything to do with stone."

"It's a library."

"Yes. I heard you." She got up and walked out to the kitchen. "Oh, this is nice. Did you do this, too?"

"No. She had the kitchen done later."

"But it's an old refrigerator," Alice said as she opened the freezer door. Nothing was inside. She opened the refrigerator door and saw a half-gallon of milk, some eggs, cheese, butter, and a few bowls with food still in them. "Leftovers," she said. "These are rotting." She took the bowls out of the refrigerator and began to scoop out the contents into the sink. Marie had installed a disposal that washed the food down into the septic system. Alice stacked the bowls on the sideboard. She then opened the oven and peered inside. "A gas oven," she said. The dishwasher held several days worth of plates and cups. Everything was spotless. Alice dried her hands on a tea towel, then walked through the rest of the first floor.

"The views," she said. "Wherever you look. Except the hall. It's too dark in there. Could you install some lighting in the hallway to brighten it?"

"Probably."

"I saw the laundry down in the back hall. I wouldn't be surprised if she still has clothes in the dryer." Alice began up the steps to the second floor. Peter watched her and decided to let her go on her own. He heard her footsteps above his head. He had never realized the house could be so quiet. All the time he had been here with Marie her music was soft throughout the house, or Marie herself would sing and play the piano. Now the silence was strange, almost forbidding. He heard Alice walk into Marie's bedroom and stop. In a few minutes she moved to the stair head and looked down. "Is this the bed you used?"

Peter did not answer. Jasper scratched at the front door and he let him in.

"I'm going to take the sheets off," she said. "And wash them."

CHAPTER NINETEEN

Peter told Stanley Staunton Ellington's news about Crown Island. Stanley had seen the island, but except for his visit as an infant, had never been on it. He asked Peter how it had come about that Miss Wainwright left the island to him. Peter told him it was as much a surprise to him as to everyone else. Stanley was also attentive concerning the entailing of the island conditional on Peter's going to college. For him it was an interesting legal point.

"Are you going to do it?" Stanley asked.

"I'm not sure I could do it. You know how many years it's been?"

"You could do it. If anyone can do it, you can do it."

"I'm a little old."

"Never too old," Stanley said quickly.

"Maybe."

Stanley promised that he and Kathleen would come up and visit the island as soon as they could. He was trying to work out the weekend and he'd call. When Peter put the phone down it rang almost instantly. It was Sybil Forstner. "I've been trying to reach you," she said. "I'm Marie Wainwright's editor." Peter told her he remembered her from years ago. "It's about Marie's manuscripts," she said. "Mr. Ellington told me nothing could be touched until the will had been read and problems of ownership settled. So that's settled, am I right?"

"More or less, I suppose."

"Well, I need to come out and see the manuscripts as soon as possible. Marie was working on a new book and we'd been talking about it right along. I don't know whether she finished revising it or not. Are all the manuscripts safe?"

"Of course."

"You haven't touched anything?"

"No one has touched anything."

"I'm acting as executor of Marie's literary estate. You know that, right?"

"She never said a word about it. It's not in the will, is it?"

"I'm not mentioned in the will, but that's not the important thing. What's important is that the manuscripts are safe and that you let me examine them soon so we can get them in shape for publication. Her estate gets the royalties, and I understand you control the estate. I'm here to make sure we all profit from the manuscripts and that Marie's memory is honored by the way we treat them."

Peter listened to her go on about the seriousness of her mission, and while he did not like her tone of voice any more now than he did those years ago when they first met, he realized he would not stand in her way. She wanted to do what was right by Marie, and so did he. He had not yet looked closely at any of the manuscript material she had left behind. They agreed to meet before Peter closed the house for the winter.

Karl Stender, one of the members of the Quarrytown Conservancy, made a point of seeing Alice in school about his son, who was in her class, but it was soon obvious that he wanted to talk about Crown Island.

"They don't think we're good enough for Crown Island," she told Peter.

"Maybe we aren't. I'm not an island person. We're not island people, are we?"

"How long have our people sat here and stared out at those islands and watched the summer folk coming up from New Jersey and New York and God knows where else and unloading their cars and SUVs and getting Steve Clements to port them out to their houses? You'd see all those children, all scrubbed and ready for summer. You saw those kids in their own boats, tying up at the town dock, going into the Quarrytown Café and ordering food like they owned the town. How long did our parents stare at them and wonder?"

Peter nodded. He moved to the sink and poured hot water over some instant coffee crystals. He put his finger in the cup to see if it was hot enough.

"You know how they told stories about Marie Wainwright standing out in front of her house in a white dress around dusk. She did it all the time, and people said she was a hermit. But we never got to see how island people lived." Alice corrected herself. "*I* never got to see how they lived. Now, I want to know what it's like to be island people."

"How?"

"I want to live on Crown Island for what's left of the summer."

"The islanders are not going to talk to us."

"They don't talk to us as it is. So nothing changes, except we get to see what life is like out on the most beautiful island of all. You already know all about it, but I don't."

"I don't already know all about it. I only saw a small part of it, and I was young. And working, too."

"Sure." She finished her coffee and stood up. Peter took his cup out of the microwave. It was too hot to drink. "I want a chance, Peter. That's what I'm saying, and I really mean it. You owe me that." Alice gave him a stern glance and went upstairs to her bedroom.

Peter wondered just what he owed Alice when all was said and done. If it was guilt, then as far as he was concerned he was finished with it. Guilt was what you felt when you did something wrong, something you should not have done, maybe something that hurt other people. But the love he and Marie had hurt no one but themselves.

Peter's views on guilt were not the same as those of Ricky Coddle, who himself took a liberal position in relation to the regulation views of the church's "Thou shalt nots." As far as Peter was concerned, the worst of the "Thou shalt nots" was the most important: Thou shalt not love one another. Sex was only part of it. What he and Marie had was not just sex, but love, and love took them to places deep in the heart and deep in life itself.

His feelings of guilt were appropriate for his misstep with Constance Faynell, but that was long ago. He had not been the predator, but the prey. A willing prey, in a sense. But prey nonetheless. With Marie there was only mutual conquest—to use her term—and from that Peter had emerged not just changed, but more deeply realized as the person he truly was. In her fashion, Marie had not altered him, but discovered him, and in discovery opened a world to him that made him sometimes feel happy with himself—and in extraordinary moments, joyful with himself.

They determined to go out to Crown Island on the weekend, but Peter first had to put in a day with Packy Caserto, who was left to re-face the house on Termite Falls Road. When he got there Packy was sitting on a pile of stones with a cup of coffee in one hand and a glistening cruller in the other.

"I could use a hand," Packy said.

"I'm late, I know." Peter studied the wall where they stopped work the day before and moved a load of stone close to the job. He made a mix of cement grout and examined the work they had already done. "Looks good, don't you think?"

"I suppose so. I just work here." Packy was busting his balls.

"Right. I forgot."

"Hey, is what I hear true?"

"Probably not. What is it?"

"That you own Crown Island. That a fact?"

Peter hauled a large flat stone into position and began working with it. It fit almost perfectly. "I guess it is," Peter said.

"How'd that happen? I knew you knew her, but how'd she ever come to leave you the island. That's what happened, isn't it?"

"Who were you talking with?"

"Beady was talking with Karl Stender."

"What's Beady got to do with Stender?"

"Stender does his taxes. He heard about the island last night. Karl says Miss Wainwright gave the island to the Conservancy. Then somehow it winds up with you. Says something fishy's going on. That right?"

"Jesus Christ," Peter said. "He said something fishy was going on? What the hell does he know? There's nothing fishy. Marie Wainwright left the island to me. Fair and square. She changed her mind about the Conservancy."

"Beady says Stender's a little worked up. Maybe he'll challenge the will."

"Let him. He can waste his time all he wants."

"Must have been something between you and Miss Wainwright. Buddy Dooley says you was both friends for a long time."

"We were friends. I did a lot of work on the island. She didn't have any family to leave it to, so she left it to me. I might have done the same thing."

Packy grinned at him. "Seein' it's that way, maybe you could leave it to me when you go."

"Sure. Hold your breath."

"What's it like living out there?"

"I haven't done it yet, so you'll have to wait."

"What's that place worth now. They tell you?" Packy tamped in a small filler stone.

"No."

"Gotta be two, three mill. Right? Maybe more. Looks like you hit the lotto. How about that? And you got that just for building that library addition out there?"

"Who knows? It was a surprise to me. I would have never guessed . . . ."

"You're not gonna tell me you and she weren't doin' it," he said with a sharp grimace.

"Packy, you got a dirty mind."

"Ain't nothing dirty. Just a little of the nasty. You know that." Peter noticed Packy's missing front tooth.

"Well, dream on." Peter put an end to the conversation by moving a large flat stone into place and fitting it properly in the puzzle that grew under their hands. Packy finally quieted down and the two of them worked to the rattle of Packy's paint-splattered transistor radio tuned to the jazz station on Long Island.

Peter came by the pier house at quarter to five and saw Alice sitting in the dim twilight with her school bags. "Did you get milk and cereal for the morning?"

"Was I supposed to?"

They got in Peter's pickup and went back to the convenience store north of the town dock and bought enough so they could have a decent breakfast, then went back and took the skiff out to the island. The moon was full and as it rose the water seemed to take on more and more brightness. It was going to be a beautiful evening on Crown Island.

Alice turned on all the lights on the first floor of the house. "I want it to be cheerful," she said. "And I want other people to see us out here."

"But a lot of people have gone. And we can't be seen from the mainland."

"There are people in boats."

Alice made a simple dinner of chicken, mashed potatoes, and broccoli. They forgot to buy coffee, so they had tea. They ate at the same table where Marie had entertained her publisher and editor years before.

"Does it feel very different to you?"

Peter couldn't tell what Alice was hinting at, if anything. He studied her face before answering.

"The fact that we own it?" he asked.

"The fact that I'm here at the table instead of Marie Wainwright."

Peter did not think her question implied hostility. "The whole thing is unreal to me."

After dinner Peter went out on the verandah and stared off at the water. In the distance he saw the lights of Long Island. Far to the east he caught sight of a lighthouse blinking at him every minute or so. It had been so long since he'd spent an evening on Crown Island that he had lost sense of what it was like. The moon had risen higher in the sky, its faint reflection rippling toward him on the water, covering an immense stretch almost from Long Island itself. He saw off to his left a light on Extra Island, which told him that the good weather had brought people out for the weekend. He had no sense of how the island people lived, what their expectations were, or how they shaped their lives. All he knew was that, except in some explicitly legal way, he was not one of them.

Alice came out on the verandah when she finished the dishes.

"It's beautiful," Peter said.

"And it belongs to us."

"For the time being."

"What are you going to do about the University?" she asked.

"I'm a little old for stuff like that."

Alice almost responded as if to take issue with that statement, but she seemed to think better of it. "Let's go for a walk," she said.

They went down the porch steps and took the walkway back to where Peter had hauled the skiff out of the water. They stood there listening to the water lap against the stone dock. Lichen and slippery seaweed had invaded the bottom steps, but otherwise, his youthful work was still functional and seemed destined to remain so. They walked along a little-used pathway covered in leaves from autumns past. It led along the periphery of the island and in some places rose fifteen or twenty feet above the water. Everywhere, the light from the moon cast shadows before them as they walked. They were silent. They did not hold hands. Alice was only a step behind him and occasionally she stopped to snap a twig from the new trees beginning to clog the path.

Apart from Jasper, birds, and a few rabbits, there was no wildlife on the island. They were surprised by the sudden movement from a tree over head. Alice gave a slight cry in alarm. "It's nothing," Peter said. "Just an owl. Probably hunting for mice."

"Would there be mice out here?"

"Could be. This is a pretty large island, and nothing ever comes out here to disturb anything, except for Jasper."

"He should be out here with us," Alice said. "Doing guard duty."

"He's okay up at the house."

The moonlight made it seem brighter here on the island than it was on the town dock. The tree frogs and crickets sounded steadily around them. The shapes of the stunted pines ahead of them on the old pathway resembled figures of men in various stages of contortion. Peter saw why Marie had imagined ghosts on the island.

"How long would it take us to get all the way around?"

"About half an hour," Peter said. "Maybe a little longer in the dark. This path is a little tricky up ahead. The undergrowth gets thick. Slows you down."

"That means we can't use much of the land, then."

"Right. Most of it is overgrown like what you see on both sides. There's a little meadow on the other side of the ridge, but most of it is just woods."

They heard Jasper barking inside the house. They turned and began walking back. It was cool, but not too damp. The moon overhead seemed enormous, an almost incandescent white. Away from the lights of the town, the stars seemed sharper, more intense, more powerful. A twig snapped against his face as Alice made her way along the leafy path. Peter rubbed his cheek and followed her back to the dock, then up to the house. The lights on the first and second floor made the great house seem more like a hotel than ever before. Alice went up the steps and quieted Jasper when she went into the hallway. Peter stood outside and looked up at the building. It was impossible to think of it standing here without Marie waiting inside, without her music drifting across the waters.

On that Saturday they had their breakfast out on the verandah. Peter sat there nursing his second cup of strong black coffee. He was beginning to feel relaxed. Alice had suffered a minor crisis when she began to get ready for bed and discovered there was no television in the house. She couldn't believe it at first and came to Peter insisting that it must be hidden it in a specially designed piece of furniture. "No one can live out here without a TV," she said. "What in God's name do you do out here?" But Alice got by. She went to bed early, tired after a tough week in school. Peter stayed up reading. He had found a copy of *Metamorphoses* with Marie's notes in the margins. Some notes read simply, "Read this aloud to Peter." He read silently until he fell asleep.

CHAPTER TWENTY

They stayed on the island for two weeks, commuting to the mainland each weekday. No one came to visit, and they saw none of the other islanders. Alice busied herself by gathering all Marie's clothing and packing it in large cardboard boxes. She was determined to give it away to Good Will or the Salvation Army, and only Peter's protests stopped her.

"I don't think we should do anything with her belongings until later."

"Why?"

"I'm not sure. It's just that if you give things away, that's final. You can't tell who might want some of the clothes."

"Peter. She hasn't got anyone else. Who would want her clothes? I don't understand you."

"Please. Pack things up, but let's hold off on throwing things out. For a while. Maybe by next season we'll know more."

Alice shook her head. She wanted to get things cleaned out, to change the way the rooms were decorated, to erase all the touches that Marie had lived with through the years.

When the telephone rang Alice answered. It was Sybil Forstner calling back. She had a difficult time explaining who she was, but eventually Alice understood. Peter had taken Jasper outside for a run. When Sybil spoke to her as if she were the new owner of the house, Alice told her to wait and speak with Peter.

"I can come out on Sunday, will that do?"

"We are going to be here only until Monday," Peter said. "We're closing the house up for the winter."

"Didn't Marie keep it open in the winter?"

"Yes, at the end. She liked it. Almost everyone except

Marie wintered on shore. We're only here a couple more days."

"I really must be there before you close things up."

Peter told her to wait a moment, then spoke with Alice and explained things.

"Let her come," Alice said. "We won't have that much left to do on Sunday."

Peter gave her directions and said he would not touch any of Marie's papers before she arrived, but the truth was that he had already begun looking through them to see what was there. She had manuscripts of her published novels, sometimes in three or four versions. They were neatly wrapped and placed in boxes in cabinets he had built for her in the library. The manuscript on the editing board near the computer was definitely a memoir of her childhood and it may have gone on into later life, but he couldn't be sure because there were several versions of that book, too. He had no idea how to use her computer, so he could not check to see how far she had got with it. On an open shelf nearby he had found two manuscripts with titles that he did not recognize: *Stolen Moments* and *The Lonely Sea*. They were novels that Marie was working on when she died.

At first, Alice missed her television programs on Crown Island. But soon she began to fill her evenings with work from the classroom and the committees that she served on. She learned to tune in FM stations from Long Island and the surrounding area on Marie's sound system. Sometimes she played one of Marie's CDs or one of her old LPs. Peter took a walk around the island with Jasper every evening. Sometimes Alice came along with them.

Their entire lifestyle altered absolutely for being on the island and not having the conveniences that they took for granted. The kitchen stove used propane gas, which Alice had never tried before, and, in the process of learning, Alice cursed its slowness and its chugging sounds. In the house on Haycock Street, she relied on an electric stove and a microwave oven.

Marie had no microwave, and Alice scoffed at the old adage, "Now you're cooking with gas." She hated its stench and asked Peter to install a fan and vent next year.

Peter read in Marie's library in the evenings. Alice was determined that she was going to get the most out of their ownership of Crown Island. She was going to become an island woman no matter what. She seemed to keep her irritation under control and her criticism of the limitations of cistern water, the older refrigerator, the ugly stove, and the drafts around the windows to a minimum.

Alice kept herself distant throughout this period. He expected it, given the situation, but, considering how she had first reacted to discovering that Peter and Marie had been lovers, her behavior was almost forgiving. Peter had long since forgiven himself.

Peter took Jasper along to pick up Sybil Forstner at the town dock at ten a.m. It was a brilliant Indian Summer morning and Jasper stood in the bow of the skiff enjoying the white scuds that came up over the sides. Peter would not have recognized Sybil. Her hair was gray, her shoulders rounded with age, and her sense of glamor dissolved. She looked like a bookish old orphan. He remembered her as so fashionable, so intense, and so bright and cheerful that he was disappointed when he saw her waiting there for him. He felt an irrational sense of loss.

"You're both very good to have me at such short notice," she said when she met Alice. She took her long coat off and placed it on a side chair in the hall. "I remember this house so well, and the island is still magical, isn't it?" She turned and looked out through the front door to the water. A few adventurous souls were sailing in the distance. "And you built this magnificent library," she said, walking into the open room. The sun had only just crested the ridge in the rear of the house, so the light in the library was soft and even. "And her books," she said, pausing by the shelf on which her published novels sat. "What wonderful books. I'm sure you've read her books."

"Of course. But Marie and I never talked about them. At least not often."

"Too bad," she said. "I know she talked with almost no one about her work."

"We talked about other literature. We sometimes read together."

Alice stood in the entry to the library. "I never really knew her," she said. "Peter, of course, knew her well."

"Marie was wonderful," Sybil said. "An amazing woman, considering what she went through. I have an immense pile of mail for her. I mean, mail that her fans have written after she died. They felt very close to her, you know. She got the most remarkable mail from people who loved her books. I'm trying to figure out now what I should do with it. I used to show some of it to her and she would sometimes answer, but I can't do that now. Would you have any coffee?"

Peter apologized and went into the kitchen to make fresh coffee. As he got things together he heard Sybil tell Alice how Marie had once described Peter as a "Roman hero."

He wished she had not repeated that.

"So Marie left you the island on condition that you get a degree at the University?" Sybil said when he sat down with his coffee. "That's so amazing."

"She said I should have returned to the University when I was much younger. I couldn't. But she kept saying I should think about going back."

"Are you going to do it?"

"We're looking into it," Alice said. "Peter couldn't start until next semester."

"What an opportunity," Sybil said. "Are you excited?"

"Apprehensive," Peter said. "I have to go and talk with people. I don't have to do anything for a while."

"Lucky you. Can we see Marie's manuscripts? I take it that you've found them all?"

Peter led her to the cabinets in which Marie kept the

piles of manuscript for the two novels she was working on. When she saw them, her face brightened. "Good," she said. "These are the things I was most concerned about, especially *The Lonely Sea.* I know she finished at least a second draft. Then the other book was *Stolen Moments.* I don't know if she ever reached the end of the first draft. Would you just let me look through these for a while on my own? I'll call you when I'm done."

"There's also this," Peter said, pointing to the manuscript that was her memoir.

"Oh, yes. Good. I'll look at that, too. And did you find her journals?"

"I'm not sure. I really haven't looked."

"All right. I'll call for you."

She was basically telling him to leave, so he got up and went back to the kitchen. Alice had gone upstairs to finish packing her own clothes and necessaries. The shutters were closed in the upstairs rooms, so the lights were on throughout the second floor. Peter had his suitcase near the door. He went down to the furnace room and drained the water out of the system. They planned to leave the electricity service as it was. The propane tanks were shut down. When Sybil finished with the manuscripts, he would close the shutters in the library, put the shutter on the front door, and they would have the place secured for the winter. While he waited, he took Jasper out for a walk around the island.

They had walked only a few yards before Jasper ran off after a rabbit. Peter watched. He wondered how rabbits could have gotten here. He called to Jasper to stop the chase, but he carried on until the rabbit was safe in its hole. Down in the meadow on the north side of the island, the air was cool, but the sun was warm. Jasper ran through the meadow at a leisurely clip, then circled back and rolled in the long grass. Peter sat beside him and stroked his head. "You miss her, don't you?"

Marie and Peter had sometimes walked in this meadow

and sat and talked the afternoon away. In places, the granite showed through the topsoil, and now that the leaves were beginning to thin out, he had good views of the water in several directions. When they sat, or sometimes stretched out looking up at the sky, he wondered just how he had gotten here. What magic had transformed him into a man who could lie in the grass on Crown Island on a lovely afternoon and talk with Marie about life and love and the world outside Quarrytown?

Jasper and he walked along the path overlooking the water below. A small powerboat moved steadily around the island and someone waved to him. Peter waved back because he thought it was expected of him. When he returned to the house Alice was busy upstairs and Sybil sat at Marie's editing board reading.

"This is quite something," she said when Peter and Jasper came in. "She'd been talking about doing this for some years now, but I never thought she'd get it done."

"An autobiography?"

"Of sorts, but remarkable. She's got at least three new books here. I've been used to the way she liked to work, but this is even more than I expected. She's so meticulous about all her manuscripts. I think it's a wonder in its way. We need to talk."

"Okay."

"You've got to let me take this material with me. I'm acting as her executor, but I need to go over all this material in detail."

"I'm sorry," Peter said.

"What do you mean?"

"I can't let you take the material with you."

Sybil turned sharply toward him. "What are you talking about? I have to take the material with me. I have to read it carefully. And I want you to send me her computer when I get back to New York. Don't you realize how important this is?"

"I haven't been able to look at the manuscripts yet."

"What does that matter? These are important literary

properties. For God's sake, you don't seem to understand anything about what we have here."

"I think I do. I just want to read everything before it leaves the house."

"That's ridiculous. What would you know about the literary value of this material? Don't you see that I'm her literary executor. You'll receive a handsome royalty from this material no matter what. I'm really shocked at what you're saying."

"Just stop. I told you what I want. This is my material now."

"No. No it isn't. It's Marie's. How can you talk that way? You're beginning to sound ridiculous. You're a carpenter, not a literary expert. Why don't you recognize your own limitations?"

Peter stood up. "I'll take you back to the dock now."

"Do you realize what you're doing? What all this means?"

"I'll take you back."

Sybil sat looking up at him. She seemed to have aged even more in the brief moments in which they talked. Alice came into the room behind him. "What's the matter? Why are you arguing?"

"Talk some sense into him," Sybil said.

"I'm taking her back to the dock," Peter said.

"Why don't you let her take the manuscripts?" Alice said. She had been standing there longer than Peter realized. "What possible problems could that involve? She's her editor."

"I want to read the manuscripts first."

"Fine," Alice said. "Fine. Read them. Then send them on."

"Look," Sybil said, finally rising. "Let's do it this way. I'll pay to have the manuscripts photocopied. You can have that done on Monday or maybe Tuesday. Then, you send me the originals–so I can read all the pencil marks–and you keep the copies. They we can both read them. Then we'll know what we have and I won't have to wait until winter is over."

"That sounds fine," Alice said.

"I'll decide," Peter said.

"You mean you'll do it?" Sybil asked.

"I'll have copies made. I'll send you what you want, but I want to read things first."

"I'll pay for the copies."

"I can pay. I'll do it at my own speed."

Sybil came very close to him. "What is it? What are you afraid of?"

"I just don't want to be told what to do," Peter said. "It's that simple. You come in here and then you start telling me what to do, and I won't have it."

"Are you afraid of what Marie might have said about you? Is that it? Are you in her books somehow? I know she sketched local characters into her books. Is that what's holding you back?"

"I'm not being held back from anything. I think I have a right to read this material before you take it away from me."

"I'm her editor. If anyone has the right to read this material I do. You're going to profit from this material, but I need to read it and edit it so that it can be published in the way Marie would want it. I've been doing just that for thirty years."

"Peter knows that. I'm sure you'll see the material soon."

"You're in her books, aren't you?" Sybil said. "That's the only thing that could explain this situation. How you ever inherited this incredible island. It had to be. I've been so blind. You are Carpenter Halliwell. And who else? Hallstatt Stone. That's it, isn't it?"

Peter walked out on the verandah and left the door open. He heard Alice ask Sybil what she meant.

"What I mean is that your husband is a character in some of Marie Wainwright's books. I should have known right from the first that she was alluding to someone she knew. She always tried to give interviewers the slip on whether her novels were *romans a clef*."

"Which means?"

"Novels based on real life, with identifiable characters."

Later that week at home, Alice avoided TV and went to her room to read the novels Sybil Forstner mentioned. She did not discuss what she read with Peter, but Peter knew she was looking for references to him–and possibly to herself. When she finished the books she came into the living room and put them on the sideboard. "These are interesting," she said. "That editor is right."

"I'm not so sure I see that," he said. He didn't want to go into the question of how his own words found their way into Marie's dialogue.

"I'm sure you do," she said. "And anyone who knows you would see you in them. What is it?   What is it that bothers you so?"

"Nothing bothers me."

"It certainly seems as if it bothers you."

"I'm going back to the island later. I want to go through some of the manuscripts."

"You're avoiding my question."

He turned to her. "I don't like to be studied," he said. "Simple as that."

"Don't you like the way she portrayed you?"

"I hope she didn't portray me. I didn't want her to portray me."

"Well, she did. Are you embarrassed by it?"

He didn't know how to answer her. In some ways he was embarrassed, but what really bothered him about his role as Carpenter Halliwell was that he could not ultimately understand what Marie's portrait of him meant. What was she driving at in using his words, his skills, and some of his demeanor in these people?

She had always said she loved him in a special way, but he was not entirely sure that the portraits of the characters that were most like him were as sympathetic as they should have been. The problem was that he had no idea how sympathetic he ought to have been if he were portrayed in those novels. Maybe it was fine. Maybe he was just not smart enough to be able to interpret the portrayals as Marie intended. There were so many things that he disliked about Carpenter Halliwell and Hallstatt Stone. They were limited people and they did not seem to know their own trades as well as Peter thought they should. On the whole, he would have wished to be left out of those books entirely.

"I don't know what they mean," he said.

"In the books?"

"Right."

"I don't think they mean anything special. They are characters. They mean themselves, I would guess. You don't like them. Is that it?"

"Yeah, I guess that's it."

"Maybe you don't like yourself," she said, and left the room.

CHAPTER TWENTY-ONE
November 2001

That next Saturday, Peter went out to Crown Island with a thermos of hot coffee, and a quilt for his knees. He knew he could turn the heat on in the kitchen, and even though it was mild outside, the house was going to be damp. When he found the manuscript of Marie's memoirs, he read through several sections. What surprised him was her forthrightness in describing how lonely much of her childhood had been.

He thought she might have been more cautious, but she was outright in her description of the coolness and distance of her parents, despite the fact that she loved both of them. It was touching to see how she tried to make them understand her better, while she always knew that they were so self-involved that there was little room in their lives for her.

Even more surprising was the description of her first marriage, which sounded ideal in its early stages, but which became progressively more problematic. Her husband, Paul Montgomery, was a Wall Street broker for the Friedman Group. Apparently, he spent most of his time in New York making considerable amounts of money. It seemed to Peter that Marie had married a man who resembled her father.

There had to be more of the manuscript because it ended in the middle of a sentence. He went through the drawers and cabinets in which he had seen paper and supplies. Then he went through the manuscripts that were stacked in the cabinets he had built under the bookshelves. The manuscripts of the two novels Marie had been working on before she died were tied with twine and sometimes broken into smaller "installments" with rubber bands. In none of the cabinets did he find more pages of the memoir.

But as he was scouring through stack after stack of papers, he came upon something even more interesting. It was Marie's journal. Sybil Forstner implied that she had kept a journal, and Peter knew that writers usually did, although Marie had never mentioned anything to him about keeping notes in the years when they were very close. He took out three boxes containing a variety of small books, odd sheets of paper, some of them from hotels, and typewritten pages that seemed hasty and smudged. Peter studied the boxes to see the dates and found that Marie's system was actually very clear. The first box dated from 1967, but it ended in 1975 and the earliest entries were in a small black notebook that Marie may have carried around in her pocketbook. Some notes were sketchy, quickly jotted down, and not very systematic. Marie talked at first about missing her daughters and wondering how she was to fashion a new life now that her family was dead. Occasionally the handwriting seemed mildly hysterical, certainly disturbed. Some of it was water-stained and smudged as if she were trying to wipe out a word or two, or as if she might have shed a tear on the page.

Her daughters names were Liz and Kara and when Marie began writing about them, she chronicled a story of pain and loss that seemed overwhelming. She talked about how they had loved their father, how they had longed to go sailing when they were in St. Barts. Paul Montgomery had surprised them all by having their boat sent on ahead by a service that took it out of winter storage and placed it on a freighter so that it was waiting for them when they arrived. It had seemed such an imaginative touch, such a remarkable gift to all of them, but when it came time to take the terrible sail that snatched away her family, Marie was in her hotel room editing an article on Crown Island that was to be published in the New York *Times* Connecticut Section. *The White Wraith,* published the year before, in 1966, had made her a local celebrity and she thought her article important enough to dedicate to her parents. Had it not been for that strange obligation, Marie Wainwright would have died at sea, and Peter would never have found himself sitting there reading the inmost thoughts of a woman he once loved.

Periods of time were missing in the journals. After February, 1967, there was a gap. Marie began entries again early in December, 1967, but she broke off in the middle of the month. She must have had a difficult time facing Christmas without her children. She made an entry in January, 1968, describing a party she went to in France, where she visited friends. But there was very little in the entry apart from names and a description of a house settled into a cliffside that needed great skill approaching down a steep staircase. The advantage was in the view over the startling blue ocean.

The rest of 1968 was essentially a blank. The first entry in her book for 1969 had several exclamation points. *I've begun writing again!!!* The journal entries were sparse, but a few of them revealed some of her feelings about having come out of a deep depression. *They call it a dark monster and I now know why. My soul all but withered in those months in Cherry Hill. So many lost people and I was one of them. Such darkness engulfing all, a slough of despond such as I never hoped to find. Dreadful nights.*

He looked through the rest of the year 1969 and saw similar comments. He read some of her notes on her daughters and on her husband, small scribblings that recalled pleasant times, that brought back to mind some of the ambitions and hopes of Liz and Kara. Many of these broke off abruptly as if she were unable to continue. She recorded how, when they went to New York on a sight-seeing trip and went to the observatory on the Empire State Building, Kara stood and looked out at the haze in the distance and said, "We must be close to heaven."

Other entries recalled moments of intense pleasure, and then of intense pain. Peter was surprised to see how many entries meditated on the peculiar accident of Marie's not being with her family on their boat when it went over and threw them in the sea. One entry reviewed the arrangements she made to have the boat repaired and returned to Connecticut. It had been one of her father's prize possessions and she had agonized over what she should best do with it. *It is not an instrument of death!!* she said in one entry.

Peter pulled the quilt more tightly around himself and poured the last of the remaining coffee. It was growing tepid. He decided to go right to the journals for 1971. The January entries were from London when Marie stayed with her English editor, a woman who loved theater and lived in Sloane Square near the Royal Court Theatre, where they saw some of the work of Edward Bond and Joe Orton. Peter did not recognize the names. Marie described some of the plays she saw. However, from her descriptions, he thought they must have been dark and unpleasant affairs.

The entry for February 2 struck him as strange at first, but once he had read it and thought about it, he was stunned to realize that she was writing about him long before they had actually met on Crown Island.

February 2. It's Joyce's birthday again. He always liked to have new beginnings on his birthday. I was thinking about Joyce when I saw him again this morning. He was dressed in a heavy woolen shirt. I must find out what they are called. He must be back from the University. I know his name now, Peter, and I saw him with some other young men I've seen there before, other stone builders in town. The Quarrytown Café is manageable in the dead of winter these days. He has a beautiful face and the most wonderful hair, curls upon curls upon curls. I saw so many of those faces in the British Museum's Roman busts. He might be a heroic athlete. His shoulders are wide and his manner gruff and intense. He laughs loudly and with such abandon.

Peter looked further to another entry.

February 10. I may be crazy to stay on the island in the

winter. Mr. Clements has been good in ferrying me back and forth. I pay him, but it must be a chore for him. He says almost nothing as we go back and forth—the cold air virtually prevents conversation. Today was bright and the sky such an intense cerulean that I was pained to think I cannot paint. Peter was there again having coffee. I think I have some of his routine down. He was there at lunchtime on Tuesday, then in for a muffin at 11 on Wednesday. His father was hurt in the quarry. Is that why he is in Quarrytown when he should be at the University? I'm my invisible self these days, huddled in the back. I bring my book and continue with notes for the new novel. Will he be in it? Would he ever speak to me? Today he laughed again and I found myself smiling as if I were part of his audience. His eyes are a deep hazel or perhaps a blue. His lips are sensual and full. I've seen his hands. They are powerful and huge, but I think he is a sensitive soul. He seems unlike some of the young men, the other carpenters he jokes with. They sometimes tease him because he has an aesthetic sense. How wonderful for him.

Until he read that entry, Peter was not entirely sure Marie was talking about him. It could have been another Peter, but when he saw her writing about his father and about his laugh, which was the object of jokes on the part of Buddy and Packy, he knew she had noticed him—but why? What was it about him that made her aware of him? When he stopped and thought back to those days in the Quarrytown Café, he could barely recall any but the most infrequent lunches with Buddy Dooley. He was working all the time and usually ate on the job, or skipped eating entirely.

Marie occasionally spoke to him in the Quarrytown Café. He hadn't thought about that for years, but he remembered seeing her with a notepad sitting at one of the tables by the windows. He tried to think of something clever to say, but what came out was almost simple-minded, "What are you writing?"

"Words, words, words," was all she said, and he laughed.

When she asked after his father's health, he told her about the accident. She seemed thoughtful and sympathetic.

He remembered Marie's novel, *On an Island of Hope*, had still been a best-seller and people were talking about it. He even went to the library, but the waiting list was so long that he figured it was a lost cause. He'd wait. But he once overheard a conversation at a nearby table between two women from upstreet who worried that the novel was going to attract the wrong kind of people to Quarrytown. They were sure that the summer tourists were already ruining the town, what with the buses and parking problems and all the kids they brought in to use the beach. They didn't need any woman writing books about Crown Island, no matter how many best-sellers were involved. That issue never bothered Peter, but he'd heard complaints from his own parents as well as from the Carlsons. Everyone was worried that Quarrytown would somehow be ruined by letting people know where it was.

Peter read the scraps of entries for much of the rest of February, then came to a longer entry for the first week of March. *March 5. A nice day, but one of those steely skies and cold mornings. Responsibilities in town today. I stopped at the Café and had breakfast. He was there with his friends. I sat at a corner table in the back and I think he noticed me. Later I asked him if he thought it would rain and he turned to look at the sky before he answered. I loved that about him.*

Peter remembered that day. Marie was right. They all noticed her, but she was sitting so close that they couldn't say anything directly. Packy made some remarks in her direction when he was sure she was deep in the newspaper and couldn't see him. Buddy Dooley made a few rude comic gestures, but Peter had not recalled that moment until reading about it just now. At the time he thought her willingness to talk with him was an example of how wrong his father was about the islanders. They were just like everyone else once you got to know them.

He remembered being friendly toward Marie when she

came to the Quarrytown Café for breakfast or lunch. He would say hello, sometimes tip his cap, and she would smile back at him. He grew to love that smile when he worked on the island, but he never dreamed that she had really taken notice of him as a person until he read in her journal. He was curious at the time to know how she got back and forth from the island when the ferries weren't running. It was Steve Clements, using his small skiff as a taxi on call.

The next entry was even more interesting. *March 7. The house speaks out and intones in this wind. Will March go out like a lamb? Were these the sounds my mother heard in the house before she left? When I play my own music I sometimes hear the staccato settling of the house, punctuating Satie or Debussy. I have the feeling that Crown Island accompanies me when I play my piano and strike a tone. I am never alone here. They are all with me and all sing in their way, on the wind, in the bushes outside, in the creaking eaves, in the rattle of the windows. I hear their spirits. They only leave when I am deep in my writing, lost to the conscious world and lost to my own self–if only for a few hours. Then I sit and look at the sea, the nickel-silver whitecaps that stretch now across to Long Island. The wind scuds the water away from the island at an intense rate, yet the tide draws the water up the steps at the dock and up the dark stones by the meadow. I thought of him today. For a long time. I was frustrated with my writing all day, and I sat there wrung out and saddened by the closing clouds and early darkness. When I thought of him, he brightened my spirit so much I was surprised. His smile is so authentic and so joyful. He wore a watch cap today and looked rugged and beautiful the way I imagined him, as if he were captaining a boat across the channel. He had a heroic carriage when I saw him on Granite Avenue walking away from his truck. But it seems to be an unselfconscious bearing as if he were unaware of anyone near him. He has a bearing one trusts. I heard Franny Bond say a few words about him. He must have done some work for her. She found him perfect for what she needed done. I wonder how I could get him here.*

Marie once asked him late on a windy afternoon when they were reading in the kitchen what it was that caused the house on Crown Island to make so much noise, so many different tones, so much music and percussion, as she called it. He was by no means sure, but he said it might be settling, although the house was really too old to be settling. There had to be more to it, something about the construction, the way the rafters were fixed, the way the siding held like skin to the bones of the building. It could have been so many things, but he knew it had nothing to do with the spirits of the past or those who had lived in the house when it was a hotel. People thought such strange things sometimes.

Subsequent entries implied that Marie was coping with loneliness. *March 10. I've learned to be alone at last. I see a dark blue bird at the window and think he is a friend. The crows sit on the patches of snow in front of the house. I leave them crusts of bread and leftovers. They are the watchdogs of the island. I hear them in the morning calling for me. My ravenous friends. If I open the door they sound the alarm and wait for food. If I disappoint them they assemble to scold their strange friend. Do they think I am some fashionable bird who hides in her house? Am I somehow a goddess they pay homage to on my lawn? Is this a temple for such wanderers?* He was surprised and amused at the way she regarded the crows. The crows on Haycock Street sat in the snowy boughs of the oaks and squawked loud and sharp for reasons that eluded him. Were they sounding alarms? Were they calling to other crows to assemble for a parley?

When he looked up, he saw that the crows were outside the windows even now. He saw them settling near the verandah. They walked about noiselessly, gathering their energies. Like Jasper, they missed Marie. Their silence was the dark silence of mourners. The light outside began to dim and he felt his energy draining away. He wanted to read more in the journals, but he wasn't sure he could. Marie had seen him and noticed him long before he had known her, and that thought, strange and surprising, made him think back to times when he had walked along Granite Street past the Café, down past the church to the post office, or out to the end of the town dock where he kept his skiff. He thought of the rare late afternoons when he sat in the pier house and watched the bright, preppy islanders assembling on the weekends, waiting for Steve Clements to ferry them over to their homes.

During her first years in college, Alice worked at the Café in the summer and was not free until it closed. And when the Café closed, her mother needed her help in the house. The weekends had been their own, but the only time they spent their evenings on Granite Street was when they were in high school, and, then, they congregated with friends beneath the street lamp on the steps of the Quarrytown Church planning impossible adventures. In the summer, when Peter was working full time for his father, he and Alice went to Elm City on weekend evenings to dance or get pizza on St. Ann's Street where the cherry blossoms fell by the thousands in the spring around the square park that had been saved from development.

Peter had worked on St. Ann's Street refurbishing an old stone building and had come to love the Victorian homes and the Federal houses that were now two- and three-family buildings. And during some of that time could Marie have known who he was? Did she congregate with the other islanders waiting for Steve Clements while Peter sat in the pier house completely unaware?

Peter put the journal away, careful to note where he had ended his reading. He was anxious to read the entries for the beginning of April, but he did not want to rush. He wanted to have those entries all to himself. He had no idea what he would find, and no idea how he would feel, realizing that he had thought of himself and Marie in one way, and that Marie may have thought of them in an entirely different way. The world was much larger than he had thought, much more subtle than he had imagined. As he looked out at the darkening water, he knew he had to leave now or he would stay the night and suffer the same loneliness that had marked so much of Marie's life.

He left Packy to finish the house on Termite Falls Road alone. Buddy Dooley was overseeing another remodeling job in Elm City on St. Ann Street. Peter went to the library in North Franklin with Len Moore to do some figuring on how they would start redoing the building. He wanted Len to act as foreman and get some of his men in Quarrytown on the job as soon as possible. Peter had drawn up the designs when he submitted plans and made his bid for the job, and Len had a hand in all that from the first. Len was happy to take the job himself and, unlike Packy, he'd not given Peter any grief about his owning Crown Island. Len had other things on his mind, and Peter was not so sure he really owned anything yet.

It was Alice who made the clearest gesture toward ownership when she began to talk about what Crown Island was going to mean to Stanley. At dinner she said having the island was going to guarantee that they would actually see Stanley and Kathleen. "Don't you see," she said. "It's a destination. It's someplace for him to bring Kathleen and his children when he has some, and it would mean that we would see them. They wouldn't be going off to Maine or the Carolinas or wherever they think might be wonderful. Crown Island would be an ideal place for vacations. It's large enough for all of us. And think of what it would mean for Stanley to inherit it when we're gone. It might even bring him back to Quarrytown."

"He may not want it."

"Oh, he'd want it," she said. "You can be sure of that. You know how those people out there fight for their few weeks on the islands? I hear stories when I get my hair done. There's a lot of in-fighting and jealousy. Stanley would have it all to himself."

"Maybe."

"Have you asked him to come see the island?"

"Sure. He said he'd call."

Alice had buttered her roll and set it down on her plate. "Do you think you should call?"

"I'll ask him when I talk with him next."

"What are you going to tell him? Will you tell him about you and Marie?"

"That's not his business."

"He'll want to know."

"Yes, maybe. But it's not going to come from me."

Alice picked up her roll and Peter began eating his macaroni casserole. He could not avoid talking about the island when they had dinner. He knew it was on Alice's mind much of the day, and when he went through Marie's journals and read the entries that seemed to apply to him, the thought of ownership was far from his mind. Working with Len Moore was an even greater distraction, but when he came back from North Franklin he had driven his pickup to the end of the dock and sat there for a while staring out at the setting sun and the silhouette of the ridge on Crown Island, barely visible behind Kidd's Island. He parked his truck next to Tony Morello's new F-150 and watched Tony working on a cigar, staring out at the empty water. Tony had worked for Peter for a while a year or so ago, but he was out on his own now, refurbishing kitchens and bathrooms, the way Peter had begun. He wondered if Tony knew he was the owner of an island. He wondered if Tony would treat him any differently if he knew.

That Wednesday, Stanley came home for Thanksgiving. He brought his wife, Kathleen, with him. Just as Alice feared, after law school Stanley and Kathleen married and stayed in Washington. Stanley joined a firm that represented international lobbying interests. Stanley was making enough money to begin thinking about buying a house in Georgetown. He tried to explain the commuting problems in Washington, but they were of a magnitude that approached myth, and Peter took his word for it.

The bedroom arrangements for Stanley and Kathleen were never easily solved. When Stanley was still in school and before they got married, he managed to insist on sharing his old room with Kathleen. Alice was intractable at first, but Kathleen took charge and just came out with it clearly. "We sleep together now," she said. "So it's really no different. We think we should be open about it."

Peter was surprised at her directness. She was much more direct than Stanley, who tried to insist on convenience as an excuse. But then Kathleen did not really know Alice, and her very forthrightness settled things and left Alice with nothing to say.

But now, things were different. When Stanley and Kathleen came to stay, they did not share Stanley's old room. It was much too small. They stayed at the new motel up on Route 1 where they could be "comfortable." Peter was surprised to see that Alice did not challenge them when they used that expression. Later, of course, she complained to Peter that it was not exactly pleasant to hear that Stanley's bedroom, which she had kept perfectly as a guest room for him, was no longer comfortable for her own son. Peter tried to smooth things out, but it was useless. He, too, felt a slight sting because Stanley was really saying not just that he had outgrown his old room, but that he had outgrown his old house and his old family. Ironically, it was exactly what Alice had feared and Peter had hoped for him.

"So when can we go out to the island?" Stanley asked. He looked over at Kathleen, who sat on the edge of the couch with her arms resting on her knees. She was a lovely looking woman, but it was clear that she was tired. She had worked with Children's Aid for only a semester before she, too, entered Georgetown Law School. Now she worked for a firm that specialized in children's law. She had very little in common with either Alice or Peter, and Peter could see that she was sweet, but somewhat impatient. Basically, she put up with them both for the sake of Stanley, and it would always be that way. Kathleen was from another world, and so, now, too, was Stanley.

"We could go out tomorrow," Peter said. "It's mild enough so we won't get too cold."

"Stanley says it's a beautiful island," Kathleen said.

"Have you been out there?" Peter asked him.

"I've been around it on a boat. Lots of times. I meant that you can see it's a beautiful island. It's incredible that you inherited it. That's a real kick. I never dreamed you'd made that much of an impression on Marie Wainwright. I used to see her in the Café. She was very nice to me and we'd sometime sit and talk. She was really smart. Do you know any of her books?"

Kathleen shook her head. "Best-sellers, aren't they?"

"Yes, but they're pretty good. A lot of them are set right here on the islands or places that are symbolic substitutes. They used to say that she used Quarrytowners for her characters. Was that true, dad?"

"Sometimes. She never talked about it."

"You know what I think the best part is?" Stanley said. Peter looked at him. "It's that you'll be going to the University. Isn't that fantastic?" he said to Kathleen.

"They've admitted you?" she asked.

"Peter had to drop out during his second semester. When his father had the accident," Alice said. "Miss Wainwright knew that. Peter hasn't talked with the admissions people yet. But he will."

"I think that's great," Stanley said. "You are really going to love it. Dad loves to read," he told Kathleen. "Greek tragedies, believe it or not."

"And Roman poets, believe it or not," Peter said, hoping that did not sound too unbelievable to Kathleen, who seemed skeptical.

They went out to the Lobster Place not far from Stanley's motel and had a meal memorable primarily for

Stanley's excitement at the prospect of seeing Crown Island. He was filled with questions about Marie Wainwright and the friendship that she had with Peter. Peter did not like dancing around the issue of how and why Marie Wainwright thought to leave him the island. He tried to tell the truth without admitting that he and Marie had a longstanding love affair, although in a way he wanted to tell Stanley the story as it really happened.

He wished he could explain what Marie had meant to him and how she had helped him see himself in a new light. He thought there was a chance, however slight, that in time Stanley would have come to understand him better and understand the power of affection and what it meant to Peter. But he knew that Stanley would be shocked. And he would undoubtedly reject him and comfort Alice. So it was impossible.

"I really don't know why she left me the island," Peter said. "It was a complete surprise, a shock, really. She was going to leave it to the Quarrytown Conservancy and had all the papers drawn up and signed contingent on the terms of her will. That's basically what I know. Ellington got us down there and told us just what she did, and not much more. He had no idea why she left the island to me."

"She left it to Peter, not to us," Alice said. She looked at Stanley.

"So it's not community property," Stanley said. "That's interesting. What do you think prompted that?"

"I couldn't tell you," Peter said honestly.

"Maybe she thought it would be more wonderful to give another person the chance to enjoy the island, if it's as nice as you all say," Kathleen said.

"Well, you've actually seen it," Stanley said. "When we went out on the Granite Islands tour with Steve Clements in the Lost Penny last summer. I pointed it out."

"There were too many islands. I couldn't remember. They all looked interesting."

"It's a great getaway," Stanley said. "I've always wanted

to be able to spend a summer on an island. You can't imagine how much fun they have out there. Kids just love it. Boating, swimming, and you can get across to Long Island if you want. It's going to be great."

"Must be isolating, though," Kathleen said.

"I felt a little of that when we were out there in September," Alice said. "There's no TV or anything."

"That'd be a relief," Kathleen said.

"There's music," Peter said. "Plenty of good music. Nice to hear when you're looking out over the water in the early morning, or in the evening."

"You could have a rock band out there and never disturb anyone," Stanley said.

"The music carries over the water," Peter said. "Besides, I meant classical music."

The next morning they took Jasper in the skiff out to the island. It was a bright morning, but rainy, the first rain in several weeks. The leaves were gone from the maples, but the pines on the ridge still protected the house, so that as they rounded the north side of the island it was still a surprise to suddenly see it bright in the reflections from the water.

"It's like the Eastern Shore houses," Kathleen said. "Isn't it beautiful?"

"See the section to the right," Stanley said. "My father built that. It's the library. She told my father that she loved it. It's where she wrote all her novels."

They took the walkway slowly up to the porch and stood before the house and admired it for a few moments. "It looks better when the shutters are open," Peter said.

"I think it's beautiful," Kathleen said. "It's amazing that this is the only house on this island. It's really pretty big in comparison with the other islands we passed. How did she manage to keep it so pristine?"

"Her family had it since the late 1800s," Peter said. "They always had money, I guess, so they didn't have to sell it.

Some of the smallest islands did get sold to new people. And the houses come on the market every once in a while."

"In a blue moon," Stanley said. "We used to sit on the dock back there, where the pier house stands, and fantasize about living on an island when I was a kid. I had some friends who came up in the summer and we'd go hunting for treasure on Kidd's Island."

"There's treasure there?" Kathleen asked.

"I think so, but nobody's found it."

"I even dug for it when I was a kid," Peter said. "They chased us off the island like we were rats. All anyone's ever found is some old silver coins. I think they were planted."

"Wait until you see the kitchen," Alice said. "She had a gas stove."

"We have one, too," Kathleen said. "We had to get a special hookup, but it's great."

Peter opened the large shutters over the door and Jasper barked anxiously. When Peter opened the door, Jasper ran into the kitchen looking for his water bowl. He sniffed in the corner near the refrigerator, then turned and ran into the library and stood wagging his tail. He turned and raced back to the hallway and barked once, sharply. Peter watched him. "He misses her," he said. Stanley nodded. "I've turned the water off," Peter said. "I think he may be thirsty." Stanley took a bottle of water from his backpack, poured some into a bowl, and watched Jasper drink.

"How long has he been here on the island?"

"I'm not sure. A few years, I think. Marie always had a dog for company. It wasn't for protection or anything."

"What a stunning room," Kathleen said, when she went into the large living room. "And look at that fireplace."

"Useless," Peter said. "It just sucks the heat out of the house. I closed the flue."

"But look how grand it is," Kathleen said. "And these paintings are beautiful." She went up to a portrait of a woman wearing a red shawl. "Was this Miss Wainwright?"

"No, I'm not sure who it is. I think the paintings belonged to her grandfather."

"She must have bought some herself," Kathleen said.

"Well, I suppose. I don't know which ones."

"This is real period furniture, too," Kathleen said. She looked at Stanley. "Don't you just love it?"

Stanley smiled at her. "It's like the old hotels in the southwest a bit."

"It was a hotel," Alice said. "I want to modernize in here. Get rid of some of the old junk."

"Oh, that would be sad," Kathleen said. "It's so perfect in here."

"It's dark and gloomy," Alice said. "I've had enough dark and gloomy in my life. I don't need more. You need something to brighten this room. A lot of work is needed in here. Of course I'm like the cobbler's children. We don't get new shoes or much remodeling time, do we?" She laughed, but Peter knew it wasn't funny. Alice had a number of ideas for how they should redo the house, but he was not sure any of them were quite right. More than that, he wasn't sure he should change anything. The Conservancy wanted to preserve the building in the fashion of the Crown Island Hotel, so it was obvious that they'd be grieved if he redid this room, the one room that was closest to the original plans.

"I like it," Kathleen said. "It's rugged, like the island."

"Let's go upstairs," Stanley said, moving to the staircase. Jasper moved along with him and ran up a few steps and paused on the landing, looking back at them.

"Okay."

They mounted the steps and looked in the bedrooms and the bathroom. They stood by the windows and looked out on the calm water. "What a view," Stanley said. "Isn't it beautiful."

"I love it," Kathleen said.

"There's another level?" Stanley asked.

"The attic. It has a couple of gables, but it's pretty dusty up there. They used it for storage."

In the attic, the roof was hipped and the windows pressed slightly outward admitting considerable light. The ceiling was eight feet high, and the views were even more remarkable looking out toward Long Island and some of the other Granite Islands to the east and west.

"This could be a great space," Stanley said. "We could finish this off, Dad."

"I thought you were a lawyer."

"Yeah, but I didn't forget how to tape sheetrock. I got taught by a pro, remember? This could be a great playroom for kids, or maybe a couple of bedrooms if we had guests. How many bedrooms are downstairs?"

"Six. One big one, the rest not so big."

"That's great."

"Look at this," Kathleen said. She had found a small sewing mannikin in the corner. "This must have been for when they made children's clothes. It's probably for a seven year old. It's ancient, too." She opened a large wooden chest and discovered a collection of children's clothes and old dolls. The dolls looked up at her with blank stares. Their dresses were yellowed linen. Some had colorful hats and ribbons. "And look at these. They're amazing. They must go back to the nineteenth century, some of them."

"Some were probably her dolls," Stanley said.

"I'm freezing," Alice said. She turned and went down the stairs to the second floor.

"Look at the way they built this attic, Dad. It's almost like an upside down bridge. It must be unbelievably strong."

"It's withstood a lot of hurricanes, including 1938."

Kathleen looked blankly at him.

"In 1938 a lot of these houses were swept off their foundation. Some were lost into the sea. It was a wall of water when the surge hit Quarrytown. This house held on. They made it right. They made it to last." Peter held open the door to the stairway.

"She has a real widow's walk," Stanley said.

"She was a widow most of the time she was out here, so she needed one."

"I bet you get an intense view up there." He pointed above his head.

"So you like it," Peter said.

"I love it. How about you?"

"Yes," Kathleen said. "It's astonishing. Imagine if you could have this in Washington. I think it's wonderful."

"When we can get away in the summer I'll help you out with it," Stanley said. Peter looked at him. He hadn't been this enthusiastic about anything in Quarrytown since he was in Little League. "We've got to plan a vacation, don't we?"

"Sure," Kathleen said.

Peter went downstairs while they talked. The chill and the damp had gotten to him. Alice was standing in Marie's bedroom looking out the window. "Is my taste just rotten?" she asked.

"No. Why?"

"Everything I want to do is wrong is why."

"They're just kids."

"I don't want this place to be an antique store. I want to make it liveable. Is that so bad?"

Peter could see that she was hurt. "They're young."

"Well, I'm not so young any more."

Stanley and Kathleen left on the Acela train late on Friday afternoon. They were full of admiration for the house on Crown Island. Kathleen even vowed to read one of Marie's novels and asked Peter for a recommendation. He told her any one she chose would be fine.

"So what are you going to do?" Alice asked him when they were gone.

"About?"

"About making sure the island is ours. Permanently."

"Is that what you want?"

"It's what I deserve, don't you think? Considering?"

They walked back to the garage and their car, ready to drive home. "I'm thinking about it."

"Well, think seriously. We've got some time, but you're not getting any younger, and if you're going to go to college you've got to start now. Before your brain dries up."

He stopped and looked at her, but she kept walking. He was not going to let his brain dry up and as far as he could see, he had always been working on keeping it fresh and active.

On the highway back home, he thought about Stanley's enthusiasm for Crown Island, and how Kathleen had seen so much beauty in it, so much potential. But more important, he responded to the way she liked the house just as it was, how she valued the spirit of the house as it had articulated itself over time.

On Monday, Peter made sure the jobs that Len and Beady worked on were going well. He wasn't anxious to get any new business for a while because he wanted to focus on his next move in relation to the island. The weather was holding up. He made an appointment with the Director of Admissions at the University for Tuesday morning, but he said nothing to Alice or anyone else.

Coleman Warburton was a tall black man probably ten years younger than Peter. He winced when Peter shook his hand. "We have your file out," Warburton said.

"Should I call you Doctor?"

"God, no. I'm an M.A. In history. Besides, everyone is Mister or Ms. Or Professor. But no, never Doctor. You only call professors Doctor at second rate schools. Or in hospitals." He laughed. "Your file has a note saying you were going to try to return. You dropped out because of your father?"

"He had a bad accident. I had to help him. We're in the

building business."

"Aha. Lucrative, I'll bet."

"We made a living."

"You know, Miss Wainwright communicated with me about you several years ago. I didn't know why then, I thought it was just because you were friends. But she left you Crown Island, didn't she?" He didn't wait for a reply. "Marie Wainwright didn't go to our University, but she was on our Board of Trustees. For quite a while. A very valuable mind, too. And I love her books. I'm sure you did too. We'll miss her. She wanted you to come back to the University. Is that why you're here now?"

"I thought I should talk about it."

"You're not sure?"

"At my age? How could I be sure?"

"I suppose you can't, but maybe we could ease you in."

"You have some suggestions for me? I've been out of school for a long time."

"Well, one idea is to get your feet wet. You've already got some credits. We could start you off with a couple of courses and see how you do. You wouldn't be the only overage student, you know."

"There can't be too many like me, though."

"Well, no. But every so often we get people in their seventies and even into their eighties who just want a University degree, and they really go at it. I think they have a good effect on the average age student, too."

"What kind of tests do I have to take?"

"Actually, none. I've gone over your file since Mr. Ellington told me about the terms of Miss Wainwright's will." He smiled at Peter. "I expected to see you even sooner."

"No tests?"

"No, you're a special student. We will try to get you started in two courses that will give you a chance to see how you fare. Then we'll review things and decide how to go from there.

You're a very fortunate man to have Marie Wainwright as a patron. She must have thought highly of you to leave you the island. It was in her family for generations. She must have trusted you. I know she regarded you as a very worthy person. She told me so herself."

"You talked about me with her?"

"Yes, when she was drafting her will she came to speak with me about her desires, and I reassured her. We make a number of special arrangements for our admissions decisions, as I'm sure you understand. This was the most original arrangement in my tenure as Director, but some of my predecessors have had interesting adventures as well. I'm very much looking forward to your being with us. I imagine you'll not be interested in our clubs or secret societies, but then you never know."

"You still have secret societies?"

"The old buildings without windows?"

"Yes, I remember them. They're like mausoleums."

"Very old traditions," he said confidentially. "At the heart and soul of the University."

Peter left with a thick catalog and a folder of papers that had to be filled out and returned. In the waiting room sat several anxious young women and men. Parents were there as well, and one of them smiled and said hello as if he were an admissions officer just coming out of a conference with the director. The assumption made him feel uncomfortable.

He drove to the town dock and took his skiff back to the island so he could read more of Marie's diary. His visit to the University was not as difficult as he feared it might be. He felt out of place, because of his age, and he wondered what people would think of him when they realized that he was a new student, not a professor. He had a hard time believing that people in their seventies and eighties were actually undergraduates at the University and that he would not be regarded as unusual. After talking with Coleman Warburton,

Peter was not sure what to expect at the University. Warburton was enthusiastic, but unctuous. He implied that admission to the University was an honor reserved for the very few, the right people.

Back in Marie's library, Peter went to the journal where he had left off. He went through the entries for the rest of March and then turned to April. He found the very entry he hoped for. *April 3. It was a beautiful day in every way. Peter called to say he would come to the island and I watched from my window as he pulled up his skiff and went down to look again at the steps up from the water. He knocked at the door and I hardly knew what to do. I was not really in control. I wanted to open the door and sweep him in, but I resisted. I went downstairs and looked out the tiny window beside the door and watched him as he walked off the pattern he imagined for the walkway. Then he drove some wooden stakes into the ground and tied white string to them. He stood again and looked around and then came back to the house. I knew then that he was like a God walking up and out of the sea. Of course I'm being ridiculously romantic, but I can truly understand how the ancients were beguiled into thinking that such beautiful figures were divine and not mere mortals. I had that feeling looking at him. He was tan, but almost marmorial, as if already immortalized statuary. I held my breath. And then I went out the back and swam around the island so I could greet him the way I wanted to. If he could arrive like a heroic God, then I could do the Botticelli thing and arrive before him like a Goddess. He seemed almost embarrassed when I offered him coffee. I have no idea if he takes coffee breaks, but I insisted and he complied, and we spoke. It was the first time I was close to him, and for a moment I wanted him to kiss me there and then, but I controlled myself and pretended to be fascinated with his plans and we talked as if there were nothing special about our meeting. I touched his arm, and he hardly noticed, but I felt an electric charge. His skin was soft, but the muscles beneath were strong. I wanted to touch his chest, but I restrained myself. We walked along the pathway as he explained his plans, which are extraordinary, I must admit. He understands Quarrytown stone. I wonder if he will come to understand me as well?*

April 6. We have talked a great deal, and I begin to see how he thinks. He is eager and excited about books, and that is promising. He has one of my books in his lunch box. Very sweet. He's very young in some ways, but he is not simply an innocent. He understands feelings and emotions more than I would have thought from looking at him. He is really a sensitive plant and I was right in choosing him. I must have seen that about him unconsciously. He is not just a wonderful physical specimen. He is a worthy.

Peter puzzled over that entry. To be a worthy was something important to Marie, but what could she have meant? And how had he surprised her? He read through a few more entries that meditated on the issues that confronted Marie in the book she was writing. She had several variations on a specific scene that had given her trouble. She wrote it first one way, then in another way, then again in a third way. Then she tried a fourth variation that seemed to borrow a bit from each of the earlier versions. She careted in words where she had struck out inappropriate phrases, circled phrases and indicated where they should go with lines and arrows. Beneath that she wrote yet another version of the scene, and in this one all the words seemed to belong together perfectly in the order in which they appeared. He went back to read the first version and saw how inadequate it was in comparison with the version she ultimately reached. Her comments on the exercise told him how much energy such an enterprise involved.

Most of the entries for the month seemed focused on her writing, while at the same time taking note of the weather, the books she was reading, and the books she was reading with Peter. Her comments on the books were like miniature book reviews and indicated her responses to the ideas that struck her as important. Every so often, she connected her reading to her life. But more often, she connected her reading with the world around her, marveling at the ways in which classic authors seemed to be speaking in a modern voice about modern concerns. Then he came across another entry that mentioned him.

July 27 Tuesday. We made love! I don't know how much guilt Peter feels, and if he does feel guilty I hope he does not also feel pain. I feel guilty myself because I feel so much like the predator. Peter's innocence was very touching. I don't think he had really made love before. Certainly, he did not seem very experienced, and he did seem very nervous. He was good in not pretending and he let me help him. I confess I enjoyed showing him how to please me. And he was a very quick study. I've read so often of such love-making in literature, and now I have the living example. His very clumsiness is touching, and his excitement is as flattering as other women have said in their own sexual memoirs. I shall not write a sexual memoir. I should need to take dozens of lovers, and the world is not large enough nor my patience great enough for such a task. Today was amazing in so many ways. I was able at last to set foot in the Petrel. I had to conquer my fear, and with Peter there it was much easier. He is a good sailor, as I knew he would be, but he could not have known the emotional baggage I carried on our excursion to the Eagle Yacht Club. The Petrel had been there many times before, and I knew it was essential for me to touch shore there once more. Peter seemed to enjoy it all, and I think he is truly in love with me. I'm terribly flattered. But it is wonderful to look into his wide, lovely eyes and imagine his feelings. He is so emotionally honest. The storm was something I could not have anticipated. The sky seemed untroubled when we began, although I did see the first darkness touching the clouds in the distance out toward the end of Long Island. Like Peter, I thought nothing of them, but they unleashed a torrent of rain and took out the electricity on the shore and tore his boat from its mooring. *We had to swim ashore and when we got there we were all in darkness and I knew it was my chance.*

Peter looked at the page and brought that day back to him, recalling the crackling of thunder, the pitching of the sea, the way the Petrel homed toward the island, and how Marie had seemed energized by the storm. She had not seemed fearful despite his own terror. That evening had been among the most memorable of his life and he had felt then that he was taking advantage of her loneliness and fright. But the truth was quite the opposite, he saw now. It was not as it seemed, but instead Marie had taken the initiative and he was a willing lover–and in no sense a willing victim, as she seemed to imply.

Peter seemed frightened, but I tried to calm him. In the darkness in the house I lighted the oil lamp and touched his lips. It was so natural and so immediate that it seemed as if it were meant to be. We've become so close in the last months, and it has been so difficult to hold myself from him. I could not be sure he felt as I do, but I did not want to risk humiliation. Being an older woman is such a strange experience, so inherently painful in potential, and with such a young man as Peter, who, when he came to the island was really much younger than his years. He has blossomed. I am touched by his enthusiasms. He is an artisan, and a good artisan, he has the sensitivities of one much advanced in years and one whose life has been–or could be–rich. He reads poetry well, and responds to it with feeling. I would never have imagined such a response from seeing him with his friends in the Quarrytown Café. They are rough and ready fellows, and when he wishes to be, Peter is rough and ready as well, but under the powerful physical surface is an immensely powerful emotional depth. We've only begun to plumb it, but today was what I hope was the first of a long period of love-making. I don't want to frighten him, or make him feel responsible. And I don't want to have us the center of a scandal of any kind. I know I can trust him. The question is, can I trust myself?

It never occurred to Peter, even years later, that Marie and he could have been at the center of a scandal. He never even imagined that what they did could be considered scandalous, yet in Quarrytown what could have been more so? He felt foolish at not having considered such a fate. Marie's discretion had protected them. He read further.

In some ways Crown Island is an unreal world. I know that, and I have known that since I was little, since I began to see the way the world on shore seemed to be lived so much differently there. I have walked the streets of Quarrytown and I have seen the way people look at me. We do not know one another. It is as simple as that. I retreat into my books and my thoughts and I cannot imagine what they, who have neither as their comforters, must do when I am gone, when I am out of their sight. When I was a child I imagined Crown Island was enchanted, that the sounds in the meadow were those of souls lost at sea, souls that protected me from catastrophe and change. But I soon learned that change is the essence of the life I am to live. Painful though it may be, and there are days when I find myself almost unable to think clearly with the pain of loss. But change is inevitable, and I must learn to cope as I have done. Peter has brought the magic back into the island for me. Those who think of me as a hermit on Crown Island simply do not understand. It is here that I am in most comfort, despite the times of loneliness that I sometimes feel.

July 31. It has been a week. Peter has been tender and a delight. We read in Ovid today and I hope one day we will read Propertius. He seems to take to the classical authors. A wonderful bonus of sorts. I had not expected this, yet his nature is such that it should be no surprise. It is painful to me to think that he had to drop out of the University. How many such young men must there be in the country, in the town? Perhaps not many, but even one is a tragedy of sorts. I have to work on this. It will be my project. He is young and he can grow enormously if he has the chance. I can give him the chance.

Peter sat back. He closed the journal notebook. He did not wish to read more. He looked at the notebooks and saw that there was more than enough left to read to keep him occupied for weeks, perhaps months. But he had discovered things that he felt he probably should not have known. That Marie had seen him and chosen him, that she was aware of his total innocence and that she thought so long ago that she could help him go to University, all this was more than he needed to know. T h e thought of his being a "project" for Marie was difficult for him to accept. Why would she think of him as a "project?" And what had he done to give her the idea that he could achieve the goals she set for him? Peter closed the house and set out for shore.

CHAPTER TWENTY-TWO

Buddy Dooley lounged on the dock. "I'm not gonna say nothin'," Buddy said.

"What do you mean?"

"You know. Now that you're an islander you don't need any shit from me."

Peter watched him carefully. "What's up?"

"I just been wondering where you been? I expected you to check on the job on St. Ann's Street this week, and you don't show up. What's happening?"

"Is the job okay? You having a problem?"

"No, Christ no. Everything's hunky dory. It's just you usually check in and I thought I better run you down before I get a message saying you don't like the way things have been going. That's all. Shit, Pete, you been a little odd lately."

"I'm not odd. I'm just tied up."

"So what's it like out on the island there? I didn't know when you'd be back. Alice told me you go out there now and then and sit there all by yourself. What's up with that? Didn't you close it up for the winter?"

"Yeah, but I ran into a few problems."

"Want me to come out there and give you a hand?"

"Thanks, Buddy, but it's not those kinds of problems."

"So what is it, then?"

Peter thought about how he might put things. "It's kind of complicated in a way. Has to do with some things that Miss Wainwright was working on. I gotta go through some of her papers is all."

"That's hard work?" Buddy grimaced at him.

"Sometimes, yeah. Weighs me down."

"I'll trade ya."

"Sure. I wish I could."

"So, now you own an island. You gonna move out of Haycock Street?"

"No."

"Didn't she live out there year 'round?"

"Lately, yeah. By herself."

"Not all the time, I bet." Buddy smiled. "Must 've had some company now and then. I'd see her every so often, you know. I'd wave to her from Len's Novi when we'd come in from emptying his pots. Len's catches have been lousy, incidentally. She still looked pretty good, at least from out there."

"She was a good woman."

"She just left it to you in her will? Just like that? God, that's some luck."

"She liked my work."

"I'll bet she did. I got a few people in town liked my work, too, but I didn't so much as inherit a bird house. What's the trick there, Pete? You got some golden touch maybe?"

"I wish I knew. She surprised the shit out of me with that. I got the call from Ellington and I thought he was suing my ass about something and he goes and tells me I inherited Crown Island."

"You know what they're saying about you in town?"

"I really don't give a shit what they're saying in town."

"They say you been planking her for years and worked on her until she left the island to you. She was supposed to leave it to the Quarrytown Conservancy I heard. Until you worked on her and changed her mind about all that."

"You believe that?"

"I'm just saying what the talk is. I'm not saying I believe it. 'Course I seen you out there from time to time."

"She was a friend of mine."

"Oh yeah, friends is friends. I know that, Pete. That's what I said. Friends is always hanging out. But, hey, what do I know? You never talked to me about how you were friends."

"No, I never did. And I'm not gonna start talking now. She's gone. She was a lady. I always respected her."

"Sure."

"You almost finished at St. Ann's Street?"

"No, not almost finished. But it could stand a look if you've got time."

Peter took Buddy in his pickup into Elm City and went into the large old Federal building they were redoing. Tony Manassas, a house painter from Guildford, had inherited the house from his uncle Sallie, who'd lived in it for fifty-one years without doing much of anything with it. Now Tony hired Peter to make the house into a four-family dwelling. It was big enough and the shape of the house was such that it was a pretty simple job. Peter had Buddy take on the job as foreman and gave him the plans and oversaw the beginning of the job when they gutted the house and checked it for its general integrity before taking out walls and putting in stair cases. Peter liked the way these old houses were made, and he liked the idea that they were flexible in design and could adapt easily to the kinds of change Tony Manassas wanted.

The house was brick outside, but the stair case to the porch was Quarrytown Stone. Peter took a special interest in the stone and when they washed down the brick Peter supervised the washing of the steps until the stone came back to its original blush. Buddy was a good man and Peter relied on him even more than he did on Beady and Packy and Len. They had become a good team, and Peter made sure over the years that they shared in the profits of his company. They were friends, not just employees, and Peter made it clear how he felt. But now, it was starting to seem that Buddy didn't quite know how to take Peter's good fortune. Was the fact that he thought Peter was an islander now going to change things? Peter had a feeling it might.

"Is this wall okay?" Buddy said, when they got upstairs

to what would be the third family unit. Peter wasn't sure how to take the question. Was Buddy playing some kind of game?

"What's the matter with it?"

"No, I don't mean there's something wrong. I just wanted to get an okay before we paint it. I decided I had to move it a little. See what I mean? You got the heating duct here and I had to move it about four inches."

"Sure. Yeah. So it's okay. I didn't figure on the duct originally. It's only four inches. Is that why you got me down here?" Peter studied Buddy, trying to figure out what the problem was. This wasn't the way Buddy usually worked. The wall was a few inches off, and in a job like this, it was nothing. Peter wanted Buddy to get to the point and stop this run around.

"No, no. Well, yeah, a little. But really I just wanted to be sure you were happy with the way the job's going. You haven't been here in a while. I just didn't want you to get pissed or anything."

"Jesus, Buddy. I'm gonna get pissed over a four-inch difference in a wall? What's got into you? You got this job and all you got to do is finish it off like we said when we first talked about it. You know what the hell you're doing. You don't need me for this."

"I just thought because we were out of touch."

"We're not that much out of touch, Buddy. Put that out of your mind. Let's go down to Carmine's and get a couple beers."

Peter took Buddy down to the end of St. Ann's Street, near the overpass back to Quarrytown and went into Carmine DeVoto's lounge. It was a large dark-paneled room with several old men sitting at a corner table playing cards and drinking beer. It was six o'clock when Buddy ordered two boilermakers. Peter went to the pay phone and left a message telling Alice he'd be home for dinner around seven or seven-thirty.

"Thanks," Peter said when their drinks came. Carmine served them himself and looked at them oddly.

"This the boss?" Carmine asked Buddy.

Buddy nodded.

"Pete Chello," Peter said, holding out his hand. Carmine shook it.

"Knew your father, Tom. Came in here for a couple of shots every so often."

"I've been in here, too."

"Funny, I don't remember. How's business?"

"Not great, but we're still working. Small jobs these days."

Buddy ordered another boilermaker and had one set up for Peter. Peter didn't like to drink the way Buddy did. He'd watched his father sometimes tie one on, and the sight was rarely pleasant. But this time, because it was Buddy, and because he wanted him to feel okay about their working relationship, he said okay, and he matched Buddy drink for drink. But after the fifth round, Peter began to feel the kick from the booze and he decided it was time to get on. "Let's go," Peter said.

"Shit no, you owe me a round."

"Come on, Buddy. Time to go."

"Jesus Christ, what's got into you? I bought three rounds and you bought only two."

"I gotta drive us home."

"Fuck that. You owe me a round. You getting cheap as well as snooty?"

Peter was off the barstool. Carmine came near and waited as if he expected Peter to order another round. "What the hell are you talking about? What do you mean snooty?"

"This guy owns one of those islands. The Granite Islands?" Buddy said to Carmine.

"Yeah, I seen 'em," Carmine said.

"So now he's a big shot and too cheap to buy another round."

"Damn it, Buddy. We don't need another round."

"Don't tell me what the fuck I need."

Peter was unsteady and as he turned to Buddy he bumped his stool and Buddy reacted by pushing him back. "What the fuck?" Buddy said loudly. He was off his stool and pushing Peter roughly. "You think you can shove me around?"

"Take it outside," Carmine said sharply.

Peter lost his balance and stumbled against a table. He heard the old men in the corner snort at them as if they were amused. Finally some action in the place.

"Think you're better 'n me," Buddy said, and with that he slugged Peter in the face and knocked him down. Peter hit the floor head first. He didn't feel it right away, but when he pushed himself to get up he realized he was drunk and fed up with Buddy's bullshit. Buddy was just about to hit him again when Peter stepped inside his left and creamed him with a sledge hammer punch that broke his jaw. Buddy yowled and grabbed his face, and the blood from where he bit his tongue poured over his lips. He fell down in a squat and Carmine was over the bar with a short bat, waving it at Peter.

"Get the fuck out," Carmine said. "Now. Or I'm gonna clock you. And don't ever bring your ass in here again. And take him with you," he said, pointing to Buddy, whose eyes were open in shock.

Peter looked down at Buddy and knew things had gone too far. Buddy sat with one arm holding himself up and the other holding his jaw. "Jesus, I'm sorry," Peter said. Peter leaned down and held out his hand to help him up, but Buddy muttered indistinguishably and knocked his hand away. "I'm sorry," Peter said again. "Christ sake, let me help you up." But Buddy rolled over and got up on one knee while Carmine pushed Peter from behind and kept telling him to get him and his friend out of there. Finally, Buddy was on his feet, wobbly, holding his face, the blood dripping out of his mouth. He tried to say something, but his jaw wouldn't work and whatever it was he said was so unclear that Peter just came to him and touched his sleeve as a gesture to help him out of the bar, but Buddy shook him off.

"We gotta go," Peter said. "Or else Carmine's going to brain us one. So let's get in the truck." Buddy staggered out into the street. It was dark and the truck was parked on the gravel next to the bar. Peter opened the passenger side door and watched Buddy climb into the seat. "Let me see your face," he said. "Christ. Can you talk?"

Buddy shook his head.

"I think we better get you to the emergency room." Buddy protested, but it was a weak drunk's protest and Peter drove them over to St. Michael's and helped Buddy, who now was feeling the pain seriously, into the bright waiting room.

A heavy black woman looked up at them briefly as they came in. "You boys been playing?" she said.

"I think I broke his jaw."

"Assault and battery," she said. She sat in front of a typewriter and Peter thought she was typing out those words, but she was just readying an admission form. She took their information and told them to wait. Buddy sat down and groaned for more than an hour. Finally, a young guy in a green hospital shirt brought them over to a curtained-off area and examined Buddy.

"We need a picture," he said, and led him off to another room. They were back in twenty minutes. "X-Ray shows two breaks in his jaw. I'm going to have to wire it." Buddy yowled when he examined the jaw and tried to examine his tongue. "God," the doctor said. "I'm going to have to stitch that tongue. What the hell hit you, another drunk?"

Peter raised his hand. "Yeah. Two drunks. Bad ass drunks."

They were out of the emergency room after midnight. Peter was sober, more or less. The doctor cleaned up his face where Buddy had mauled him and he now felt the pain and knew that Buddy's pain was going to be fierce after the anaesthesia wore off. His face and right hand were bandaged and there was no way anyone would understand what he was saying, so when

Peter left him off at his truck down by the Quarrytown dock he asked him if he was okay to drive home and Buddy gestured with his free hand. He couldn't nod his head because of the pain and he couldn't say anything that made any sense. But even so, Peter told him again that he was really sorry he hit him so hard. Buddy mumbled something in return, almost as if he were beginning to get sensible. "Look, I'll come by tomorrow. At your place," Peter said. "Stay home tomorrow. I'll be there."

He sat and watched Buddy clamber into his Chevy and slam it into gear and burn a little rubber on the way out. He felt like shit. He'd known Buddy Dooley almost all his life. The last time they got into a fight was in fifth grade and that ended with them being best friends for the rest of that year. Peter was not sure it was going to work out that well this time.

"Where in the world have you been?" Alice was pissed. "I called Beady and Packy and they didn't have a clue as to where you were. I had dinner ready at seven-thirty the way you said. And it's all ruined. I didn't even eat until about midnight. Look at the time. It's almost two a.m. What happened to you?"

Peter tried to explain, but it sounded pretty lame when he spelled it out. What he didn't convey was the sense he had that Buddy thought of him as an islander now, a person apart. When they were kids they'd always scorned the people living out on the islands, the way they seemed so preppie, so fay. Islanders were always the butt of their jokes, but now that Buddy considered Peter one of them, they could no longer share that contempt. Peter was no different from what he always was. He was the man he always thought himself to be, and Buddy was the one who changed. Buddy was the one who saw him as some one he was not. But how would he explain that to Buddy, or anyone else?

In the morning, Peter tried to tell Alice what happened. She couldn't listen for more than a few minutes because she had an early meeting with a school counselor, and when she left she told him it was all in his mind, that Buddy Dooley had been one of his best friends for his whole life and that the two of them were acting like school-ground toughs and that they ought to be ashamed of themselves for carrying on like that in Elm City. He was lucky, she said, that the cops didn't run him in for brawling.

Peter got himself together and went over to Termite Falls Road where Buddy had bought the old Castlevetro house and added on a new kitchen. It was a square white house with a flat roof, set back from the road across from the railroad tracks. Nearby was an open marshland meadow that had just begun to turn brown.

He knocked on the door and Laura Dooley, with a cigarette in the corner of her mouth, opened it and looked at him. "Well, now maybe I can get some information on what happened last night. What the hell were you two thinking?"

She let him in and he explained as best he could how they got to drinking and how before you knew it they were slugging each other. "It was all stupid," Peter said. "I don't know how the hell things like that happen."

"I couldn't understand a frigging thing Buddy was telling me. I was gonna call the cops just about when Buddy pulls in still drunk. He wrote me a message, said his jaw was broken. They got it all wired up and I gotta fix him soup for a couple weeks or so. Pete, did you go and break his jaw on me?"

"I didn't mean to, but he was pissed off that I wouldn't buy another round of boilermakers, and he slugged me and knocked me down. It was instinct is all I can think. Hitting him back like that. I wouldn't want to hurt Buddy. You know that. Jesus. It's the last thing I'd want to do." Peter sat in the kitchen wringing his hands. His own head still hurt, and he could imagine what Buddy must have felt like. "Is he in bed still?"

Then he heard some grunting from the hallway. Buddy came in and sat at the table. He grunted at Peter and grabbed a notepad and wrote a simple statement: "You owe me!"

"You're right. I do. How the hell did all this happen?"

He realized Buddy couldn't be understood. "Look, I'll pay for the medical bills."

Buddy scribbled again, "I'm covered."

"Christ, remember how we did this in fifth grade?"

Buddy took his pencil, "You weren't so big then. I whipped your ass."

"Yeah, well, we're both bigger now. We better cut this shit out or somebody else is going to get hurt."

Laura came over to the table with a cup. "You want some stale coffee?"

Peter nodded. "I'm really sorry about this, Laura. I'll try to make it up to you."

Buddy passed him another piece of paper, "Just put it in the Christmas bonus."

"Sure. I wasn't so sure there'd be a Christmas bonus this year, but yeah. I'll put it in your bonus. It's a shitty thing to have to deal with through Christmas."

"Except for the soup, it'll give me a rest," Laura said. "You should hear him sing all those reindeer songs. I'm getting used to the peace and quiet already."

Buddy grunted and tried some guttural expression, something like "Shut up now." But it was essentially good-humored. Peter held out his hand in a gesture of friendship and Buddy looked at it for a moment before taking it. They were both sober now, and even if they were in pain, they were more themselves. Buddy might forgive him. He could be sure that he wasn't going to noise all this around with the other guys, so it had to stay between them.

"How the fuck did you come to own Crown Island?" Laura asked. "That came outa the blue, far as I could see. That Miss Wainwright was a big deal. Didn't she have any family to leave it to?"

"She was the last. She told me that once, but I never gave it another thought."

"I was in the hairdresser with Molly Parady. She told me

the Conservancy is really ticked off that you got the island. She thinks there was some hanky-panky going on. Thinks you worked the old lady over until she changed the will."

Peter shook his head. "You believe that?"

"It's not up to me," Laura said. Buddy grunted something that was indistinguishable.

"She's one of the Conservancy people. They want the whole town to be left to them. You wait and see. They'll come after your place, too. Soon as you're ready for Hollow Hills. You watch. Like they got Sandy Oster's seven acres last year," Peter said.

"I heard she actually left the island to the Conservancy in an earlier will."

"Maybe she did."

"Then she decided to change the will. That's a weird one, don't you think? Changing your will like that when you've got everything set. Doesn't make a lot of sense to me. Buddy said he thought you and the old lady were doing it." Laura was a blousy woman who seemed to want nothing more than a juicy bit of gossip to bring back to the hairdresser. She leaned over and lit another cigarette, blowing the smoke up toward the ceiling in consideration of Peter.

"She wasn't an old woman," Peter said.

"Far as I could see she had a few years on her. Paper said she was sixty-eight. I figure that's pretty old. A lot older than you. So, did you two get it on?"

"Laura, you and this town got a lot to learn about people."

"That right?"

"Look. I told Buddy. I haven't got clue one as to why Miss Wainwright left me the island. We were friends, and for a while there we were pretty good friends. But that's not a good enough reason for her to turn around and leave me the whole damned island. I can't figure it. She never said a word to me about it, and if she did I would have told her I didn't want it."

He heard Buddy grunt noises that sounded like "Ha, ha."

"What are you talking? That's gotta be worth a couple million by now. What do you mean you wouldn't want it?'

"What I said. I got a house on Haycock Street. I don't need an island. I don't know anybody out there."

"Yeah, well I got a house on Termite Falls Road and I'd take the island anytime. You can give it to me if you don't want it. Christ, I'd like to know what it's all about out there with the water all around you. I was on Extra Island that time with you and Buddy. All I could say is, 'This is the life,' you know what I mean? The kids could go swimming and diving and running around. What a way to grow up. And those houses out there are big and terrific. It's like a big party out there most of the time. Sure, I'd take it. I'd be crazy not to take it. Trouble is, I don't have anybody out there who's likely to remember me in their will, if you know what I mean."

Buddy grunted. He agreed with her.

"Those Conservancy people," Peter said. "They made me think twice."

"What about Alice? Now, I'll bet she's wondering how you inherited that island."

"We're all wondering. But Alice wants to live on it."

"Good for her. Maybe she'll ask us out there once in a while. Special occasions, like."

"Sure. You can count on it."

"Molly Parady told me something crazy."

"Something else?"

"Said you had to get a degree from the University in order to keep the island. Now, that sounded crazy to me. What's up with that?"

"Yeah, it's true," Peter said.

Buddy grunted, then groaned in pain. He pushed a note across, "Don't make me laugh!"

CHAPTER TWENTY-THREE
December 2001

When they heard what happened to Buddy Dooley, Beady and Packy Caserto kept very quiet around Peter. He tried to explain that it was a stupid thing, a drunken thing, but both Beady and Packy were standoffish in a way that Peter had never seen before. Buddy was back at work and his swollen tongue had recovered well enough so that he could talk and be generally understood. He still had to confine his meals to soup and anything else he could get through a straw, but whatever he had to say, it wasn't said to Peter. Buddy confined their conversations to the work and not much more. Peter had hurt more than Buddy's jaw.

Alice was not very consoling. She told him how stupid it was for him to go over to Elm City and drink boilermakers on an empty stomach. "What the hell are boilermakers, anyway?" she said. "My father said they were what drunks drank." Of course, she was right. But Peter could have used a little sympathy after losing one of his best friends. Buddy had been a little weird lately, true, but friendships from grade school playgrounds were usually impervious to time and even to stupid fights.

With the way things were, it was hard for Peter to decide which job to go to. He wasn't needed at St. Ann's Street, and Packy was almost finished at Termite Falls Road. Beady was working in Guildford fixing the roof on St. Martin's Church and Len Moore was still working on the Library in North Franklin. They had at least five or six months on that. The company had no new jobs in prospect, and the new secretary, Janice, was in only three days a week now taking care of paper work.

Peter decided to go back to Crown Island and try to solve

the puzzle that seemed to have no answer. He wanted to know why Marie willed the island to him instead of giving it to the Conservancy as she had planned. The answer had to be somewhere in her journal. Since the really cold weather had held off, Peter read in the sunshine comfort of the library until late afternoon.

In Marie's library, he pulled out the boxes in which she had kept her journals. There were a great many, and the answer to his question might have been in any of them. In her journals, Marie talked to herself in a way that intrigued him. He wasn't at all sure how he would write in a journal if he had ever thought of doing so, but he thought it might be different. He might keep a record of what he did each day, the job he was on, the problems he faced and solved, the people he worked with. He wasn't sure what he'd write down, but he would not ask himself questions that couldn't be answered. Marie approached life in interesting ways, but they were not his ways.

Peter opened Marie's journal for 1998. He read a few entries in which she described her travels and then he came to the entries for Quarrytown. *August 9. I came home to Crown Island exhausted and somewhat weakened. Peter surprised me with a visit and we did not have a good talk. He read* The Mention of You *and realized Cantrell was Muldoon. Now I wish I hadn't written it, or that I had hidden things better. Peter was angry that I had slept with Miles Muldoon, but Peter is still very young. He has no idea how I felt, how worldly Muldoon could be. It was such a brief thing, too. As if that mattered to Peter. But for me it was important to have a relationship with someone I need not shape and could not influence. I may have been wrong to take on Peter as I did. The question of whether one has the right to change people, to put them on a different path from the one life has set out for them, is one that I must somehow address. Perhaps in a novel? I'm not sure. But the contrast was what I was left with when Muldoon and I separated that evening in New York. He was a happy man even as he pretended to be saddened, and I was a happy woman even as I pretended to be hurt. We were both extraordinary in our capacities at pretense, and I realized later that one of the distinguishing qualities that Peter brought into my life was his inability at pretense. In part, I think it has to do with a limited imagination–Peter is as literal in his approach to life as he is in his approach to the stone he loves so well. The result is a solidity. I rather love that quality in him, but life is complex and the peculiar qualities of someone like Miles Muldoon also have their value and they satisfied me in their way. I pretended to be terribly offended by Peter's indignation at learning the truth about Muldoon. Peter was so protective I almost laughed aloud when we spoke. You would have thought I had fallen for Don Juan and had been cast aside like a serving wench. The truth was so much different. Peter might have knocked poor Miles down if he'd gotten the chance. For an instant, I felt like a wayward wife. I doubt that I made Peter aware of how preposterous his position was. He sees things from a single angle only.*

Peter looked up from the journal. It was written with a carefully articulated pen using a dark blue ink and the words flowed smoothly across the page with an almost innocent beauty. But Peter was stung by her judgments of him. He lacked imagination and he was wrong about Muldoon. Didn't Marie say they should not judge one another? When they talked about Muldoon she said something very like that. She accused Peter of judging her, and he in turn pointed out that she was judging him. Well, here it was in her journal. She judged him and judged him unfairly. She thought of him as still very young in 1998 when he was forty-six years old. Was that fair?

He wondered if he should read any more. Peter tried to understand how he could react so painfully to an entry in a journal written years ago. Was he too thin-skinned, as his father had told him when he was a young man? Or was it just that it was painful to think that the woman he had once loved so deeply had the capacity to find fault in him, even though he was willing to admit that he possessed many faults. His reaction to Muldoon's having had an affair with Marie was, as she said, protective. He would have done anything to protect her against a man like that and it pained him at the time to think that she did not want to be protected against him. She had actively courted him. And now he saw that she felt the affair had done her good. It was a bewildering world when emotions were stirred at such depths.

He decided to keep reading. *August 14. I've been thinking about our talk. Peter deserves much better than his lot in life. He still maintains that beguiling combination of goodness and naivete, a combination that in some people is fatal, but which in Peter is engaging and curious. We have not talked about literature in many years, but I had hoped that when we did he would have begun to see the complexities that lie beneath the surface of every relationship, every gesture, every commitment. I know he takes great joy in his son, as he should, and I know that he has followed out the obligations to his wife and his family that other men might not have done. It is a quality that some would condemn and point to not as a virtue but as a willing limitation. Who were the playwrights who said, sardonically, that "obligation is the deepest form of love?" I am all the more determined that Peter should have the chance to explore the world from a different vantage. He does not understand what the University can do for him. He thinks it is a matter of reading more of the same books that we discussed, and not that it implies a profound re-making of the man. At his age, at any age now, he would find himself so altered as to permit himself to understand his choices and how they have made him what he is. I will talk with the University about this.*

August 28. I finally had a talk with Coleman Warburton about Peter. Apparently it is unusual for someone to give a private scholarship to an individual. Coleman tried to talk me into just giving the University enough money to support a scholarship program, but that's not what I'm interested in doing.

I made it very clear to him that I wanted to pay Peter's way through the University. Coleman was worried that Peter would not apply, but I assured him that he had nothing to worry about from that point of view. This is my last attempt at helping Peter. There must be a way.

Peter looked at the next page, but it was blank. The later pages for 1998 were devoted to problems that Marie was having with her newest book. She was talking to herself about what she had written and how her characters had reacted to the events of the book. When Peter first read these pages, he thought that she was talking about real people, but it soon became clear to him that this was the kind of dialogue that only a novelist could have with her creations. He looked for entries that mentioned him, but if there were any, he missed them. Marie seemed to be conducting her life as if she were having an affair with the people in her book, so centered was her attention on them.

Marie's entries in her 1999 journal were more of the same. She entered the names of people he had not met, friends of Marie's in France or England. She had taken a whirlwind tour, it seemed, of places where she had spent time as a young woman. She had so many friends in these places that his head was almost dizzied with her descriptions and her responses to the calls she made to her friends. A few notes she made in these entries began to trouble him. In one she talked of visiting a doctor in London. Peter stared at that entry. It was only a line, but it was followed by a long lapse in the journal. And it was underlined twice. He looked for other entries that mentioned doctors or hospitals. He skipped through the journal looking for more such references and he found two. One spoke of a doctor in southern France who was an "expert." Marie described him as more afraid than she was and with that description Peter knew as well as one knows anything that Marie was aware that she was dying. There were many lapses in these last pages, unlike the earlier journals, which were crammed full.

When she got back from France in 1999 she went to see

her lawyer. *September 30. The young Ellington is very much like his father, but unlike his father he doesn't ask personal questions. I have told him what I want to do and while he looked at me oddly, he explained that it was perfectly reasonable to do what I intended. He does not know Peter, although he remembered Tom Chello from some work he once did on his family house on Heights Road. It may be a strange sense of satisfaction that moves me now, but the smugness of the Conservancy people had gotten to me at some level, I think. So I plan not to let them know that I have changed my plans, but let Peter and Ellington tell them. I wonder how Peter will react when he knows the property will be entailed. I am hoping that he will so much want the island that he will drop all his anxieties and misgivings and follow through with the University. It will change him, and God only knows what will happen to him and his wife. I think it will make him closer to his son, but you never know where a gesture like this will end. I may indeed be bringing a curse down on his head, although it is not my intention. That last time we spoke I saw that Peter had reached a limit, perhaps years before, and that without his doing something radical, he will never change. He always spoke with me of his fate, and in some ways I realized that he was quite right in feeling that his life was constricted and limited by the fate of having been consigned to Quarrytown as he is. His father's accident and his obligations to his mother kept Peter home. It pains me to think that he has never been to London or Paris or Rome or Athens, that the limitations of his life have been such that every move he has made to expand even a portion of his vision has been at great personal expense. I worried in the early years that I had opened not just a range of opportunities, but a door into a world that Peter could plainly see but never truly advance into. Our talk about Miles Muldoon made it painfully clear that I was right. Now that I cannot see things through, I must be forceful. Somehow I must close the door behind him and not just open it before him.*

There was nothing said in the newspaper obituary about Marie's death except to describe it as heart failure. Peter had assumed it might have been a heart attack or a sudden stroke, and perhaps it was. He had not thought that she would have had prior warning. He assumed that she would have told him if that had been the case. Who else would she have spoken with? And who else could he speak with now? He felt painfully isolated. None of the guys he worked with would listen to him. Not now. And Alice's anger still smoldered. She could hardly be sympathetic to his fears.

Ironically Marie was the only person he would have been able to talk with about his feelings and it was she who had made him feel now as if he were a terrible disappointment to her. He had tried so hard to be the person she had wanted him to be. He read carefully and thought he understood the significance of what he read. He had become, he thought, a man. Not just in terms of what Quarrytown expected of him, but a man in the sense that he was a being with a genuine understanding of life. But here was Marie saying something quite different.

Coleman Warburton had frightened Peter when they talked about his entering the University. Warburton was as smooth as young Staunton Ellington. They both dressed the same way and they both spoke with a sense of confidence and utter control of their worlds. They were secure in their belief that what they held to be true was true, that the vectors of their lives were secure and appropriate. Peter knew that such men were different from him. Peter's world was dominated by the tangible, by the constructs that had yielded under his own hands and responded to his own designs. He was comfortable in the quarry, walking around slabs of granite, watching the stone yield to explosives, selecting the pieces that he knew would fit where he wanted them. As long as Quarrytown was on the water he would make a living, his father told him, and that presumed only that he would make a living as long as he belonged to Quarrytown.

Marie had never belonged to Quarrytown even though

she paid her taxes to the collector on Main Street. She belonged to Crown Island, a world in one sense all onto itself. But in another sense it was to her what it had been to her parents: an avenue to the world far beyond Quarrytown. Her father had used it as an avenue to Washington and the center of power. Her mother had used it as the gateway to Europe and whatever freedom she had yearned for. Marie was a citizen of the world, wandering as she willed. Her friends were in England and France and, as far as he knew, in many other countries as well.

Going to the University was not going to make Peter a free man. He was, when he admitted it to himself, frightened by the prospect. When he was in high school, the sign prohibiting entrance to the University library inhibited him but did not keep him out. Later, he learned he was as welcome inside the library as anyone else, but at bottom the feeling of rejection never truly left him. The University was for other people, the kind of people who loaded their boats in the summer and motored out to Parker, Kidd's, and Mother's Islands.

No matter how you looked at it, he was a dropout. Yes, he had a scholarship to the University, but it was to play baseball. Granted, he'd seen what learning could be, and he had warmed to it. Granted, he'd done okay in his first semester in college. But for the last thirty years he'd been fixing seawalls, laying stone, putting on additions, and trying to figure out how life should be lived. His life shaped him in ways he'd sometimes struggled against, and sometimes gave into. Even Marie had understood how he was carried along in a tide of obligation. And, now, he was not entirely sure he regretted the way things had worked out for him. He could have lived a much less interesting life if he had never become Marie Wainwright's lover.

What she was saying to him in her journals is that the University would do for him what it had done for her. But could it? He didn't think so. Now that he was almost fifty-one years old, how could he sit in a classroom with eighteen year-olds and risk showing them his ignorance? How could Marie not understand his feelings of not belonging? How could she have thought that her plans for him were reasonable? How could she have done what she did without asking his advice?

It made him aware that she regarded him not as a lover, not as a precious friend, and certainly not as an equal. He remained for her a project, a person to be made over. But she had not taken into account that his metamorphosis had occurred long ago. She had changed him, true, but how much more was he likely to change and yet hold to a semblance of himself?

Did she think of him as a character in one of her books, like Hallstatt Stone or Carpenter Halliwell? He was neither of those people, and it was painful for him to sit there thinking that he had never told Marie that she had got him wrong in both those portraits. She had seen him as she imagined him to be, but not as he was. Even now, it was clear that she saw him not as he truly was, not as Peter Chello, the man who had shaped the stone walkway that took her to the water each day, but as a child to be plucked from the mainland because she thought he looked like a Roman boy in the age of Augustus. He had walked up from the sea, true, and instead of dripping the ocean's brine, he dripped possibilities, the potential to be shaped and changed into an erotic fantasy. Except that he was no fantasy. He was flesh and bone and more than that, he was ambitious to be the man Marie had envisioned.

But life intervened. If he were fated to be himself, then the years he spent visiting Crown Island were little more than intervals, like the years Oedipus spent ruling Thebes. Peter determined not to spend the last years of his life blind to the realities around him. There were some things, he said, that he was not sure he could do. One of them was going to the University as an old man. Oedipus spent his last years not in a University, but wandering blind in a desert. Peter planned to spend his last years neither blind nor as a wanderer, but as a man centered in the world that was his world and that had always been his world.

"I've changed my mind. I want us to live out there this winter," he told Alice.

"You're crazy."

"I mean it. It's very important to me."

"What kind of life are we going to live out on Crown Island in the winter?"

"A genuine life, I think."

"What are you talking about? You sound like a nutcase. You know that, don't you? Steve Clements always said only a nutcase would stay out here all winter."

"He's a nutcase himself. Look, I want to make it our home if we are going to keep it."

"We're going to keep it. You saw how Stanley and Kathleen loved it when we took them out there. I told you we're going to keep it."

"I don't want it if we can't live in it. I don't want anything to do with it if it isn't going to be a home for us."

"But what are we going to do in the winter out there? It's bad enough here in the winter. Nobody winters out on the islands."

"Except Marie," he said. "And her family. They wintered out there. And we wouldn't have to depend on anyone. My Whaler will take us back and forth."

"We'll freeze in that thing."

"It's only ten minutes or so to the mainland."

"And if it ices over?"

"We'll sit it out. Or if we need to, we can walk over the ice. People did it years ago. You've seen the pictures. We'll build a safety sled and push it over the ice the way they used to do. It's either that or we give the island back to the Conservancy."

"What? You promised me."

"I never promised anything. You said you deserved it, but that's you. Not me. I didn't deserve Crown Island. I'd like to make myself deserving of it. We can live well there. We can learn how to make it home. Don't you see the opportunity we've got here? How to make our lives much more interesting."

"By living out there with snow and ice around us? Peter. It's one thing when you can swim in the summer, when there are parties on the island and when everyone is out there with their boats having fun. But what kind of fun can you have when it's freezing? And how will I get to school?"

"We'll work it out. I'll ferry us in and out. No problem. And we'll make the island a place to have fun if that's what you want. I want to have Beady and Packy and Len and Buddy, all of them, out to the island and make them feel like it's a place for them too."

"Is Buddy talking to you now?"

"When he can talk. Right now Laura does most of his talking for him. But he'd come out if we invite him. They'd all come out. I want them to be comfortable on Crown Island. They're never going to understand the island if they don't get out and spend time there. And if they don't spend time with us out there they will always think I'm somebody I'm not. They're going to treat me just like they treat the other island people, like someone who's looking down their nose at them. I never want that. I never wanted to be like that. But that's how they see me right now. I want to change that. And if you think you want us to keep this island and pass it down to Stanley, then you've got to come along with me on this thing."

Alice had been standing there in the living room with the TV remote in her hand when Peter began this conversation. She finally put it down on the coffee table. "And if I don't go along with you?"

"I think you will. We've been through a lot of stuff that hasn't necessarily been good for us. I think this is going to be one of the best things that will ever happen to us. I don't think I realized it until I sat there yesterday reading Marie's journal. Where she talks about how she thought the Conservancy people were too smug and that they maybe didn't deserve the island and how it would affect us."

"Affect you."

"Okay. She just talked about me. It's true. But she knew you and I would be there together. If the island is going to have an effect on me it's going to have an effect on you, too."

"What's this stuff about having an effect on us?"

"That's it, don't you see? Crown Island shaped her whole family. It will shape us, too. Maybe it will shape Stanley–or probably his kids–more than it will shape us, but it will shape us just the same."

"And you think you'll really go to the University?"

"I talked with a guy there. He says I can start slow. I don't have to do it all at once. I've got ten years, remember. I can take a couple of courses at a time. I'll know in a few months whether or not I can do it. You went to college and I couldn't. At the time it seemed the right way to go. But now I want my own chance. We've got the money. And the chance. So, if you think it's for the good, then come with me to the island. I'll turn on the water and the heat and we'll have everybody out for Christmas. We can light the whole house for Christmas. What do you say? We can make it the most exciting place in Quarrytown. Wouldn't your fourth grade class love it?"

Peter gave Alice a kiss and she looked up in surprise. It would take her some time to come to terms with what Peter knew they needed to do. And in the intervening days while he worked details out with the teams he had working in St. Ann's Street, in North Franklin, and elsewhere, he explained that he was taking a back seat in the business for a while and that during that time Beady Caserto was going to take over from him but that nothing was really going to change. They were a team, he told them all. They'd stay a team. And this year's Christmas party was going to be on Crown Island and everyone they wanted to bring was welcome.

The second week of December was unnaturally warm. He heard the newscasters talk about a record-setting situation and everyone said they thought this weather was a gift. In a way it was. Peter went back to Crown Island and turned on the heat and water and all the lights. He called Sybil Forstner and told her that if she wanted to come and take the manuscripts from the island she could do so. Including the journals and the memoir that seemed half finished. But she better come soon, Peter said. Before he changed his mind.

There was much more to read in Marie's journal, but he was afraid to read another word. He had made up his mind and he thought he somehow understood some of the complexities of Marie's decision to pass Crown Island on to him even though he had not read anything about what her imagined conditions might have been. Did she want him to live here alone or with his family? Did she expect him to live on the island at all? He did not know. And at this point in his life he was more interested in what he wished for himself than in what Marie might have wished for him. She had changed him into the man he now was, and from this point on it was up to him.

If Crown Island had shaped the Wainwrights, then it was possible that it would shape the Chellos, and in turn it was also possible that Peter could reshape Crown Island and transform it from a world apart to a place of familiarity where people like him would come to hear how the water laps against the bedrock in the early evening, see how the tides rise and fall throughout the day, how the sun bathes the sea pines in the morning and feel how it warms the great old hotel in the late afternoon, and learn how the world becomes peaceful when the boats have gone off for dinner and the birds sit in the trees to watch the setting sun. If somehow Crown Island had become his fate, then Peter knew he would never let it remain the hermetic retreat it had been in Marie Wainwright's last years, but make it a welcoming and open place that would be an avenue to understanding and, yes, to love.

Crown Island is an imaginative work of fiction that celebrates a beautiful part of the Connecticut shoreline. Any resemblance to anyone living or dead is purely coincidental. This is not a *roman a clef.* Lee Jacobus is a shoreline resident and Professor Emeritus at the University of Connecticut at Storrs. Among his books is a collection of short stories all set in Hawaii: *Volcanic Jesus,* also published by Hammonasset House Books.

CPSIA information can be obtained at www.ICGtesting.com
Printed in the USA
BVOW02s0330160913

331197BV00001B/6/P